MOM'S GOT THIS

MOM'S GOT THIS

CASE FILES OF AN URBAN WITCH™ BOOK SEVEN

MARTHA CARR

MICHAEL ANDERLE

LMBPN Publishing
PMB 196, 2540 South Maryland Pkwy
Las Vegas, NV 89109

Version 1.03, January 2022
ebook ISBN: 978-1-64971-971-3
Print ISBN: 978-1-64971-972-0

THE MOM'S GOT THIS TEAM

Thanks to the JIT Readers

Misty Roa
James P. Dyer
Dave Hicks
Diane L. Smith
Jackey Hankard-Brodie
Jeff Goode

If we've missed anyone, please let us know!

Editor
Skyhunter Editing Team

From Martha

To everyone who still believes in magic and all the possibilities that holds.

To all the readers who make this entire ride so much fun.

To Louie, Jackie, and so many wonderful friends who remind me all the time of what really matters and how wonderful life can be in any given moment.

From Michael

*To Family, Friends and
Those Who Love
To Read.
May We All Enjoy Grace
To Live The Life We Are
Called.*

CHAPTER ONE

Lucy Heron raced down the street, pursuing a pack of large, shaggy dogs and their Willen riders. Each of the Willen was wearing a jockey's outfit, which made them look almost like a half-size human, except for their rat-like noses pointing out from under the helmets.

"Stop!" Lucy shouted. "Come back here, the lot of you!"

The lunchtime crowds parted to let the dogs through, then the spectators pulled out their cameras and snapped pictures, capturing the moment to share with their friends. People laughed and pointed but didn't pay much attention to the two women chasing the dogs. That was something, at least.

"Are we gonna have to wipe all these people?" Jackie Kowal asked as she ran along beside Lucy. She reached around to her back pocket, and the magic wand concealed there.

"I hope not." Lucy was short on breath, but her mind was still racing, trying to work out how this situation would play out. "They only got a glimpse."

"Of rat-men riding dogs."

"Could be publicity for a film."

"In the middle of the day?"

"Weirder things happen in LA."

"What about the photos?"

"Moving fast. They'll be blurry."

"Hope you're right."

The dogs rounded a corner, and the two witches followed. Things were less busy here, which was great for containing the incident but meant the dogs could pick up more speed.

"Can you cut them off?" Lucy asked. "Direct them that way?"

She pointed down a side street toward an area of new and largely unoccupied office buildings. If they could herd the Willen and dogs into somewhere without spectators, they could finally deal with them.

"I'll try."

Jackie sprinted off, heading down one side of the pack of racing dogs. She had longer legs than Lucy and was the member of their running club who had to hold back the most to keep the group together. If any Silver Griffin agent could get ahead and steer this situation, it was Jackie.

Lucy kept running. She'd almost caught up with the rearmost Willen, but then what would she do? Grab the bloke off his dog and arrest him for a public display of magical features? That would leave Jackie to deal with the other five all by herself. They'd called for backup, but it was a busy day, and there were only so many agents available.

Jackie had almost drawn level with the lead rider. He

steered his dog to the right, across the street and away from her. The others followed, triggering a blare of horns and screech of tires as cars swerved, skidded, and braked to keep from hitting the dogs.

Lucy planted a hand on one of the cars and slid across the hood like a cop from an action movie. She grinned to herself. She'd always wanted to do that. Landing in the road on the far side, she pushed herself into a sprint to catch up with the rear of the pack again.

At the end of the short street was a shiny new office block, thirty floors of gleaming glass and pristine new concrete dotted with corporate logos. The dogs were chasing straight toward its lobby.

"Stop them!" Lucy shouted.

"How?" Jackie shouted back. "People are watching."

Glass doors slid open a moment before the leading dog would have hit them. It bounded through, its Willen rider whooping and waving a hand in the air as he bounced upon its back. Jackie, only a few strides behind, lunged at the rider, tackling him around the waist, lifting him off the dog, and slamming him into the polished floor. The other dogs streamed in behind her and began running circuits around the lobby, riders laughing and cheering as they went.

People around the lobby caught the edges of Lucy's attention, but she didn't have time to deal with them now or to worry if there were a few witnesses. They were out of sight of most of the world, and it was easier to wipe the memories of a few executives than a whole street full of spectators. This was the best chance she had.

She pulled out her wand and pointed it at the closest dog.

"Inretio!"

A magical net hurtled from her wand, spreading as it went. It enveloped both dog and rider, bringing them to the ground in a tangle of glowing threads.

Jackie had restrained the lead rider, though his mount was still charging around the lobby, yapping excitedly at receptionists and security guards. Pinning her captive in place with one hand and a knee to the back, she pulled out her wand and pointed it at the next dog to run past.

"Agglutino!"

Glue appeared around the dog's paws. It tried to keep running, but the glue stuck firmly to the floor tiles. As the dog jerked to a stop, its rider flew off its back, slammed head-first into a large potted plant, and went limp, knocked out cold.

Three down, three to go. Lucy aimed at another of the dogs.

"Dormio!" Her aim was a little off, and she hit the rider instead of his steed. The Willen slumped, fell from the saddle, and hit the floor with a thud. He lay there snoring with his paws curled around his nose as he slid into an unnatural sleep.

"Dormio!" Lucy snapped again. This time she hit the dog, which slowed, yawned, stumbled, and fell with one ear flopped across his face, as soundly asleep as his master.

The last two riders, realizing that the gig was up, made for the elevators at the end of the lobby.

"Refrigero!" Jackie called, and a bolt of icy magic shot from the tip of her wand.

One of the Willens raised her hand. Magic flashed around her claws, and the freeze spell melted to nothing.

"They're getting away." Lucy raised her wand, but one of the Willens had cast a spell at her, and she was too busy countering it to cast anything at them. "We have to stop them before they get to the lifts."

The doors to one of the elevators slid open. Both Willens turned the heads of their dogs, guiding them toward this escape route.

A woman stepped out of the elevator. She was as short as the Willens, stocky and muscular, dressed in a black suit that bulged slightly under the arm. To anyone familiar with the magical community, she was unmistakably a dwarf.

"Stop right there." The dwarf held up a hand.

The leading Willen turned his dog's head again, steering around the new arrival and toward the elevator. As he passed her, the dwarf's fist flashed out, punching him in the side of the head. He fell like a puppet with its strings cut, sliding off the dog and hitting the floor with a *thud*.

The final rider, seeing what the dwarf had done to her companion, turned her dog away and headed for the stairs. The dog's excitement level rose, and it barked loudly while its rider clung on with grim determination.

A tall, slender woman with long blond hair strode down the stairs, heels clacking with each step. She raised her hand, revealing a short metal tube, and pointed it at the dog. There was a flash of light, and both dog and rider yelped in alarm. The Willen rubbed her eyes while the dog skidded to a stop and started walking in circles, whimpering in confusion.

"Hush, boy." The woman reached the bottom of the

stairs and leaned over to pat the dog on the head. As she did so, her hair fell forward, revealing the pointed tip of an elven ear. "It's all right. Your sight will come back soon."

With her other hand, she raised the tube, then brought it down on the Willen's head, knocking her out. The rider fell to the ground, further confusing the poor dog.

"Full lockdown," the dwarf called.

"Yes, ma'am," said a man behind reception. He tapped a button, and the doors slid shut, then shutters slammed down over them. They cut off the daylight, but artificial lights immediately switched on, bathing the lobby in a warm, comforting glow.

Lucy and Jackie looked at each other.

"I thought this place was empty," Lucy whispered.

"Looks like you thought wrong."

The dwarf strode across the lobby toward them. She'd pulled a tube from inside her jacket, just like the one the elf had used to take out the Willen, and she was pointing it at Lucy and Jackie.

"What are you jokers playing at?" she asked sharply. "This is private property."

"Silver Griffins." Lucy pulled out the amulet that hung on a silver chain around her neck. "I'm Lucy Heron, field agent number 485. This is Jackie Kowal, agent 782. We're here on Griffins business, as you can see."

She gestured to the fallen Willens and the dogs that were still roaming the lobby, looking for attention or anybody with an interesting snack.

"Yeah, right." The dwarf snorted. "Since when do the L.A. Griffins hire Scots?"

"Actually, I'm English."

"Whatever. Eduardo, call the Griffins, check those badge numbers."

"Yes, Ms. Helmsguard," said the receptionist, who now had a wand in his hand.

As she looked around, Lucy realized that everyone in the room was a magical of some sort, whether witches and wizards who had pulled their wands out when the shutters went down, or dwarves, elves, and gnomes dressed to pass as humans. In one corner of the room, a disrupted illusion flickered, briefly revealing the Kilomea beneath a magical shell of humanity.

"Halldora, please, these are clearly legitimate agents." The elf walked over, wearing a smile that could have melted icecaps. "We have a responsibility to help the authorities."

"Fine." The dwarf snapped her fingers. A dozen magicals in black suits appeared from the corners of the room and gathered the fallen Willens, securing them with cable ties. The security guards were all blond, and with skin so pale it almost glowed.

"Welcome to Nuada Industries, agents." The elf shook hands with each of them in turn. "My name is Elethin Tannerin, and I'm the director of public relations. This is Halldora Helmsguard, head of security."

Elethin's smile made Lucy feel calm and comforted. Halldora's handshake, on the other hand, made her feel like she might be lifted over the dwarf's head at any moment and flung out the door.

"Sorry," Halldora muttered. "First day open. We're all a bit jumpy."

In the time it had taken to do introductions, Halldora's

people had assembled the captive Willens in a neat line, as well as finding leashes from somewhere and getting the dogs under control. It was a level of organization and professionalism that Lucy envied.

"I didn't think anybody was working here," she said. "Might have led this a different way if we'd known."

"Mr. Nuada recently purchased the building as part of our expansion effort here on the West Coast," Elethin said. "I'm sure that he would want to meet you personally to show his gratitude and our commitment to supporting the Silver Griffins and the local community, but unfortunately, he's tied up in meetings all morning. Perhaps another day?"

"Sure." Lucy pulled her phone out of her pocket. "We should get this lot back to HQ anyway. Is it all right if we bring a transport van around, or would you prefer a portal?"

"Please, allow us to help. This will be the perfect opportunity to try out our new solar-powered transport vehicles."

"Plus, the drivers need to learn these streets," Halldora said.

"Well, if you're sure..."

"Of course." Elethin beamed. "I'll bring the vans around directly."

"Thank you."

"Don't mention it. We're always happy to help."

CHAPTER TWO

Nuada Industries' vans provided a smooth and quiet ride through L.A. and Griffith Park, where a magically camouflaged driveway led to a hidden underground parking garage behind the Griffith Observatory. In the cool concrete darkness, Lucy and Jackie led the Willens out of the vans, all of them now conscious and complaining bitterly about their incarceration.

"You can't do this to us," said one of the captives. "We have rights."

"No magical has the right to show humans that we exist," Lucy said. "I don't believe for a minute that you're not smart enough to know that."

"I'm being repressed!"

"Boo freaking hoo." Jackie rolled her eyes and pushed the Willen toward the team of Griffins waiting to take him for transportation to Oriceran and a long stretch in Trevilsom Prison. "Keep moving, or I'll repress you so hard your grandkids feel it."

Halldora Helmsguard tugged on a collection of leads, and the dogs followed her out of her van.

"You sending these across the gap too?" she asked.

"I don't think Trevilsom has kennels," Lucy said. "Well, except for the shifter cells. We'll check this lot over in case they're somehow magical, then try to find them new homes."

"If you can't find anywhere, let me know. These good boys don't deserve to end up taken around back of the farm just because their past owners were irresponsible rats." Halldora handed Lucy her business card.

"You have dogs of your own?"

"Currently between pets. That's part of why I took this job in LA. Good time for me to move. I'll be looking for company once I settle in, and every dog deserves someone to love them, you know?"

For a moment, Halldora's stern expression faltered, showing something tender underneath. It reminded Lucy of how she felt when she got home to her dog, Buddy.

"We'll probably still need a home for one of these lads in a few weeks' time."

Halldora smiled. "Thanks." Then she got into the van, nodded at the driver, and they headed off.

Each wrestling with the leads of three large and excitable dogs, Lucy and Jackie made their way in through the rear entrance of the Silver Griffins' L.A. headquarters. Reception here was more functional than in the observatory, with only a metal bulkhead embedded in concrete walls. Each witch in turn pressed her wand against a panel next to the bulkhead. Once it recognized their magic, the steel sheet slid back, and they walked in.

"She seems all right," Jackie said. "For a corporate security stooge."

"You don't like private security?"

Jackie shook her head. "My family has too many stories about private magical security ops gone wrong. You give those guys a wand and a couple of rules to enforce, they end up going John Rambo in the middle of Melbourne. Then there are all the private companies that keep trying to change the Silver Griffins' rules, saying we need to open up to the market." She laughed bitterly. "Uncle Harold has some stories from Washington that would make you spit out your tea."

"I'm very protective of my tea."

"That's how bad they are."

"Well, those Nuada people seemed all right to me."

"Yeah, I guess." Jackie shook her head. "That Elethin..."

"Wait, do you have a crush?"

"You don't? I mean, did you see her?"

"I'm straight and married."

"Everyone has exceptions."

"Not everyone."

"Yeah, right. Now, where are we stashing the doggos?"

"Well, we need somewhere secure, with space for them to run around in, and given their energy, somewhere practically indestructible."

"I see where this is going." Jackie laughed. "All right, but if Jenkins turns them all into newts, you get to explain it to our new dwarf friend.

Halfway up the headquarters complex, they took a turn off the concrete corridors, through a reinforced door, and around a corner into a long room filled with strange machines and tattered targets, its walls scorched and scratched. The dogs looked up in confusion at the sound of grinding death metal emerging from a customized speaker system, then started bouncing in time to the beat.

"Jenkins!" Jackie shouted.

Halfway down the hall, two men in lab coats turned. Toliver Jenkins, the ginger-haired head of the Special Equipment and Weapons department, waved, but his younger companion stood looking nervous while a variety of fruit orbited his head. The music turned down from a deafening roar to a background growl.

"Stay there, Nigel," Jenkins said, then walked over to the witches. "What can I do for you ladies today?"

"We need to ask you a favor," Lucy said, then held out the leads to him. "These dogs need a temporary home, and this seemed like the best place."

Jenkins shrugged. "Why not. I've wanted to try some behavioral experiments, and apparently, it's unethical when I do that on Nigel."

"I'm not sure any of your experiments on Nigel are strictly ethical."

"He agrees to them. Don't you, Nigel?"

"Well, I..."

"Exactly!" Jenkins grabbed both sets of leads. "Come on, let's see what treats Uncle Toliver can find for you lot in the back office. I have a pig cadaver I was saving for a weapons test, but I didn't have any plans for the bones..."

He headed off, the dogs swirling around him in an excitedly barking cloud of fur, while Nigel stood in the middle of the firing range, fruit floating around his head.

"Hi, Jackie," he called and waved.

"Hi, pale guy. Nice banana you've got there."

"Are you sure they'll be all right here?" Lucy whispered.

"The dogs? They'll be fine. If they keep Jenkins distracted, the rest of the world might be safer for it."

Together, the two witches headed out of the lab and up the stairs to the main office floor. There, dozens of witches and wizards sat at their desks, doing research, writing up reports, or drinking coffee and discussing cases. Between them, administrative gnomes scurried back and forth with piles of paperwork in their hands while pigeons flapped past overhead, carrying small objects around the office and mission briefings out to agents in the field.

"I didn't know Twylan was coming in today." Lucy gestured at the teenage witch who sat by their desks, her brown coat hanging loose around her and magic flickering from her eyes.

"I must have forgotten," Jackie said. "Never mind, it's always good to have the kid around. She's going to make a great Griffin one day."

"All the better because you're training her."

Twylan stood as they approached.

"Hey, kiddo," Jackie said. "Did I forget an appointment?"

"No. I hope you don't mind, but the rest of the Underfoot Brigade are studying some low-level enchantments today, and, well..."

"That's a bit basic for you." Jackie nodded. "Glad you've come in. You missed a really fun chase and a bunch of cute dogs, but the day's still young."

"Dogs?"

"I'll explain once I have a coffee." Jackie grabbed a stained mug off her desk. "First things first..."

"Agent Kowal, Agent Heron." Sam, the personal assistant to the regional manager, had appeared as if out of thin air, though Lucy was sure there hadn't been any real magic to it. "Mr. Applegate said to send you both to his office when you got back in."

"Let me just—"

"He said straight away."

Jackie snorted but put her mug back down on the desk. "Can the kid come with us?"

Sam considered this for a moment, then nodded. "I don't see why not. It's nothing confidential."

They trooped into the regional manager's office. Roger Applegate smiled at them from behind his desk. Across from him sat a short, gray-haired witch with a narrow face and piercing eyes. Next to her was an older man in a three-piece suit every bit as dapper as Applegate's, but with the addition of a watch chain dangling across one side.

"Uncle Harold!" Jackie strode across the room to hug the older man. "You never told me you were coming to town."

"It was a last-minute decision, favor for a friend, and all that. Good to see you though, little Jack-Jack."

"How many times do I have to tell you not to call me that?"

"Always one more."

Applegate cleared his throat. "Agent Kowal, Agent Heron, I believe you're both familiar with Director Sunder, our head of security for North America."

"We've met," the older witch said. "Who is the other young woman?"

"This is Twylan," Lucy said. "Jackie's teaching her about how the Silver Griffins work."

"She seems a little young." Sunder raised an eyebrow.

"Too young to recruit," Applegate said. "But not too young for us to show her why she should be interested in the Griffins. Twylan is a young woman of great potential."

"Your office, your choice." Sunder's tone said she didn't believe it.

"Did you want to see us for something in particular?" Lucy asked. Sunder's attitude toward Twylan had her feeling defensive, and she wanted to get this done before she was career-crushingly frank with a superior.

Applegate looked at the more senior Griffins expectantly.

"We're going around several of the offices," Sunder said. "The Silver Griffins have recently entered into an agreement with a magical-run company called Nuada Industries, who are expanding their North Americans operations. It's an important relationship to all of us, right up to Lacey at the very top, and we want to make sure it goes smoothly."

"Really?" Jackie shot her uncle a questioning look. "Corporate collaborations now?"

"Finn Nuada is a fine fellow," Harold said. "We have a lot of faith in the company. We believe they're going to do good things for the whole community, particularly here in L.A., where he's making some big investments. We want to make sure that all goes smoothly."

"Well, it went fine this morning."

"This morning?"

"The incident we were chasing down ran into the Nuada building. It's all cleared up now."

Harold and Sunder exchanged a look.

"Perhaps you could tell me more later?" he said. "For now, the important thing is this. Nuada are our friends, and the Silver Griffins will extend them every courtesy. Is that clear?"

"Crystal clear, Director." Applegate smiled. "Got that, agents? Now, get out there and make our new friends feel at home."

CHAPTER THREE

There was frantic activity all around as Lucy, Jackie, and Twylan emerged from Applegate's office. Lucy grabbed Jim Lamont, a junior wizard, as he hurried past.

"What's going on?" she asked.

"Troll attack in West Hollywood," Jim said. "They've called out half the office to deal with it."

Twylan glanced at Jackie. "Should we go?"

"They've already got half the office. They don't need us too."

"Surely it's better to have more people?"

"Then what happens if another emergency comes up?" Jackie shook her head and picked up her coffee cup. "If they need us, they'll call us. For now, it's time to get caffeinated."

They headed to the break room, which was still in top condition after a recent redecoration. Jackie and Twylan got coffees from a shiny new machine while Lucy brewed herself a cup of tea.

"Nearly fifteen years over here, and you're still acting

like one of the invaders." Jackie shook her head. "Maybe we should take you up to Boston and drop you in the water."

"Maybe I should start taxing you without representation, a dollar for each stupid comment about my Englishness, and no place in Parliament for you."

The *clack* of high heels announced Kelly Petrie approaching the break room. Lucy fished her teabag out of her mug and added milk, hoping to get out before Kelly arrived, but she wasn't quite quick enough. Her least favorite agent walked in, dressed in a tailored suit, perfect makeup, and a look like she'd stepped in something unpleasant.

"Oh good, you're here," Kelly said. "Mr. Applegate said you were around."

"Which of us was that directed at?" Lucy asked. "It's hard to tell past the sneer."

"I need to talk to both of you." Kelly ignored both Lucy's comment and Twylan's presence. "I have to ask..." She grimaced. "...a favor."

"You do it with such good grace," Jackie said. "How could we possibly refuse?"

"It's not for me," Kelly said as more footsteps approached down the corridor. "It's for my husband."

Max Petrie walked in, dressed as smartly as Kelly, but without the superior sneer. In his presence, something shifted in the atmosphere. Kelly became less uptight, and Lucy felt more forgiving. If a guy as nice as Max loved Kelly, she couldn't be as bad as she seemed.

"Hi Max, how are you doing?" Lucy asked. "Haven't seen you at the dining room business meetings lately."

Max chuckled. "Sadly, no. Corporate work has kept me

busy, but I'll be back with the guys soon, I promise, and not only for the sake of your cookies."

Lucy had seen a lot of unlikely things in the past year, from a smog monster to a knightly order to a creature of nightmare stalking people's dreams. Out of it all, the part that had most caught her by surprise was her husband teaming up with Max and the disreputable bounty hunter Ringo Fuller to form their own company. Not that she objected, especially given their environmentally friendly work, but it still felt more than a little unreal.

"It'll be good to have you back," she said. "If corporate work is keeping you busy, what brings you here?"

"Nuada Industries."

"You have a case against them?"

"Quite the opposite." Max gestured at a table in the middle of the room. "Shall we?"

While Kelly fetched coffee for herself and her husband, the rest of them sat at the table. Max opened a folder and spread paperwork out across the surface.

"Obviously, this isn't my full case file," he said. "Client confidentiality means a lot, even in the magical world. Heck, especially in the magical world. When the opposing firm has scrying lawyers, it's all the more important to put your paperwork away. Still, this will give you some idea of what I'm dealing with."

The witches looked at the papers he'd put out. There were legal contracts, photos of factories, and diagrams that might have meant something to Lucy if she'd paid more attention in high school chemistry class instead of wishing she was in art or English.

"Pretend for a minute that we're not all lawyers," Jackie said. "What is this mess?"

"It's a court case, one worth a lot of money, and is due to reach court in the next few days. Because of a reorganization in my firm, it landed on my desk on short notice." Max shook his head. "Very short notice."

"What's it about?"

"You've heard of Nuada Industries, right?"

"Met them today, but I have no clue what they do."

"Seriously?"

"Seriously."

Max looked at Lucy. "You know about them, right?"

"Should I?"

"Well, Charlie's really into magical tech, so I figured he must have talked about them."

"Possibly." Lucy blushed. "I have to admit, sometimes what he's talking about stops making sense to me, and I zone out a bit."

"I know that feeling." Kelly squeezed her husband's shoulder, then set a cup of coffee in front of him. "Assume for a moment, honey, that not everyone you meet lives in the intersection of technology, law, and environmental salvation."

Max laughed. "Okay, that's fair. So, Nuada's a big deal in magical tech. They've been around for years in various incarnations, but the current name and corporate structure is relatively new. They made a lot of their money in the past by working in lights: bulbs, fittings, research into better filaments, things like that.

"Recently, they've taken a few steps sideways. Making

headlights led them into car electronics, led to self-driving and electric vehicles, led to an interest in green tech. Now they have a new division that's flipped their position around, from turning power into light to turning light into power."

"They're making solar panels?" Twylan asked.

"Exactly! Great to see that everyone around here's so smart."

Twylan blushed and focused on her coffee.

"Now I see why this would be Charlie's bag," Lucy said. "Where does the court case come in?"

"Nuada has a competitor, Leader Luminosity. They both front as mundane companies while using magic in the background of their tech. Kind of like the changes Charlie and Ringo make to clean up the fumes from cars. To a casual observer, it's a normal vehicle, but under the hood, there are all sorts of spells and runes. In this case, they're used to make solar panels more efficient, among other things."

"This is making me feel better about helping them."

"That's exactly what I want to hear because Nuada needs your help."

A pigeon fluttered in and landed on Kelly's shoulder. She frowned at it.

"Really, now?"

She untied the message from the pigeon's leg and read it. As she reached the end, the slip of paper turned into a handful of worms, which she dropped onto the table with a look of disgust.

"They want me down at this troll thing." She took a napkin off the counter and wiped her hand. "Max, sweetie, don't forget to pick up the kids from soccer practice. I love you, and I'll see you at home."

Without even a word to the others, she headed out the door.

Max shuffled his papers around to get them out from under the worms. The pigeon hopped onto the table and started pecking away, gobbling up its wriggling reward.

"Why does Nuada need our help?" Lucy asked.

"Because Leader Luminosity has been cheating." Max slid one sheet out from the rest. It was the front of a submission to a magical court, and it had a long list of charges. "Infringing on intellectual property, undertaking monopolistic practices, fraud, slander, intimidation, pretty much any dirty trick they can think of. We'll never be able to prove all of it, but if we can prove a decent part, we can force them to back off."

"I still don't see how we can help."

"Two things. First, the Griffins must have information about Leader Luminosity. No magical organization can exist for long without running into you folks. I'd like to see what you have in your archive."

"You're in luck. We wouldn't do that normally, but we've just been told to help Nuada however we can. Though that begs another question: why couldn't Kelly sort this out?"

"It would look shady legally, using my wife as my contact here. Also, there's the second thing, where you'll have insight she doesn't. I believe that you know Leader Luminosity's lawyer, Gruffbar Steelstrike. I'd like you to tell me everything you can about him."

"Of course, Gruffbar's their lawyer. Who else would a

shady company turn to?" Lucy got out of her seat. "Let's head to the archives. I can dish the dirt on Gruffbar on the way down." She picked up her tea, then looked at Jackie and Twylan. "This won't need three of us. Can you write up the great Willen dog chase, and I'll catch up with you in a bit?"

"Ha!" Jackie said. "She acts so helpful, but it's all a ruse to get out of paperwork. Shameful, Agent Heron."

Lucy shrugged. "What can I say? I'm a monster. A terrible, colonial monster that's coming for your taxes."

"Huh?" Max looked confused.

"Never mind. Let's go nose around in the archives."

When Lucy and Max were gone, Jackie turned back to the coffee machine.

"Gonna need more fuel if I'm stuck doing the paperwork," she said. "You want another?"

"I'm okay, thanks," Twylan replied. "Does it seem odd to you that this Nuada company is suddenly turning up everywhere?"

Jackie shook her head. "Seen it before. A big company decides to set up shop in LA, or a small company gets big. Suddenly, all their messy business goes from a minor distraction to something we have to deal with right now. Give it a month, and they'll be background noise again.

"The only odd thing is Uncle Harold being cool with it. Guess he's going soft in his old age if he's happy to see the Griffins work with big business."

She turned to Twylan with an apologetic look.

"Sorry, kiddo. Looks like today's going to be a dull one, all politics and admin. How's your typing? Only I hate filling in report forms..."

CHAPTER FOUR

The elevator stopped at the twenty-fifth floor of the Nuada Industries building. Instead of the bright *bing* that sounded on most floors, there was a soft, expectant *click*, and a pad next to the door lit up.

Halldora Helmsguard pressed her hand against the sensor, and light beams started crisscrossing the palm of her hand. She was particularly proud of this part of the security array. It was good, modern dwarf craftsmanship, seamlessly melding magic, technology, and a touch of subterfuge.

On the surface it was only a palm scanner, relying on a physical print to let people pass. Underneath, the device also read the target's magical aura, creating both an extra layer of security and an opportunity to learn more about visitors. They'd learned the powers of several competitors through these devices, then turned those powers against them.

Now came the *bing* and the doors slid open. Halldora

stepped into Finn Nuada's office. The CEO stood at the window, an elegant figure in a white suit, looking out possessively across the city. Elethin Tannerin sat in a chair close to his desk, one leg artfully crossed over the other like they were an advertisement she wanted the whole world to see.

Another chair sat empty close to her, but Halldora didn't sit. Instead, she stood behind the chair, stiff-back at attention. Old habits died hard. Military habits died hardest of all.

"Well?" Finn didn't look around, but while his tone was casual, Halldora understood how serious his inquiry was. "How did it go?"

"Close to perfect," Halldora replied. "The Griffins have no idea that we hired the Willens and no way of finding out. As far as they're concerned, a bit of L.A.'s wild magical mess crashed into our office, and they had to clear it out. Agent Heron was particularly apologetic on the drive to Griffith, talking about how they'd hoped to avoid disrupting anyone's day."

"We made ourselves helpful?"

"Yes, sir. Helpful enough to create a good impression without overdoing it. Your idea about asking after the dogs was a particularly nice touch."

Finn turned his head slightly, and she saw the edge of his smile, perfect teeth gleaming. "It was, wasn't it? Remind me again, why did we arrange things so they had to clear up a mess for us, instead of us going in and doing something for them?"

"It's the psychology of the thing," Elethin said. "If you've helped someone out, you tend to like them more."

"Seems counterintuitive. Shouldn't they like people who help them?"

"I could explain the theory behind it if you want, Finn, or we could get on with work."

"That's what I like about you two, always ready to get down to business."

Finn turned to face them, his face illuminated from within. That was something Halldora could never quite get used to, however long she worked for him. It was one thing to know that her commander was pure elemental power, another to see it radiating from him in the moments when his guard was down.

"The other thing I like is how well you work together. Who else could have combined security and PR thinking so seamlessly? You're a perfect team."

Halldora didn't look at Elethin, who didn't look at her. It was easier to hide the hostility that way and much easier for both of them if the boss kept assuming that they got along.

"Thank you, sir," Halldora said. "I'll pass on your compliments to the rest of this morning's team."

"Of course, of course. Now, what's next in our conquest of L.A.?"

Elethin tapped a slender tablet and scrolled down a list.

"You have a public appearance at an orphanage this afternoon. We're providing solar panels and science education for the children. Local press will be along, of course, and some of the tech magazines. It's possible we might get some national coverage too. My friend at CNN has been very helpful lately."

Halldora stifled a comment about how helpful that

friend had been and why. Maybe Elethin was sleeping her way to success, perhaps she was just flirting her way there, but however distasteful Halldora found it, that work was paying off for their side, and she had no reasonable cause to complain. Still, she shifted a little farther away as the elf continued.

"Tomorrow should be the trip to the Silver Griffins' headquarters. That won't be so good for broad publicity, but it's crucial in the magical community. The Griffins have saved L.A. from several disasters recently, and they're generally well-liked and respected within the city."

"Really?" Finn laughed. "I suppose they have to be popular somewhere."

"Of course, that one's not only about the publicity. We need to reinforce our positive relationship. The court case will help, and we've already started building up that line, but I want you to meet as many of the Griffins as possible. Turn on the charm. Use their names. Show them you care."

"I know how to do my job, Elethin."

On the surface, his voice was still warm, but there was a firmness behind it. Elethin shrank back into her seat, and those oh-so-elegant legs pulled tighter together. Halldora smiled inside at her rival's discomfort.

"Of course, Finn, I didn't mean to--"

"It's fine." He settled into his seat behind the desk and steepled his fingers. "Now, let's talk about the real battles. Where are we at on the court case?"

The tiniest flicker of a frown crossed Elethin's face at the suggestion that her efforts weren't the real deal. By now, Halldora was struggling to keep her smirk inside.

"Our original lawyer started asking some awkward

questions," Halldora said. "We arranged a disruption at his company, and they transferred the case."

"Won't that set us back in case prep?"

"Not to our detriment. The new lawyer, Petrie, is as experienced as they get in our little niche. I've given him all the evidence we created and not enough time to find the holes. The case will be over before he has cause to get ethical qualms, but perhaps next time we could use a less reputable firm, someone whose lawyers aren't so firmly wedded to the truth?"

Nuada looked at Halldora, and it was her turn to shrink back a little.

"You know that won't do," he said. "We have to shine."

As if to make his point, the glow from his face intensified until Halldora, whose eyes had developed in the shadow world of a dwarf mine, had to look away to stop the pain.

"How is the PR side of the case shaping up?" he asked.

"I've planted stories in the local press and some of the appropriate discussion groups," Elethin said. "Judging by our incoming inquiries, some of the big outlets are starting to take an interest. You know how they love a battle between tech companies, that whiff of wealth and scandal. By the time you get into court, we'll have all the attention we want."

"I will appear in court? This Petrie isn't going to change that?"

"Even if he doesn't call you as a witness, the other side will. The truth will have its day."

"Excellent. I love it when the truth shines bright. Our parts of it, of course." The glow of Finn's face faded a little as he brought himself back under control. "You've done shining work, Ms. Tannerin. We're making exactly the sort of dazzling display I hoped for."

"Thank you, Finn."

"Now I need to talk with Ms. Helmsguard. Alone."

Elethin's face stiffened, but she had too much self-control to let her disappointment show.

"Of course, Finn."

Those legs unfolded, then her ridiculously impractical heels *clacked* across the floor. Doors opened, then she stepped into the shadows of the elevator and was whisked away. As she'd hidden her discomforts and disappointments, Halldora hid her smug satisfaction again. It was enough to know that she was the one doing the real work, the soldier in the field, the general rallying Finn Nuada's forces. It wouldn't be professional to gloat.

"Now that Leader Luminosity's well in hand, we need to move on to the others," he said. "You have a plan of campaign?"

"Yes, sir."

"If you won't sit, at least stand at ease, Ms. Helmsguard. You're not on parade."

"Yes, sir." Embarrassed, she clasped her hands behind her back and set her feet apart. She knew that she didn't fit in here, and in many ways, she took pride in that, but she wished that her commander could take more pride in her.

"You've identified our key targets?"

"Yes, sir. A dozen leading companies in L.A. whose interests intersect with ours, whether it's lighting, solar power, or magi-tech."

"No small fry. I don't want you chasing after three-man

businesses working out of some suburban dining room. Those wannabes can waste their own time, at least until they're big enough for me to care."

"Yes, sir. These twelve are all significant players. If we can take them over or shut them down, we'll be without peers."

"Good. And the strategy? Espionage, sabotage, some unfortunate accidents for them and their customers?"

"Best if you don't know, sir. Plausible deniability."

"Ever the professional, Ms. Helmsguard. I like that you protect me like this."

"Thank you, sir."

"Remember, no need to pull your punches. Nothing turns people off a brand like a disabled kid."

"Of course, sir."

"You'll want the services of the boys?"

"Yes, sir. If I could."

"Of course."

Finn Nuada drew a deep breath, and Halldora hastily closed her eyes. Even with them squeezed tight shut, the light was so bright that dots danced across her vision long after the moment had passed, and she opened her eyes again.

A dozen men stood in the room, all with skin as luminous as Finn's and features much like his. Their suits were black instead of white. No one else was allowed to match his brightness.

"Boys, you'll be working for Ms. Helmsguard again. Go down to the second-floor security room, and she'll brief you there."

Without a word, the men walked over to the elevator

and formed an orderly queue. As its doors opened and the first three stepped in, the elevator's shadows vanished, banished by their light.

"Thank you, sir," Halldora said. "I won't let you down."

"I hope not." Finn smiled brightly. "You may go."

Halldora joined the queue of shining men. She was about to step into the elevator when her commander called from behind her.

"Remember, Ms. Helmsguard, disabled kids. The press loves disabled kids."

CHAPTER FIVE

"I'm home!" Lucy called as she walked through the front door.

Buddy rushed out to meet her, his paws pattering against the hallway floor. He jumped up and down, then stopped to sniff her, catching the scent of other dogs. There was a long moment of hesitation as he tried to work out what this meant, then a return to barking and jumping. The last of his humans was home, and that was all that mattered.

The smells of food drifted out of the kitchen. Tomato sauce, maybe, and something that smelled a little charred. That didn't alarm Lucy. She had faith in Charlie's culinary abilities. If her husband had burned something in the kitchen, it would be deliberate, like charring the skins off peppers. Even their day-to-day dinners were tasty.

She put her backpack down under the table in the hallway and walked through to the living room. To her surprise, Charlie was sitting on the sofa, with his laptop perched on his knees. Three-year-old Eddie, their youngest kid, sat curled up next to him, his hair in disarray and his eyes half-closed as he watched cartoon characters punch and quip their way through a rainbow-colored adventure. On the floor, Ashley, the eight-year-old girl genius, was disassembling an electronic device that looked familiar, but Lucy couldn't quite identify.

"Hi guys," Lucy said. "How's everybody doing?"

Eddie gave a half-hearted wave and curled in closer to Charlie.

"Somebody's had a busy day," Charlie said, wrapping his arm around the little boy. "First an outing with the nursery, then a solid hour of practicing shape-changing. Isn't that right, buddy?"

Buddy the dachshund, thinking he'd heard his name, came around to look up at Charlie expectantly, his tongue hanging out.

"Sorry, not you, Buddy," Charlie said, leaning forward to pat the dog's head. "This little guy. Why don't you tell Mommy what you did?"

"I was a dog," Eddie said. "And a cat and a pig and a monkey and a snake and a... and a... and some things."

"All at once?" Lucy asked.

"Silly mommy." Eddie shook his head. "Can't be a cat and a snake."

"Have you tried?"

Eddie sat up, blinking and trying to think that one through. The possibilities for mismatched animal parts were clearly racing through his tiny mind.

"We'll regret that later," Charlie said.

"Maybe. Or maybe the thought will keep him distracted from changing at the dinner table. Speaking of which, how come you're in here and not slaving over the stove like a good little housewife?"

"Dylan's cooking dinner."

"Dylan? Does he know how to cook?"

"You raised them all as bakers, remember, so he's pretty confident in that space. Plus they've been doing some cooking at school, so now he's got the idea firmly in his head."

"What's he cooking?"

"He wouldn't tell me. Said that he wanted it to be a surprise."

"Okay..."

Charlie grinned. "I can hear the fear in your voice."

"It's no judgment on Dylan. I just..."

"You're very attached to your kitchen, and now there's a twelve-year-old causing chaos in there."

"I'm not being overly possessive, am I?"

"You didn't object when I called it your kitchen instead of ours."

"Oh." Lucy shook her head and smiled. "All right, I need to let this one go. I'm not even going to set foot in there. If Dylan wants a chance to cook, we should let him. It's very helpful."

"You know you can't see through the dining room into the kitchen from where you're standing, right?"

Lucy brought her head back in from trying to peer around the door.

"Fine." She sat on the sofa, gave Charlie a quick kiss, and nestled in next to him. It wasn't all bad, having someone else cook the dinner for her. Not bad at all.

On the carpet, Ashley finished dismantling and

reassembling her device. She turned and held it up for her parents to see.

"Look, Dad, I've halved the size of my portable N64."

"That's great, Ashley. Now what are you going to do with it?"

"Disassemble it again so I can show the process on my YouTube channel."

A *clang* rang through the house as something metal hit the kitchen floor. Lucy jerked to her feet.

"If he needs you, he can call for you." Charlie tugged on the back of her jeans. "Let him make his mistakes. It's the best way to learn."

"I know, I know, I just..."

Lucy sat back down and drew a deep breath. She wouldn't have worried half this much if Dylan had wanted to paint his bedroom or replant part of the garden, but this was the kitchen, and she knew she could help him, and...

No, Charlie was right. She needed to let it go.

On his side of the sofa, Eddie pulled a face. The air around him shimmered. A moment later, the little boy was replaced by a cat, then a snake, then a cat again, his body flickering between the two.

"Careful, sweetheart," Lucy said. "You don't want to strain something."

Dylan appeared in the doorway, wearing an apron covered in flour and red stains.

"Dinner's ready," he announced with pride.

"Brilliant." Lucy leaped up from her seat and kissed him on the top of the head. "Thank you so much for this. It's great of you to help out."

She walked past him into the dining room, peering

around in curiosity. Through the hatch in the kitchen, flour covered half the counters, and the sink was piled high with dirty dishes, but she wasn't going to worry about that. Definitely not. Instead, she focused on the dining table, where three large pizzas lay on wooden chopping boards. The bases were misshapen, the sauce lumpy, and the cheese unevenly spread, but there was no denying what Dylan had made.

"This looks delicious." Lucy ignored the burnt smell that drifted in from the kitchen.

"That one's pepperoni," Dylan said. "That's mushroom, and there's a vegetable one at the far end. Help yourselves."

"Fantastic."

The family took their seats, and Lucy took up the pizza cutter. The top of the vegetable pizza gave way with surprising ease, while the bottom was brittle and took pressure to break through, but she told herself it would be all right.

"Eddie," Charlie said as a cat sat up in the youngest Heron's seat. "You know the rules. Please turn back into a boy."

The cat waved a paw as if trying to make some point, but none of them could understand.

"Now, please."

The air around the cat shimmered, and Eddie reappeared, legs dangling from his chair.

"Rules say no changing at the table," he said. "I wasn't going to."

"The rules say no magic at the table, and being an animal is your magic."

"But..."

"No buts. Here's some pizza. Why don't you give it a go? It has cheese on it, your favorite."

Eddie took a bite, frowned, then shook his head. "Want cat food."

Charlie and Lucy exchanged an amused look. They'd been through this "I am the animal, I want its food" routine before, and it wouldn't last long. Hunger could trump any game for Eddie's attention.

Lucy took a bite of her pizza and immediately decided that Eddie might have a point. The bottom of the crust was burned to hard blackness, the top somehow damp and undercooked. The sauce had too much sugar and more chili than she looked for in a pizza. Still, Dylan had made an effort, so she smiled and took another bite. She wasn't sure what vegetable was in that mouthful, but it was overcooked.

"Mm," Charlie said. "That sure is some pizza."

He swallowed a mouthful without properly chewing it, then took another bite.

"I'm really proud of how much work you put into this." Lucy smiled at Dylan.

"Thanks, Mom. I didn't have a teacher to help me this time, but it all came out okay, right?"

"Are there supposed to be holes?" Ashley prodded a gap in her slice. "That seems like a flaw in the structural integrity."

"There'll be plenty more holes once you start chewing it," Charlie pointed out.

"I suppose."

Looking relieved, Dylan himself finally took a bite from his slice. He frowned.

"That's not how it tasted at school." He took another bite, then set that slice aside and reached for the mushroom pizza. The whole family watched as he took another uncertain bite. "That's not right either."

He turned the slice over. The bottom was black. A slice of mushroom fell onto his plate with a soft *splat*.

"Maybe you had a different recipe there," Lucy said.

Dylan shook his head. "I followed the same recipe." He hesitated, then looked at her. "Except I was trying to do it from memory, so maybe I got something a bit wrong."

"I wouldn't say wrong, sweetheart. Things don't always work out perfectly the first time. Especially not the first time we do them by ourselves."

"Thanks, Mom." Dylan sighed and pushed the plate away. "This is awful."

"You're right," Ashley said. "But I thought this was one of those times where we all have to lie, like when Daddy—"

"Let's not worry about when we do and don't lie," Lucy said. "Which we mostly don't. The important thing is that Dylan tried to do something nice, and it didn't work out. We should all still appreciate his good intentions."

"What will we eat?" Dylan's cheeks blazed with embarrassment. "This pizza's inedible."

"But these aren't." Charlie grabbed a takeout menu off a nearby shelf and waved it. "What does everybody want?"

"Wait." Lucy got out of her seat and took out her phone. "If it's all right with Dylan, I'd like to get a photo of this moment. It might not have worked out like he wanted, but it was a heroic effort."

Dylan laughed. "Okay, Mom, you can add it to the wall."

They all glanced over at the display case Lucy and

Charlie had made, full of family photos and souvenirs. Then they gathered at one end of the table, Dylan holding up a charred slice of pizza.

"Everybody say cheese," Lucy said.

"Burnt cheese," the Herons called, smiling together for the camera.

CHAPTER SIX

"How do I look?" Ellis straightened his tie.

"The same as always" Sarah smiled at him across the restaurant table. "Utterly charming."

She leaned forward and kissed him. Ellis seemed more tense than usual, but she didn't want to comment on it, in case that made him tense up even further. She was pretty sure it had to do with the woman they were waiting for, but even asking about that seemed likely to make things worse.

Instead, she sat back and straightened the skirt of her floral sundress. It was a warm L.A. evening, and she was glad of the opportunity to get the dress out. Amazingly, Ellis was in his usual suit, red tie, and matching sneakers, with no concession to the weather at all. Habits could be a hard thing to break.

"You know, now you're living in one place, maybe you could have different outfits," she said. "Get a wardrobe to fill a corner of that big empty bedroom."

"You don't like my look?"

"I love your look. It's distinctive and very dapper."

"You sound like you're describing a character from a British costume drama."

Sarah laughed. "Guess I've been hanging out with Lucy too much again."

"Is this gonna happen to me now I'm working with her? Lose the accent as well as the tie?"

"Honey, I think you're safe. Those Yorkshire vowels don't stand a chance against a Texas twang."

"Glad to hear it."

The waiter appeared and set a bottle of *sake* down on the table.

"For three, yes?" he asked.

"That's right. Our friend is just..." Ellis looked past the waiter. "Well, she's here right now."

"Then I'll leave you to it." The waiter smiled and backed away.

Margaret Sunder strode up to the table. She was dressed in a carefully cut suit and a white blouse, with pearls around her neck. As Sarah stood, the older witch fixed her with piercing eyes.

"Director Sunder, this is Sarah Smith," Ellis said. "Sarah, this is Director Sunder."

"You can call me Margaret." Sunder shook Sarah's hand. "As can you, Ellis, given the circumstances. Director feels more than a little too formal for this."

She gestured around them at the brick walls and wooden furniture of the hip, informal Japanese restaurant. Ellis looked around, and Sarah caught the doubt in his eyes, the fear that he'd picked badly.

"Lovely place, isn't it?" Sarah said as she and Sunder sat

next to each other. "Tsubaki's one of my favorite restaurants in L.A."

"It's charming," Margaret said. "Far nicer than some of the places I've passed on Sunset. I have high hopes for the food."

"Ellis didn't know if you liked *sake*, but I thought—"

"When in Los Angeles, do as the Japanese do." Sunder gave a small smile, picked up the bottle, and poured for the three of them, then raised her cup in a toast. "Here's to seeing you again, Ellis, and to your new position in L.A."

They all sipped. Under the table, Sarah rested her feet against Ellis's, reassuring him.

"About that..." Ellis looked down at his tightly clenched fingers. "I'd understand if you were still disappointed at me leaving the security division. I mean, you supported me since I joined the Griffins, and I've come a mighty long way thanks to you. I guess I wanted to say that I'm sorry if..."

"Nonsense." Sunder gave a brisk shake of her head. "You'd learned everything you could in that position and were well due a chance to expand your horizons. I'm glad that this charming young lady gave you the motivation to make that leap."

"Really?"

"Really. Now, let's order some food. I've been stuck in meetings all day, and nothing builds up hunger like resisting the corporate snack tray."

By the time they'd chosen and placed their order, Ellis looked a lot more relaxed. He smiled at Sarah, who smiled back at him, then turned to Sunder.

"So Margaret, you've known Ellis for over a decade. You must have some good stories about him."

Ellis's face fell. "There's no need to bother her with questions about me."

"Oh, there is." Sunder's smile was small but mischievous. "I'm pleased to find that you've picked a partner who gathers intelligence at the first chance she gets. Informed decisions are important."

"I ain't an enemy agent."

"No, but she still needs to know what she's getting in for." Sunder sipped her *sake*. "Do you remember your second day on the job?"

Ellis put his face in his hands. "Please don't."

"Oh, I think she should hear this one." Sunder turned to Sarah. "On Ellis's first day, he had a run-in with a rogue witch who had been causing trouble around Dallas. He didn't follow procedure, and she got away while his partner had her back turned. When they got back to the office, I reprimanded him in strong terms. I think it's important for recruits to understand what's at stake.

"The next morning, my assistant's phone kept ringing. It was a call from a woman who insisted that she needed to talk to me about Ellis. Eventually, I gave in and took the call, only to receive an earful of criticism from Ellis's irate grandmother."

"Your grandma called your boss to tell her off?" Sarah stared at Ellis, struggling not to burst out laughing as he sat there red-faced.

"Of all the opponents I've faced," Sunder continued, "none was more fearsome than old Mrs. Ellis. She lectured me on what a good boy her grandson was, how hard he had worked to get where he was, and how he'd let the captured witch go because someone was blackmailing her into a life of crime. He got information from her that would let him capture the real criminal behind it all but didn't want the witch to end up in jail too. He'd broken procedure to ensure justice, and because the witch had promised to bring the evidence he needed, but he'd been too scared to tell me."

"You broke the rules on your first day?" Sarah laughed. "You're more of a rebel than I thought."

"He has his moments," Sunder said. "That one was a big risk. I would have fired him, except the fugitive witch walked in at that very moment with evidence that let us shut down a whole people-smuggling ring between Dallas and Oriceran. The boy had done good."

"I still ain't over that day." Ellis shook his head. "Can't believe Grandma called you up like that."

"She was a fearsome woman, and if she were still around, she would be proud of what you've become."

"Thank you, ma'am."

Ellis's eyes sparkled with unshed tears. Sarah reached across the table to squeeze his hand. It felt odd to do that in front of his former boss, but she wasn't going to let that stop her.

"Not ma'am," Sunder said. "Margaret now, remember?"

"You know that ain't ever gonna happen." Ellis smiled. "Habit's too strong. Habit and respect."

At that moment, their food arrived, giving Ellis a moment to compose himself. By the time Sarah had tried a piece of her tofu, he was more like his familiar, relaxed self.

"Did you hear that they caught Ost Van Grinder again?" Sunder asked.

"About time," Ellis said. "It ain't good for anyone, having that guy on the loose."

"Who's Ost Van Grinder?" Sarah asked. Her food was delicious, distractingly so, but she didn't want to miss out on the chance to learn more about Ellis and his work.

"Case from a few years back," Ellis said. "Rogue wizard running a crime gang out of ships off the Atlantic coast. I helped bring him in."

"That would be an understatement." Sunder pointed at Ellis with her chopsticks. "This young man spent ten months infiltrating Van Grinder's operation. He lived undercover, five months of it on a cramped boat being blown around by Atlantic storms.

"He won Van Grinder's trust, broke into his office undetected, and gathered intelligence that let us both build a case and plan an ambush to capture Von Grinder. Then, before he got out, he sabotaged the mystical generator powering half of Van Grinder's systems. We brought that whole gang down thanks to Ellis."

Ellis blushed bright enough to match his tie. "If I'd done a proper job, there wouldn't have been enough of them left to bust him back out."

"Nonsense. You completed a hazardous assignment to the highest standards. You earned that medal."

"Medal?" Sarah stared at Ellis. "You never told me you had a medal!"

He'd also never told her that he'd played the super spy, infiltrating the operations of a criminal mastermind, carrying out break-ins and sabotage, bringing down dangerous men on the high seas. This wasn't like when she had found out about his past marriage. This time she was eager for more details and more stories. Ellis was even more of a hero than she had realized.

"It ain't that big a thing," he said. "Grandma done told me not to show off."

"You think she wouldn't have been telling all her friends about it if she'd still been around to see the president hang a ribbon on her grandson?" Sunder laughed. "She would have been showing off like no one's business, and so should you." She sipped her *sake* and raised a questioning eyebrow at Sarah. "Honestly, if he hasn't been telling you about his achievements, what did draw you to him?"

Now it was Sarah's turn to blush, with her love life suddenly under the microscope of this intimidating stranger.

"He's sweet," she said. "Funny. Kind. One of the most thoughtful men I've ever met."

"Thoughtful I'll accept, but hearing one of my most devious and tenacious field agents described as kind and funny? That might take some getting used to." Sunder raised her cup in Ellis's direction. "Either this woman has transformed you, which I doubt, or you have hidden depths even I didn't realize."

"Guess we've all got our secrets," Ellis said.

"Not for much longer." Sarah grinned at Sunder. "Tell me all about his early years in the Griffins, and please don't spare any awkward detail."

CHAPTER SEVEN

Heather Fields stomped through the tunnels beneath LA, a swarm of fireflies lighting her way. The tunnels were a strange and irregular assortment, from drains to communication connections to secret basements and former speakeasies, and that was just the human-built part. Once you got into the deeper darkness, into the places where magicals had made their own spaces, things could get seriously weird, and in some cases, seriously unstable.

She didn't have to worry about that instability. Her tribe of witches and wizards, the Tolderai, had learned from nature, taking their tunnel-building techniques from ants, worms, and moles. Root-lined shafts of carefully packed dirt made a safe, solid space connecting human spaces to the places that mattered most to Heather.

As she strode down the tunnel, she drew a deep breath, relishing the clean air. She loved working with the Underfoot Brigade, but teenagers were never going to be the most fragrant of company, and cramming them into a concrete tunnel didn't help. Down here, in contrast, the air was as fresh as in a forest. Instead of the musty, smothering smell of the earth, she breathed the scents of flowers, leaves, and fresh water.

Light emerged around a bend. She dismissed the fireflies and stepped into the light, then from there into the open of the forest cave.

The place was exactly as spectacular in reality as in her mind. Perfectly positioned clusters of trees, their leaves running the range from green through silver, gold, and red, were planted across the cave so that their colors created a pleasing patchwork effect. Around their roots grew flowers, bushes, sweet-smelling herbs, and stretches of long grass. A pool bubbled out of the ground in the middle of the cave, and magical lights shone down from a roof of interlaced roots, beneath which birds swooped and sang. Simply standing in the entrance filled Heather with a glow of pride. She and her people had built these places, secret lungs for the city hidden deep under the ground, and with the help of the Underfoot Brigade, they had shaped them into something truly stunning.

Normally, it was the most calming, placid space to step into, one that grounded Heather back in nature after dealing with the sounds and smells of the city, nature's space of safety. This time, as she stepped into the cave, raised voices set her teeth on edge.

"I don't care how good it looks," someone growled. "They don't belong there."

"But the fragrance as well..."

"Are you in charge of this planting? No. So we're doing it my way."

"Even though there's a better way?"

"Don't you tell me what's better..."

Heather strode through the long grass toward the sounds of argument. The last thing she needed was Tolderai tearing into each other, especially down in the forest.

Mackam and Carol were standing in the patch of open ground created by a recently fallen tree. Nature might be perfection, but it wasn't perfectly controlled. The Tolderai let these things happen. Plants weakened and died, fell back to the ground, and fed the ones that followed.

Mackam, wearing a sweat-stained t-shirt and jeans, clutched a saw, which he'd been using to cut the trunk into pieces. They'd be scattered through the forest to decay slowly. His braided gray beard shook as he talked, beads rattling against each other. Facing him across the fallen log, Carol wore a long green velvet skirt, a loose blouse, and no shoes. Her toes sank into the soft ground. She held a basket in which a cluster of flowering plants grew.

Both Tolderai turned to face Heather. Mackam looked annoyed; Carol relieved to have someone else there.

"Heather, can you please talk to Mackam," Carol said. "He's being stubborn again."

"Mackam, stubborn?" Heather raised an eyebrow. "Who could have seen that coming."

"Don't give me your attitude." Mackam waved the saw at her. "You might be my chief, but I bow to no masters, and this space is mine to define."

"No one's telling you what to do, you crazy old bastard. Now tell me what this fuss is about."

Mackam glared. "See, there it is, making demands."

Heather pressed her fingers against her temples. She'd thought that she'd finished dealing with teenage tempers for the day, but perhaps she was wrong. "Do you want to be heard or not?"

Mackam scowled and waved the saw, but apparently, he wanted his say more than he wanted to be defiant.

"Just because she's started selling sketches to big city folks, this little girl thinks she knows better than me how I should lay out a patch of land."

"Don't call me a little girl," Carol said indignantly. "I could beat you senseless if I had to."

"Oh, yeah? You want to settle things that way?" Mackam dropped the saw and shifted into a fighting stance, his hand going to the knife at his waist.

"No, she does not," Heather snapped. "None of us do. We're one tribe, and you will act like it." She drew a deep breath. "Carol, tell me about the sketches."

"Not that it matters to this, but I've sold some pictures at last. Some sketches and prints."

"I thought you'd sold pieces already in that local gift shop back in Alaska?"

"This is different. I've sold them to collectors through Penley's gallery. They're paying ten, twenty, thirty times what I could get before."

"Because of the fashion for Tolderai art?"

"Exactly."

"Congratulations."

"No, not congratulations!" Mackam snapped. "She's drawing more attention."

"How else am I supposed to survive as an artist?"

"By getting a proper job as well!"

"That's great, coming from the man who lives in a shack in the woods, talking to his tin foil friends!"

"Enough!" Heather snapped. "Mackam, you know that things have changed. We're not living in secret like we were. More and more people in the magical world know about us."

"People in a hole shouldn't keep digging down," Mackam said.

"Not everybody thinks this is a bad thing."

"Not everybody has a brain cell in their head."

This was stupid and futile. None of it was bringing Heather any closer to settling the current argument, though it at least helped her to understand what was behind the row. Tensions had been rising among the Tolderai in recent days, as the sudden pressure of public awareness took its toll. Whether or not they liked it, not everyone was adapting well to change.

"What does any of this have to do with this part of the forest?" she asked.

Mackam pointed at Carol. "She thinks she knows better, and now she's using it to tell me how to manage the woods."

"All I said was that we have a chance to make this spot look nicer. That's part of the project here, remember, to find ways to grow woods that will appeal to humans, so they're less likely to chop them down."

"It doesn't sound like she said anything unreasonable, Mackam." Heather wasn't surprised. The older Tolderai was prone to both paranoia and moments of high temper. That was fine as long as she could turn him against an outside target, but there was no one like that now.

"It was the way she said it."

"Okay, well, perhaps, for the sake of peace, Carol could apologize for that."

Heather turned her gaze to Carol and raised her eyebrows, then waited expectantly. This wasn't the first time they'd played the Mackam management game.

"What? No!" Carol folded her arms. "I'm not going to apologize because I've not done anything wrong. You might be spending all your waking hours around children, Heather, but we're not kids, and you can't treat us that way."

Heather took a step back, caught completely off guard. "What are you talking about?"

"Ah, don't give us that," Mackam said. "Everyone knows that's where your mind's at, dealing with those Underfoot kids. That's why you let them come in and help pretty up this place, so you wouldn't have to turn your attention off them and back onto us."

"It is disappointing in a chief," Carol added. The fact that she and Mackam were finally agreeing gave Heather little comfort. "We need you to be focused on the tribe and our needs, especially when we're going through so much change."

A red wave of indignation rose through Heather, making her heart dance to an angry beat and her cheeks flush red. She clenched her fists by her sides.

"I have been focused on the tribe," she snapped. "What do you think I'm doing here now?"

"Now that the school day's over?" Mackam sneered. "Probably filling time while you think about your lesson plans."

"I made this happen." Heather waved, taking in the cave

around them. "I found the tribe new purpose. I rescued our lost artifacts. I arranged for them to be displayed, bringing in money and respect."

"Where were you when Nathaniel started channeling the forest spirits for the first time? Where were you when Godswill and Lister came to blows over the cherry blossom ceremony? Where were you when we were deciding what to do with this here spot that you now want to play judge over?"

Heather strode over to Mackam and grabbed him by the t-shirt. "If you want to challenge me for chief, old man, then stop pissing about and do it."

"I don't want to be chief. I want the chief we've got to do her job."

Heather forced her fist open and let him go. She was as angry at herself as she was at him, and she knew it. But she was in no state to deal with that now.

"This is me doing my job," she said. "Mackam, what gets planted here is your decision, but Carol has earned the right to be heard. So we're going to sit down now, the three of us, and she's going to spend five minutes explaining her idea. At the end, if you don't like it, she won't mention it ever again. Got that, both of you?"

They nodded. "Yes, chief."

Heather let out a long breath, then sat on one of the chunks of fallen tree.

"All right, let's get this done."

CHAPTER EIGHT

Lucy walked through the Silver Griffins' office, her backpack over her shoulder. The bustle of activity around the place wasn't unusual, but something about it seemed off. The office gnomes were polishing furniture instead of fetching and sorting paperwork. The pigeons weren't fluttering back and forth but were magically tethered at one end of the room. Even the other Griffins looked smarter than usual, with shirts ironed, makeup carefully applied, and significantly more neckties than usual.

She reached the cluster of desks that she shared with Jackie and Ellis. At least they weren't any smarter dressed than normal, Ellis because he always wore a suit and tie, Jackie presumably from some stubborn act of resistance. Lucy set her backpack down and pulled out a tub of home-made cookies.

"What's going on?" she asked. "I haven't seen the place this smart since, well, since forever."

"You didn't get the message?" Jackie asked. "We have a celebrity guest."

"Is it one of those elf boy bands? My kids aren't really into them, but they'll still want me to get a selfie."

"Oh, it's better than that," Jackie said, her voice heavy with sarcasm. "We're getting a visit from Finn Nuada."

"As in Nuada Industries?"

"The very same. Only a day since we saved his company from wild Willens, and the man himself is coming in. Do you think we're going to get a special prize?"

"Nuada Industries do make a mighty fine flashlight," Ellis said.

"Seriously?" Jackie raised an eyebrow. "Just how much of a tech nerd do you have to be that you can have a favorite flashlight?"

"Don't knock it. If you're creeping around some criminal's lair, wanting to find the evidence without drawing attention, then a tight beam and good battery life can make all the difference."

"A tight beam and..." Jackie shook her head. "I knew Sarah had lousy taste in men, but seriously, she should see if she can trade you in."

A few feet away, Sam picked up a buzzing phone, made a couple of noncommittal noises, and went into Applegate's office. A moment later, the regional manager strode out, straightening his tie as he went.

"Just keep on with what you're doing," he said, a little too loudly. "But sit up while you do it. The cameras are on their way."

"Looks like the circus is about to start." Jackie shook her head and hunched deliberately over her keyboard. "Let's hope it doesn't last."

The door to reception opened, and a small crowd of

people came in. First were the journalists, a gnome and an elf, both with cameras levitating by their shoulders and microphones in their hands. They walked backward to keep their attention on the other guests. Then came the familiar figures of Director Sunder and Harold Kowal, their every footstep radiating authority. Between them came the man all the fuss was about: Finn Nuada.

After dinner the previous night, Lucy had taken the time to learn a little about Nuada and to appreciate how big a deal he was. The genius magi-tech entrepreneur and philanthropist, the bright rising star of the magical world.

His physical presence matched that reputation, his face beaming not only with a smile but with the light that radiated from it, like sunlight from a summer sky. Even his pale suit seemed to shine, creating a halo around him. No wonder they'd tethered the pigeons. If one had left a deposit on that suit, it would've been a vision no one ever forgot.

More journalists followed, and Elethin Tannerin. The elf looked more comfortable in her PR role than knocking out Willens in the Nuada Industries lobby. She smiled almost as brightly as her boss. Behind her were a pair of pale-skinned men in black suits and wraparound shades, both of similar height and build to Nuada, presumably his bodyguards. Lucy was disappointed not to see Halldora Helmsguard among the security detail. Despite her initial hostility, the dwarf had turned out to be the comforting face of her company.

They stopped just inside the office while Sunder introduced Nuada to Roger Applegate. The regional manager pumped the CEO's hand and talked too loudly while the salamanders on the journalists' cameras flashed, and Elethin held a whispered conversation with Sunder.

"It's a great place you've got here," Finn Nuada said, and though he didn't raise his voice, it somehow filled the room. It helped that everyone except Jackie had stopped working, the better to watch what was going on. "And such vital work that you do. That's part of why I wanted to visit today, to say thank you, and to offer a small token of my appreciation."

He clicked his fingers, and Elethin held up a briefcase, then flipped back the lid. Inside were two orbs, each the size of a golf ball.

"These are two of our latest products," Finn continued. "Neither is on the market yet, but we're donating the first batch off the line to the L.A. Silver Griffins to help you keep the rest of us safe."

That brought a round of applause from around the room.

"Idiots," Jackie muttered. "They don't even know what it is yet."

"Like partners in a perfect marriage, these orbs are complementary opposites," Finn said. "This one will create perfect darkness when you want to stop a criminal seeing what they're doing." He touched one of the orbs, and all the light vanished from the room. Even Jackie's typing stopped as her monitor vanished from view.

"This one produces clear white light." Everyone blinked as the room suddenly illuminated, revealing Finn's finger on the other orb. He tapped it, and the light receded, returning them to the disappointing glow of strip lights. "Equipping every Griffin with these should provide some small assistance in your work and some comfort to my colleagues and me, knowing that you're out there, fighting the good fight."

Again came the applause. By the time it died down, Elethin had handed the case to Applegate, who was gesturing toward a handful of carefully selected employees lined up along the wall. At the front was Kelly Petrie, perfectly turned out and beaming with pride. She glanced for a second at Lucy, in her jeans and Green Lantern t-shirt, then turned her smug expression back to the approaching guests.

Elethin tapped her boss on the shoulder and pointed down the office.

"Uh-oh." Lucy kicked her bag out of sight under the desk. "I think we're about to piss all over Kelly's chips."

"Really?" Jackie looked up, grinning. Then she looked around, and her shoulders slumped as the crowd of visitors walked toward them. "Oh. Great."

"Finn, these are the agents who were so helpful to us yesterday," Elethin said. "Jackie Kowal and Lucy Heron."

"It's a delight to meet you both."

Even Jackie reluctantly got to her feet as Finn held out his hand to shake. As the journalists swarmed around them and Kelly glared from the side of the room, Lucy reached for something familiar, something comforting, something that would help her feel in control.

"Biscuit?" she asked, holding the tub of cookies out to Finn. "They're homemade, oat and chocolate chip."

"Sounds delicious." He took one and took a bite. "Tastes that way too."

Judging by the laughter from the assembled managers

and journalists, this was the height of hilarity, though Lucy wasn't convinced. Going by the small twist of his smile, neither was Finn, and Lucy liked him more for that.

"I'm sorry I wasn't there to thank you personally yesterday," he said. "Sadly, the move to L.A. hasn't left me with a lot of time to spare."

"Moving house is always a pain," Lucy said. "Moving a whole magical business must be ten different sorts of pain wrapped in an agonizing bow."

Finn chuckled, so everybody else did too.

"You're not wrong, Agent Heron." He held up the remaining half of his cookie. "Treats like this help." He looked at Jackie. "I was wondering, if it's all right with your bosses, whether you two could show me around? I feel like we already have a connection."

Lucy glanced past Finn at Applegate, who looked at Harold Kowal, who looked at Margaret Sunder, responsibility passing so fast it could have been a ticking bomb. Sunder gave a small nod.

"Sure," Lucy said. "What do you want to see?"

"Maybe your tech team? I promise not to steal your ideas while I'm there, at least not the good ones."

Again, Sunder gave a small nod.

"Okay, sure. Follow us."

Lucy and Jackie hurried off down a corridor and a stairwell. Finn followed, the journalists and their salamander flashes cutting him off from the agents, the rest of his entourage following behind.

"What's he doing?" Lucy whispered, leaning close to Jackie so no one else would hear. "This is going to drive Applegate bonkers."

"It's a power play," Jackie whispered back. "Getting people to do what he wants on their turf, proving who's in charge."

"And senior Griffins are going along with that?"

"Apparently."

"Weird."

"You're telling me."

They stopped outside the reinforced door of Special Equipment and Weapons.

"This is the lab where our new equipment and spells are designed and tested," Lucy said. "It can be a little chaotic, so please don't judge us by the mess."

"You should see our labs," Finn said. "I like to tell my research teams, you've got to break old things to make parts for the new ones."

"How often do your research teams levitate fruit or summon custard pie imps?"

"Depends. Is today a Tuesday?"

That got another round of laughter. While everyone was in a good mood, Lucy opened the door.

"Jenkins," she called. "We've got a visitor for you."

She rounded the corner into the sound of wailing guitars and the sight of flying llamas, a whole herd of them hurtling around the room. In the middle stood Jenkins and Nigel, waving a glowing net and a tranquilizer gun.

Lucy whipped out her wand and silenced the music so that she could be heard. A tranquilizer dart hit a llama, which fell to the floor with a *thud*.

"One down," Jenkins said. "Twelve worms to go. What happened to the music?"

"Jenkins," Lucy called again, "There's a guest here to meet you."

The researcher turned, pulled back a pair of goggles, and lowered his gun.

"Toliver Jenkins this is—"

"Finn Nuada." Jenkins grinned so wide his face seemed about to split in half. He took one wobbling step toward them, then fainted clean away.

Nigel looked down at him and sighed. "It's the Ginger Spice incident all over again."

CHAPTER NINE

An hour later, Lucy sat with Jenkins in the Special Equipment and Weapons lab. He rested against the wall with an icepack clutched to the back of his head, which he'd hit in his fall. Everyone else was long gone, except for the llamas, which kept drifting around the room, looking very confused.

"I can't believe I met Finn Nuada." Jenkins was still smiling.

"Does it really count as meeting him if you never even said hello?"

"Oh, it counts. A Spice Girl told me so."

"Are you sure you don't have a concussion?"

Jenkins got up, held his arm out in front of him, and waved it back and forth. "Quite sure."

Lucy watched him, still not completely convinced. Surely he should be dying of embarrassment right now. After all, he'd met one of his heroes, and instead of having an insightful conversation, he'd fainted. The journalists had taken photos and asked for Jenkins' details, ensuring his place as a comedy footnote to their articles about the visit. Jenkins didn't care. He'd gone from flat-out fainted to his normal self, his ego completely unbruised, unlike his head.

Nigel emerged from the back room, carrying two cups of coffee, and handed one to Jenkins.

"Thank you." Jenkins sipped. "I needed that."

"Thought you might."

"So we had Finn Nuada in this lab." Both men grinned like kids at Christmas.

"Yes, boss."

"Tell me everything. Did he talk about his new solar panels?"

"I should get going," Lucy said.

"Really?" Jenkins looked baffled. "Don't you want to hear about it all?"

"Thank you, but I've had enough Finn Nuada for one day."

Lucy made her way upstairs. The office was quieter than it had been before, and not only because of the lack of guests and journalists. With Finn's visit over, a lot of agents had left, heading out to deal with the cases they'd been ignoring while they waited to meet him. Jackie was one of the few who had remained, and she was waving to Lucy from the doorway of Applegate's office. Lucy followed her in.

"Thank you for your assistance earlier," Applegate said, once they were both in the room. "And for your work at Nuada Industries. You clearly made a very favorable impression."

"We were only doing our job," Lucy said.

"And doing the Griffins proud. In recognition of your efforts, I'm giving you both the afternoon off."

"Is this so we don't distract people?" Jackie asked. "I bet a lot of Griffins have questions about Nuada."

"That's also a factor," Applegate admitted. "Ironically, this office will function better without two of its top operatives today. Enjoy this moment while it lasts."

Lucy grabbed her backpack from under her desk. Together, she and Jackie headed out of the office, through Griffith Observatory, and down the hidden stairwell to the magical transit station below. The only other person on the platform was Normandy, the gnome station keeper, who was polishing the brass departures board.

"Agents." He nodded at them. "Always a pleasure to see you."

"And you, Normandy." Lucy handed him a small bag of cookies. "Here, I saved you some."

"That's very kind of you, Agent Heron. Thank you."

Jackie looked at him suspiciously. "Did you hear about the visit today?"

"Of course."

"Don't you want to ask us about Finn Nuada?"

Normandy shook his head. "Mr. Nuada and his entourage all drove to Griffith. If they don't have time for trains, I don't have time for them."

"You know, that's not the stupidest thing I've heard all day."

"Was that meant to be a compliment?"

"I don't even know."

"Then thank you, just in case."

A gleaming subway train emerged from the tunnel and

halted, steam hissing from its pistons. The doors slid open, and Jackie and Lucy got on board.

"Did you think today was odd?" Jackie asked as the train rattled through the darkness under L.A.

"Did you think any part of it wasn't?"

"Fair point. Why is a guy like Finn Nuada so keen to make friends with the Griffins? It's not like we're another business he can take over."

Lucy shrugged. "Maybe he did appreciate our efforts."

"Maybe I'm the undead queen of Arkansas."

"Your majesty." Lucy gave a little bow.

The train pulled into a station, and they both got out.

"Even your Uncle Harold has decided that this Nuada lad's sound," Lucy said as they climbed the spiraling stairs up from the station. "Let's not go looking for problems where there aren't any."

"I guess," Jackie said. "Cramps have probably put me in a shitty mood."

"Good thing we have an afternoon off then."

"Yeah, maybe." Jackie grinned. "I was looking forward to taking my pain out on criminals."

They emerged through a magical doorway into the back room of a Starbucks. A staff member was mopping the floor, but he didn't notice them, his mind befuddled by the chocolate-scented magical mist hanging around the door.

"You want a lift home?" Lucy asked as they emerged into the sunshine.

"No, I'm parked nearby. You go enjoy your afternoon off."

"You too."

Lucy climbed into her Rivian and headed out through the streets toward Echo Park. It was a beautiful day, and L.A.'s inhabitants were out in force. People strolled idly down the streets, sat at pavement tables outside coffee shops and bars, or stood around on corners. The whole city basked like a lizard on a sun-soaked rock.

That same sunshine gleamed off an unfamiliar car sitting in Lucy's driveway and an all too familiar van in the street. At least Ringo Fuller's vehicle no longer had a gaudy eagle airbrushed on the side. Instead, it bore the name and logo of Green Machine Conversions, Ringo's, Charlie's, and Max's company.

Lucy pulled up behind the van and got out. Al, her gray-haired neighbor, stood at the bottom of his driveway, leaning on a rake and watching as Charlie and Ringo argued over an airbrush and a tin of paint.

"What's going on here?" she asked.

"I was going to ask you the same question," Al said. "Since when does Charlie renovate cars?"

"Oh, a couple of months maybe. It's a new business he's trying to set up with his friends."

She almost started telling Al more but fortunately caught herself in time. She'd gotten into the habit of enthusing about the business to any magical who inquired, as word of mouth made for good marketing. However, Al wasn't a magical, and she couldn't tell him that this paint had magic mixed with it or how it cleaned the pollution out of a car's fumes. It was a shame, but secrecy kept magicals safe. If she'd started blabbing their secrets, she would have had to arrest herself.

"Well, he and his friend aren't much good at it." Al

pointed at smears of paint on the driveway, the lawn, and the car's windshield. "Whoever that car belongs to, they're not going to be pleased."

Lucy took the tub of cookies out of her backpack. There were two left, just enough for her and Al.

"Shouldn't you get involved?" Al asked as he took a cookie.

"No, I'll leave them to argue themselves out. It's easier that way."

They munched on their cookies and chatted about Al's garden until Charlie and Ringo fell quiet. At last, Lucy brushed the crumbs from her fingers.

"That's my cue," she said. "See you later, Al."

She walked up the driveway to where Charlie and Ringo stood with arms crossed, glaring down at their airbrush.

"Afternoon, lads." Lucy kissed her husband on the cheek. "What's going on?"

"It's this thing." Ringo kicked the airbrush. "It's not built right. It's impossible to control the flow properly."

"It's not the airbrush. It's the way you're handling it."

"You would say that."

"Well, you would say—"

"Let's not head down that path." Lucy picked up the airbrush, then looked at the work the men had done so far. It was streaky and uneven and spattered across the too-thin layer of protective tape onto the windows. "This clearly needs an artist's touch."

She turned on the pump on the airbrush, crouched beside an unpainted door of the car, and pressed the trigger. Paint sprayed from the brush onto the surface. It wasn't as fine or accurate a spray as she would have liked, but neither was it unwieldy enough to explain all this mess. She wondered how the guys had got this right on a single car, never mind the whole collection they'd recently revamped. As for the waste of valuable materials in the misapplied magical paint, that didn't bear thinking about, at least not for anyone who'd seen their company's accounts.

With a steady hand, Lucy laid a layer of paint across the door, then moved on around the car's body. It was a satisfying challenge, a fun change from painting with normal brushes, and she was soon humming to herself as she worked. A little while later, Charlie brought her a cup of tea, and when she looked up, she realized that she'd done the whole job.

"Thank you." Charlie kissed her on the top of the head.

"Yeah, that's good work, 485," Ringo said. "Don't suppose you want a job with us?"

"No thanks." Lucy handed him the airbrush. "And we're not done yet."

She looked around, making sure that Al was gone and that none of the other neighbors were looking, then pulled out her wand and cast a quick cleaning spell. Paint vanished from the windows of the car, leaving the perfectly neat job she would've achieved without Charlie's and Ringo's efforts. Lucy smiled with pride as she took in her work.

"What about the paint on the driveway and lawn?" Charlie asked.

"You can clean that up. I'm going inside to put my feet up and draw."

"What about work?"

"They gave me the afternoon off."

"How come?"

"Because Finn Nuada thinks I'm great."

Charlie and Ringo looked at each other, then looked open-mouthed at her.

"You met Finn Nuada?" Ringo asked. "*The* Finn Nuada?"

"Why is everyone so excited about that guy?"

"Tell us more!"

"All right, fine. Come inside, and I'll tell you all about it. But I'm not picking you up if either of you two faints."

CHAPTER TEN

Twylan eased her hands into the dirt around the base of the miniature rose bush, moving carefully to avoid thorn pricks. The roses were like magic, full of potential for both beauty and pain. Perhaps that made them both like life, or perhaps she'd been reading too much poetry lately. Either way, the work was comforting as the soft ground of the Tolderai forest gave way to the pressure of her fingers, and she coaxed the roots loose, then eased the bush out of the ground.

"You're getting good at that." Heather was crouching nearby, overseeing some of the other members of the Underfoot Brigade as they planted seedlings. She wasn't a woman to smile often, but her lips curled up a little now. Twylan didn't know if that was a reflection of her careful gardening or how much Heather enjoyed working with the Underfoots. Either way, Twylan was happy with it.

"Have you dampened the ground in the new spot ready for it to go in?" Heather asked.

"Yes, Ms. Fields."

"Very good. We'll make a Tolderai of you yet."

That really was a compliment. Twylan knew how deeply Heather was attached to her tribe, how fiercely they guarded themselves and their secrets. While "insider good, outsider bad" was one of the most fundamental social instincts, it was particularly strong in the secretive tribe of nature witches and wizards. If they were taking Twylan to heart, then she must be doing well.

She carried the rose bush down the cave, past all the wonders of the half-planted underground forest. Rows of saplings grew a foot every day thanks to Tolderai magic. Earth-moving spells churned up swaths of ground, on which seeds were bursting into tiny green shoots. Overhead, suspended by levitation spells, a hand-picked group of magicals was shaping the ceiling. They encouraged roots and creepers to grow from the dirt and weave themselves together, creating a ceiling as strong as stone.

Twylan reached a spot by the edge of the central irrigation pool. The rose would spend the next week here, where its roots could soak up the freshest flow of magical waters. Then they'd move it out to the edge of the cave, where it would slowly release waters of its own over the next year. These were the details of magical planting that Twylan and Kix had missed when trying to rearrange a cave by themselves, which helped bring the whole thing to life. It was a wonder of nature and of magic, and the longer she spent working on it, the more she felt it shaping her magic, bending her toward the power of nature. Given the results, she was happy with that.

The rose released a tiny cloud of perfume as Twylan lowered it into its new home as if expressing its appreciation for all she'd done. She scooped soil in around it, then gently patted down the dirt. When she stepped back, it was as if the rose had always been there. It was perfectly in place.

Raised voices drew her attention across the pool. On the far bank, two of the Tolderai were arguing, Nathaniel Oakmantle and a wizard with glasses. Nathaniel flung his hands in the air, then stormed away, while the other wizard flung something down in apparent disgust.

Twylan looked away before the wizard could notice her watching. The Underfoots were guests here, and she didn't want to intrude on events among the Tolderai. If their recent tensions made her uncomfortable, it wasn't her place to complain, though she would happily offer a patient ear in the unlikely event that they wanted to talk. Best to pretend that it wasn't happening and encourage the rest of her teenage gang to do the same. Adult business was for adults to sort out.

She walked quickly away from the pool, brushing dirt from her hands onto her skirt as she went. The skirt was dirty already and a hard-worn one that she'd chosen for this work. Kix might turn up each day in a bright new outfit and accept the price of having to clean them all in the Underfoot Brigade's scavenged washing machine, but Twylan was content with a more practical approach.

Back where she'd dug up the rose, the other Underfoots were still planting seedlings. They kept their heads firmly turned down as Nathaniel and Heather got into a heated debate only a dozen feet from them. Leontine and Kix were still working at full speed, resigned to sitting through the row, but some of the younger teens looked agitated and couldn't help looking up as if to ask when the angry exchange would be over.

Twylan braced herself, then walked over to Heather and Nathaniel.

"Excuse me, Ms. Fields?" she said, just loud enough to cut across whatever Nathaniel was saying. "Is our botanical lesson perhaps done for the day? We need to do some maintenance back at our tunnel, and this seems like a good time for it."

Heather glanced from the scowling Nathaniel to the row of teens crouched tensely in the churned dirt. She made a show of looking at the time on her phone.

"You're right, Twylan. We've overrun it already. Thank you all for your help here. You can go now, and I'll see you back in the classroom tomorrow for math."

The Underfoots patted down the dirt around their seedlings, then hurried for the cave mouth, Twylan bringing up the rear. In the mouth of the tunnel, she summoned half a dozen dancing lights, which floated ahead of them, illuminating their path into the darkness.

"What is going on with those guys?" Kix asked as soon as they were safely out of earshot of the forest. "They've gotten as bad as us, constantly sniping at each other and moaning about things that have gone wrong." The little gnome pressed her hands to her cheeks. "OMG, you don't think that we're a bad influence, do you?"

"It's not us," Leontine said. "It's not our problem to fix, and it's not our place to pry." He shrugged his wings, the mechanical one glinting in the magical light. "Just get on with the work and let them get over it."

Twylan half agreed with him. It seemed unlikely that

the Underfoots were responsible for the growing unease among their magical mentors, but that didn't mean they shouldn't help if they somehow could. Not that she had any idea what they might do.

A sound in the tunnel ahead made her stop and pull her lights back.

"Someone's coming," she said.

"So?" Leontine asked.

"What if they're not a magical?"

"All the way down here?"

"You never know."

"I guess." Leontine untied a hoodie from around his waist and pulled it on, covering his folded wings. Then he dug out a flashlight and switched it on. "You lot stay here. Twylan and I will check this out."

Twylan followed the Arpak down the tunnel. As she went, she put on a battered pair of aviator shades that she kept in her coat. They weren't a perfect cover, but if she kept her magic suppressed then it shouldn't leak so far out around her eyes that it became really obvious.

Around a corner, another beam of light appeared, from a brighter flashlight than theirs.

"Hello?" a voice called. "Is there someone else there?"

Twylan and Leontine approached the source of the voice. The beam from Leontine's flashlight illuminated a middle-aged man dressed in sturdy pants and a waterproof jacket. He had a backpack over his shoulders, held an expensive-looking flashlight, and had some sort of electronic device in his free hand. He peered at them from behind a thick-framed pair of glasses.

"Just kids, huh?" The man laughed. "That's a relief. I

thought some other academic might have gotten down here ahead of me and scooped my discovery."

"Your discovery?" Twylan asked.

"The air." The academic waved his gadget around. Figures skipped up and down on its screen. "Surely you've noticed how fresh and clear it is down here? It's affecting the air quality in the neighborhood above. I have no idea what's going on, but if this offers some kind of break-through in ecological studies, I want to make sure I publish first."

"So you're studying these tunnels?" Twylan asked.

"I certainly hope to. But first, I need to demon-strate that there's something worth studying so I can secure funding. Do you have any idea how difficult that is?"

The two teens shook their heads. Academic finances were a million miles from the world they understood.

"Suffice to say that I think this could make my name." The academic waggled his eyebrows. "I need to keep pressing on while the flashlight batteries last."

He started moving past them, but Leontine got in his way. "You can't go down there," the Arpak said.

"Why ever not?"

"Private property."

"Really. Whose?"

"Friends of ours."

"I find that unlikely. Now please, young man, get out of my way."

The academic tried to step past Leontine, who once again moved into his way. They started scuffling, shoving and grabbing each other, but Leontine was far stronger. He pushed the academic, who stumbled into Twylan. Her shades fell into the dirt.

"Your eyes!" The academic stared at her in amazement. "What's happening?"

Twylan sighed. She hadn't wanted to do this, but what options did she have left? She pulled out her wand.

"Never was, never will be."

There was a wave of magic, and the academic's face fell blank. He stood with slumped shoulders, gazing vacantly at the wall.

"The Griffins taught you 'never was' already?" Leontine gaped at Twylan.

"Not exactly, but I've been hanging around with them a lot, picking up bits of knowledge here and there."

"Bits of knowledge? This isn't one of Siltor's illusions. It could help hugely in keeping us safe."

"I know. I wasn't sure I should use it."

"Too late to worry about that now. You've done it, whether you should or not."

"We should sort him out." Twylan turned the academic around and started walking him up the tunnel. "I'll plant a suggestion before it wears off, convince him that he ran into a dead end. That way, he shouldn't come down here again." She took the measuring device out of his hand. "We'd better hang onto this too, just in case."

"What if others come down here, looking for the source of the fresh air?"

"Then the Tolderai will have to decide how to deal with them, but do you want to tell Heather that now?"

Leontine thought back to the atmosphere in the cave, then shook his head. "One problem at a time."

CHAPTER ELEVEN

Lucy walked into the kitchen to find the faucet running and water flowing out of the sink, down the front of the cupboard, and across the floor. Immediately, she had flashbacks to earlier in the year, when rustroaches had ruined her precious kitchen by chewing through the pipes. She pulled out her wand and cast a spell, stopping the flow of water before she was halfway across the room.

As she approached the sink, something rose from the surface of the water, like a slender tentacle with a glowing light dangling from its tip. Wand still raised, she moved closer and peered into the water. There lay the ugliest fish she had ever seen. It looked like a single malformed head, with milky eyes, a massive mouth full of pointy teeth, and slender fins trailing off the back. The light-bearing tentacle seemed to emerge from between its eyes. It peered up at Lucy, then waved the light.

Realization seeped across Lucy's mind like the water seeping across the floor.

"Eddie?" she said. "Is that you?"

The tentacle waved again, and the fish gnashed its teeth.

"Could you get out of the sink, please?"

The fish waved its fins, demonstrating how little it could do to get out.

"Then turn back into a boy first."

The fish looked away from her.

"Now, please."

The air shimmered. There was a splash of water running down the front of the cupboard, and Eddie Heron stood in the sink, water soaking his pants and socks.

"What on earth was that?" Lucy lifted him out and deposited him on the floor.

"Angler fish," Eddie said. "It makes light."

"So I saw. It also makes a mess." She pulled the plug from the sink, then grabbed a handful of tea towels and started mopping up. "Can you please go straight to your room and change into something dry."

"Okay."

Eddie hurried off. He'd heard that tone of voice before, and he knew better than to delay or disobey.

By the time Lucy finished clearing up the mess, Eddie was back, dry and grinning.

"Look, Mommy, I'm a firefly."

The air shimmered, and a glowing bug appeared where Lucy's son had been. Then there was another shimmer, and the boy reappeared.

"You're all about the light-emitting animals today, huh?" Lucy said.

Eddie nodded. "Making light is cool. Look, I'm a glow-worm."

Again the shimmer in the air and the transformation.

This time, a larval insect lay on the ground, trailing glowing threads.

Buddy wandered in and sniffed at the glowing thing on the floor, which promptly turned back into a giggling Eddie.

"How about we do something different?" Lucy said. "Like maybe some baking?"

Eddie clapped. "Glowing cake!"

"I'm not sure I have a recipe for that, but how about an orange polenta cake? It has nice warm, light colors."

"Yes." Eddie grabbed his apron off the back of the kitchen door. "Lenta cake."

"Polenta." Lucy emphasized the first syllable.

"Lenta."

"Polenta."

"Lenta."

"You know what, never mind."

While Eddie washed his hands, Lucy measured out the dried polenta onto a baking sheet and put it into the oven to roast. A warm, comforting smell filled the kitchen as she fetched out the other ingredients and set up the battered little table on which Eddie would work.

"Do you want to use the grater?" Lucy held up the tool and two oranges.

Eddie considered this. He had hurt himself on the grater once, but scraping the zest off fruit was fun, and he didn't want to let a little hurt stand in his way. He nodded, took the grater, and started carefully scraping the orange down it.

Lucy took the toasted polenta out of the oven and tipped it into a bowl. There was a little time for it to cool while Eddie did his best with the oranges. Lucy took a moment to watch with a smile as her son worked with endearing seriousness.

"Here you go," she said, putting the bowl in front of him. "You've done such a great job with the oranges. Now can you add the zest to the polenta?"

Eddie dutifully tipped the orange scrapings in.

"Brilliant. Mix this milk in too." Lucy handed him a half-full measuring cup.

While he did the mixing, she grated the remaining zest from the oranges. Eddie had attacked that task with all the enthusiasm of a three-year-old, and the attendant level of skill, leaving the job half done in some places and overdone in others. Lucy didn't want to criticize, but she also didn't want to miss out on any of the flavor from the oranges.

Once the polenta, milk, and zest were well mixed together, Lucy and Eddie used their fingers to break the lumped-up mix into small crumbs.

"Fun!" Eddie said, holding up his polenta-covered hands.

"Isn't it! The best part is at the end, when we'll have a delicious cake we can share with the others."

Eddie shook his head. "Best part is this."

He made as if to lick his fingers, but Lucy stopped him.

"Not until we're finished, sweetheart," she said. "Hygiene is important in the kitchen."

"Who Jean?"

"Never mind. Just don't lick your fingers."

She gave Eddie brown sugar, corn starch, and a pinch of salt to mix in a new bowl while she peeled the oranges and stripped away as much of the white pith as she could.

This definitely wasn't work for the enthusiastic but clumsy fingers of a little boy, who would have ended up with juicy hands and a squashed mess of fruit. Eddie was a champion stirrer though, and he soon had the other ingredients thoroughly mixed.

"Now put that in the bottom of the cake pan." Lucy set a greased pan down on Eddie's table.

He picked his bowl up with both hands and tipped its contents in, a careful drizzle of sugar mix at first, then a big heap in the middle of the tin when care became too much effort.

"Could you maybe spread it around with a spoon?" Lucy asked. "Imagine you're coloring in and you want to fill every corner of the page."

Clattering noises followed as Eddie knocked a spoon against the sides of the pan, its base, and eventually the table, enjoying the noise he was making. Along the way, he at least spread the sugar mixture around enough for them to add the orange slices, spacing them evenly across the pan on top of the sugar.

"More mixing?" Lucy asked.

"More mixing!" Eddie held a spoon aloft. "Lenta!"

"Flour, baking powder, and baking soda this time, but don't worry, the polenta will come in soon enough."

"Lenta."

"Polenta."

"Lenta."

"Polenta."

"Lenta."

"Never mind."

In another bowl, Lucy beat together eggs and sugar.

The recipe said to use an electric mixer, but she'd long ago learned that a whisk and a little magic could do the job equally well while giving her more control. Within a few minutes, the mix was pale and three times its previous volume.

She levitated the bowl down until it hung in the air next to Eddie.

"I've measured out some oil and vanilla extract," she said. "Could you tip them in slowly while I keep the whisk going?"

Slowly was one of those words that could have two effects on Eddie: it could either be something he decided to ignore as boring and pointless or something that could lead to deliberate, exaggerated care. To Lucy's relief, she got the second approach this time. He poured the oil and vanilla in a slow trickle, watching with curiosity as the magically powered whisk mixed them in.

"Now the lenta," Lucy said.

"Polenta," Eddie said, putting great emphasis on the first syllable to make sure he corrected her.

Lucy laughed. "That's right, polenta. Can you add those slowly too?"

She kept mixing as he added the polenta crumbs and the flour mix. By then, white dust covered Eddie, but the ingredients were well mixed.

Lucy poured the resulting goo over the orange slices in the pan and, with Eddie's help, spread it into an even layer. Then she opened the heated oven and placed the cake inside. When she turned from putting the oven gloves away, she found Eddie staring intently at the oven and licking his lips.

"I'm sorry, sweetheart, but you're going to have to be patient," she said. "It'll take an hour to bake and time to cool down before we can eat any."

"Hour?" Eddie looked at her, aghast.

"I'm afraid so. How about if we lick the bowls to keep us going?"

That suggestion was much more popular. Eddie set about cleaning the bowls and spoons with his fingers and tongue, then handing them to Lucy, who gave them a proper wash in the sink, which had soap bubbles instead of an angler fish this time.

"What shall we do now?" Lucy asked once she finished the dishes and Eddie had washed his sticky, slobbery hands.

"Animals!" Eddie declared.

"What sort of animals?"

"Light animals!"

Taking her hand, he led her into the living room, where he sat her down on the sofa.

"Best light animals," he announced.

What followed was a display of the weird and wonderful, as Eddie turned, one by one, into every light-emitting creature he'd ever heard of. Unfortunately, many of the glowing creatures lived in the sea, so Lucy had to watch as a squid, a jellyfish, and of course the angler fish each lay flapping on her carpet, unable to breathe the air but determined to be seen. It was a relief when the oven timer sounded.

"Cake's probably cooked!" she said.

An uncomfortable but clearly glowing squid turned back into a small boy, who followed her into the kitchen, while Buddy went to sniff doubtfully at the fishy spot on the living room floor.

Lucy took the polenta cake out of the oven and tested it with a toothpick: perfectly cooked, of course. She chatted with Eddie some more while it cooled a little, then tipped it out onto a cooling rack, revealing an upper layer decorated with caramelized orange slices.

"Yay!" Eddie clapped. "Eat now?"

"Not until dinner," Lucy said, "but it'll be lovely with a dollop of whipped cream."

Eddie clapped even more enthusiastically. Glowing animals were all well and good, but they couldn't compete with cake and cream.

CHAPTER TWELVE

The judge was an Arpak, Justice Delvenine, which was good news as far as Gruffbar was concerned. Arpaks who went into the law tended to be stern, rigid types with a clear focus on the detail of the rules. As far as Gruffbar could tell, his client had stuck to those rules, at least far more so than the other side claimed. It was an unusual situation for the dwarf lawyer to defend someone who might be innocent of the accusations. Of course, they weren't innocent in other matters, but they wouldn't have been one of his clients if they were.

"Do we have to put up with all this?" Chuck Leader, sitting next to Gruffbar behind the defense counsel's desk, gestured over his shoulder at the people gathered in the court's small public gallery.

There were a handful of magical journalists, mostly Earth-based, although one of them wore Oriceran clothes. A dozen scruffier-looking individuals were tech and legal bloggers. In the middle of them all, smiling serenely, was that damn elf who did Nuada's PR. The trial hadn't even started, and Gruffbar was already sick of the circus she'd mustered around it.

"Can't stop them," Gruffbar said. "Though by my beard, I'd throw them all out of here if I could. Nuada's going to milk this for everything he can."

"Jackass," Leader growled.

"Don't call him that in front of the judge. It won't go well."

"She some sort of prude?"

"Protective about the respect and reputation of the court. Trust me. We'll do better by being quiet and deferential than by kicking up an unnecessary fuss."

"I didn't get where I am today by being deferential."

"Where you are today is in a court case that could destroy your company. Maybe it's time for a change of tactics."

"Ha!" Leader slapped Gruffbar on the shoulder. "This is why I like you. You're a straight shooter."

"Thanks." Gruffbar didn't like his client, a pompous wizard whose ego had risen in proportion to his multi-million-dollar business, but that was something he could keep to himself. The guy's money was good, and that was all that mattered.

Justice Delvenine banged her gavel, and the room fell silent.

"All right, let's get this started," she growled. "No grandstanding, please. I've read the briefs. You don't have a jury to impress. As for that lot..." She pointed at the assembled press. "You can sing and dance for them all you like outside, but you keep your theatrics out of my courtroom."

"Of course, Your Honor." Gruffbar smiled. This was good. It undercut Nuada's whole approach.

"Absolutely." Max Petrie, sitting next to Finn Nuada at the prosecution desk, rose to his feet. "Shall I begin?"

"Please do, Mr. Petrie."

Petrie cleared his throat, glanced down at his notes, then slid them deliberately aside.

"As Your Honor is aware from our briefs, this case is running in parallel with another in the human courts. I apologize in advance if elements touching on mundane law occasionally slip into my arguments here, but these elements can't be strictly separated, and anything with a hint of magic about it must of course be dealt with here."

"This isn't my first rodeo," Justice Delvenine said. "Nor are you the only clowns I have to supervise this month. Please cut to the chase."

Petrie looked calm, but Gruffbar figured that he had to be sweating under his suit. Petrie had been a last-minute transfer to the case himself, and now the late change of judges was throwing him even further off his stride. Gruffbar allowed himself a small smile behind his beard.

"Absolutely, Your Honor." Petrie gestured at Finn Nuada. "I'd like to start by putting my client on the stand."

Cameras flashed as Finn Nuada crossed the courtroom, then stopped flashing as Delvenine glared at their owners. The flashes probably weren't needed anyway, given the luminosity of Nuada's skin, which could have free rein here in a magical court, out of human sight. He shone as he took the stand, a blazing bastion of truth.

Nuada placed his hand over his heart. "By my soul, I

swear to tell the truth, the whole truth, and nothing but the truth."

"For the record, please state your name and occupation," Petrie said.

"Finn Nuada, chief executive officer of Nuada Industries."

"You're also the founder of Nuada Industries?"

"That's correct."

"And you created much of its technology, including the magical components?"

"Also correct."

"Mr. Nuada, could you please explain the workings of your new solar-powered lighting system?"

Nuada laughed. "It sounds counterintuitive, doesn't it, solar-powered lighting? After all, you don't need the lights on when the sun is out."

Some of the spectators laughed.

Justice Delvenine frowned. "Mr. Nuada, my guidance to your attorney applies to you as well. This is not a PR opportunity, and if you treat it like one, it will go badly for you."

Gruffbar liked the judge's attitude, but she was naïve. To a man like Nuada, everything was a PR opportunity, and even if he couldn't play the charmer, he would still use this chance to show himself in some positive light.

"I'm sorry, Your Honor." The glow of Nuada's skin dimmed. "Bad habit. This is a serious business, and I'll do my best to treat it as such." He leaned forward with a thoughtful expression. "The Nuada Nightingale system was built using two principles: that everything is better when it's locally sourced, power included, and that the application of appropriate magic can always improve mundane materials."

Nuada began a discussion of the design process behind his lighting system and how the resulting product worked. Gruffbar tried to pay the words his full attention, though he knew the details already, having read with interest about what Nuada had achieved.

Like any good piece of technology, the Nuada Nightingale held a pleasure of its own that came from seeing a good design and execution, from witnessing what human and magical crafting could achieve. It was interesting, but by now it was getting repetitive, and Gruffbar's attention started to wander.

Then a detail brought him back to reality. Had Nuada said that the Nightingale's magic used elementary micro-heating? That was part of the Leader Luminosity design and something Nuada's previous materials never mentioned. Either Nuada was lying to make it look more like Leader had copied him, or Chuck Leader had lied to Gruffbar about the origins of his technology, keeping his attorney in the dark. Technically, there was a third possibility, that of a truly unfortunate coincidence, but Gruffbar didn't believe in coincidence where legal battles were concerned.

He leaned over to whisper to his client.

"I thought you developed the micro-heating magic?"

"We did," Leader replied through gritted teeth. "Bastard's outright lying."

Gruffbar sat back. He was sure Leader was right, but who was the bastard here? From everything Gruffbar knew, Max Petrie was a straight shooter, a lawyer who worked hard to check that his client wouldn't perjure himself or use Max to depict an untruth. Chuck Leader, on the other hand, was three hundred pounds of scheming in a two hundred pound man-suit. Lies leaked from him like oil from a cracked engine. Maybe Gruffbar had misjudged this situation.

It didn't matter. Gruffbar had no qualms about misleading the court, as long as he wasn't likely to be caught out. He would stick with the strategy he had. Hell, he might as well prod at this opportunity first, see if he could catch Nuada in a lie.

"Your witness, Mr. Steelstrike," Justice Delvenine said as Petrie stepped away from the stand.

"Thank you, Your Honor." Gruffbar got to his feet. There were a few flashes from the press cameras, though not as many as for the photogenic Petrie. Not that Gruffbar was jealous. He wasn't here for the fame.

He approached the witness stand.

"Mr. Nuada, you claim to have invented this elementary micro heating magic," Gruffbar said.

"That's right." Nuada met his guess steadily with the faintest hint of a smile. His smugness grated at Gruffbar.

"The same magic that my client invented?"

"Claims to have invented, yes."

"My client has provided proof of when he developed this magical technology, while we only have your word for it that you knew about this before, oh, let's say last Thursday."

That got a few chuckles from the crowd and a raised eyebrow from the judge. Gruffbar could have kicked himself. He'd let his professionalism slip to take a dig at Nuada. This wasn't a judge he should do that in front of.

"Actually, I have proof." Nuada pulled an envelope from inside his pristine white jacket. "We never got around to writing up a patent, but I have minutes of the meeting where I first discussed this technology with my executive team, together with a signed affidavit from all those present, stating that they remember this conversation."

He held out the envelope. At a nod from Delvenine, a gnome scurried over to take the envelope and hand it to the judge.

Gruffbar stood silent for a moment, grappling with this unexpected turn of events. It could all still be a lie, one that Nuada's executives had agreed to, one meant to prove that Leader had ripped them off. Finn Nuada's small, smug smile made that seem more, not less likely. Still, to sign a legal affidavit to an untruth was a risky business, one that put a seed of doubt in Gruffbar's mind.

It had planted more than a seed of doubt with the judge. A great forest of doubt was taking over, leaving her brow creased and her expression stern.

"This doesn't look good for your client, Mr. Steelstrike," she said. "Do you want to continue with your questioning?"

"Yes, Your Honor," Gruffbar said. He mustn't look weak. He had to keep control, not just for the sake of the judge but for the sake of the press and his client's reputation. "Mr. Nuada, your company is famed for its tight security. Given that, how do you explain the presence of this technology in a rival's hands? Are you saying that your security people failed?"

It was a long shot, but maybe Nuada's famous pride would work against him.

"One of our employees left a few months ago," Nuada said. "We discovered today that Leader now employs him. We haven't had a chance to investigate fully, but we believe that he might have stolen the technology."

Gruffbar glanced at Leader, who was furiously shaking his head. Someone was lying, but who?

"And if the technology didn't reach Leader that way?" Gruffbar said through gritted teeth. He had to keep digging, had to find something to hang a defense off.

"I don't know. Maybe a coincidence, but that seems like a long shot. Do you believe in coincidences, Mr. Steelstrike?"

Gruffbar opened his mouth to say yes, but the word wouldn't come out. It was the most disconcerting thing that had ever happened to him in court. All he wanted was to tell one small, unprovable lie, yet the word got stuck.

What was going on?

"Perhaps I could ask another question," Nuada said as Gruffbar stood, mutely flapping his mouth. "Do you believe, really believe, that your client is honest?"

Now Gruffbar really had to reply, had to say that of course, he did. No one could call it perjury because no one would ever know otherwise. Again, the words wouldn't come out.

He couldn't lie. Something had ripped one of his most important tools away from him. As he looked at Finn Nuada, he realized how. Nuada's light was magical, not a spell, but something subtler, something that had twisted the tracks of Gruffbar's brain, or worse yet, straightened them.

He wanted to object, but what could he say to the judge? We have to stop this, Your Honor, as the witness is stopping me from lying? That wasn't going to make things any better. His only hope was to buy time.

He turned to Justice Delvenine. "Your Honor, the defense has provided fresh evidence. Obviously, I need time to consider this. I'd like to ask for a postponement while I get copies of this evidence from the prosecution and look into its veracity."

"That seems fair," Delvenine said. "However, this court's time is precious, and I won't have it wasted. Clerk, reschedule us for as soon as possible. Mr. Steelstrike, I am giving you days, not weeks. Use them wisely."

"I will, Your Honor."

Before turning away from the stand, Gruffbar stared one last time at Nuada. It didn't matter now who was telling the truth or why. Nuada had messed with Gruffbar, and Gruffbar was going to bring him down.

CHAPTER THIRTEEN

Twylan and Leontine crept along the concrete tunnels, trailing the academic as he made his way back toward the surface. If he'd noticed that he was missing his sensor equipment, he hadn't done anything about it. Twylan's spell had been powerful enough to chase all his previous work from his mind.

She was proud of that and a little nervous. This was the power that came with being a Silver Griffin, and it brought with it the duty to act responsibly. It was scary to think that she could wipe away someone's thoughts and memories like that. If she did become a Griffin, would she be doing this sort of thing every day? Was that the sort of duty she wanted?

"That's far enough," Leontine whispered. "We're well away from the forests now."

"Okay." They stopped and waited in shadows, watching the academic as he disappeared up an old bootlegger's tunnel. "I just realized we never found out his name."

"Does it matter?"

In theory, it didn't. What they had done didn't change with a name, but Twylan felt worse, not knowing whose mind she had messed with. It was as if she hadn't cared enough to find out, and the thought of such carelessness made her feel sick.

"Come on," Leontine said gruffly. "We should go back. The others will be expecting us."

Twylan summoned her magical floating lights, which hovered around them as they made their way deeper under the ground. Whenever a light drifted close to Leontine, he batted it irritably away. When the third one hit the wall, Twylan decided it was finally time to have a word.

"Is something the matter?"

"No," Leontine said.

"Only you seem out of sorts, and sometimes it helps to talk."

"I said no," he snapped. "How hard is that to understand?"

They walked on in silence, Twylan frustrated at herself for upsetting him. She should have known better. Leontine was a private guy, and it seldom did any good to dig deeper.

"I'm sorry," she said. "I didn't mean to--"

"Just stop it, all right?"

He picked up speed, striding away from her. Within a minute, that took him outside the range of the floating lights. He stopped, and for a moment Twylan thought that he might let her catch up, but then his flashlight flickered on and he disappeared around a corner.

She sighed and followed at her pace. She wanted to keep the peace and to keep her people happy, but when they didn't want to talk, there was only so much she could do.

When she got back to the Underfoot Brigade's home tunnel, Leontine was nowhere in sight. That came as a relief. Rather than deal with more of his mood, Twylan headed for her room. Like the others, she'd built it out of abandoned building materials and plastic sheeting, decorated inside to make it homier. There were posters of animals and elf boy bands, some art pictures, and a lovely letter from Roger Applegate thanking her for the assistance she had provided the Silver Griffins. That one took pride of place in a picture frame she had retrieved from the dump.

She sat on a beanbag in the corner, took out a sketch pad Lucy had given her and started to draw.

A few minutes later, there was a knock on the door. Before Twylan had time to answer, Kix came in.

"How are you doing?" the gnome asked as she settled herself on Twylan's bed.

"Okay," Twylan said, not looking up from her sketch.

"Really okay?"

Twylan sighed. "No. Leontine's behaving like an idiot again."

"Did he tell you why?"

"Of course not." Twylan's pencil scratched across the page a moment longer before she looked up. Kix's uncharacteristic quiet said that something was going unsaid. "What is it? He's not sick, is he?"

Kix shook her head. "A little green, I guess, but it's jealousy, not a stomach bug."

"Jealousy?"

Kix sighed. "You know how Leontine used to be the leader around here? I mean, not officially, but we all followed him."

Twylan nodded. "We still do."

"Really? Because right now, it feels more like you're in charge."

"Don't be silly, I..." Twylan thought about their recent activities, including arrangements with the Tolderai, something that had come through her and Kix, not Leontine. "Oh. So he feels like I'm taking over?"

"Kind of. I think he'd be all right with the other part if he was still in charge."

"The other part?"

"The Silver Griffins."

"What about them?"

"You know that Leontine's uncle used to work with the Griffins, right?"

"He mentioned something once."

"Leontine really looked up to his uncle, but he never thought he'd get to do what he did. Then we met Lucy, and we started helping the Griffins out from time to time, and somewhere inside, maybe Leontine thought that he'd follow in Valnay's footsteps."

"He still could."

"Maybe, but right now he isn't, while you..."

Twylan put her head in her hands and groaned. "I'm running around getting involved in Griffin cases, training with them, talking about them, casting big Griffin spells to get us out of emergencies."

"Uh-huh."

"Oh, Kix, Leontine must think I'm awful, stealing his dream and going on about it in front of him."

"Of course he doesn't." Kix slid to the floor and wrapped an arm around her friend's shoulder. "He's proud of you. He wants you to succeed. He just finds it hard sometimes when you're living his dream."

"Oh, Kix, I don't want to upset anyone. Should I stop hanging around with the Griffins?"

"Don't be an idiot." Kix cuffed Twylan across the back of the head. "You're doing brilliantly, and you shouldn't give that up because some guy can't cope with it."

"So I should talk about it less?"

"About the amazing, kickass thing you're doing?" Kix cuffed her gently again. "Same rule applies. Still, maybe you could go to Leontine, let him know you've worked it out, let him talk it through. I think it would help."

"I didn't work it out. You did."

"No need to tell him that. Just go do the thing. While you're gone, I'm going to read your magazines because I've earned a reward."

Twylan laughed, got up off the floor, and hurried out down the echoing tunnel.

Leontine's home was only a few shacks down. She stopped outside it, drew a deep breath, then knocked on the door frame.

"Yeah?"

"It's me."

"Oh. Come in, I guess."

She pushed a curtain aside and walked in. Leontine's room was more barren than hers, the battered but functional furniture doing nothing to disguise the improvised construction. He sat in the middle of the floor, an old ammo tin open next to him. It was full of photographs, newspaper clippings, and other papers. Some of them were in Leontine's hand, others spread across the bare boards around him.

"What's all this?" Twylan took care to make her tone soft rather than challenging.

"It was Uncle Valnay's." Leontine held up a handwritten sheet of paper. "He wrote about every case he helped the Griffins with. Kept a record of what he'd done, in case it would ever be useful to them."

"He sounds like a great guy."

"He was." Leontine held out a photo. Its edges were worn from heavy handling. "This was him with the old chief of the Griffins."

The photo showed an elegant witch pinning a medal to the jacket of an Arpak. The smartly dressed Arpak's suit had gaps for his wings to spread from the back. His big grin was given a quirk by the ragged scar on his left cheek.

"He looks handsome," Twylan said. "Just like you. What happened to his face?"

Leontine took the photo back and ran a finger down Valnay's cheek.

"Fight against a necromancer and his minions. That was what he earned his first medal for." He showed her another photo of another ceremony. Then he took three striped ribbons out of the tin, each with a medal hanging from it.

"Do you have a photo to go with the third one?" Twylan asked.

Leontine shook his head and looked down sadly. "That one was posthumous. The mission was so secret that they couldn't even tell us what he did. A guy turned up with a medal one day. My mom and dad..."

His voice trailed off. The Underfoots didn't talk about their parents. All of them were either orphans or runaways, and pain had raised a wall of taboo around that conversation.

Twylan sat next to Leontine and looked into the box. She started taking out photos, and Leontine didn't object.

"Your uncle would be really proud of you," she said. "You've done loads of heroic things, and you don't even have the Silver Griffins to back you up. That takes so much courage."

Leontine blinked, swallowed, blinked again as he fought back tears.

"Thanks," he whispered. "Sorry about earlier. I just..."

"I'm sorry too, I..."

Twylan reached out tentatively toward Leontine. To her surprise, he reached out too. The friends hugged each other until the knot inside her stomach unraveled and they both sat back, more comfortable with each other than they'd been in weeks.

"Check this out." Leontine flicked through a selection of newspaper clippings, revealing an editorial cartoon. "This is from the mission that got him the second medal. He got into the magical papers, and someone drew him as a superhero, showing Superman how it's done."

"That's really cool." Twylan laughed. "What's that other cutting?"

"This?"

Leontine held it up. The headline read "NKG Ltd. Corruption Allegations Grow: Nuada Ties to Silver

Griffins Questioned." Underneath was a photo of Finn Nuada. The cutting was decades old, but Finn looked the same.

"Uncle Valnay kept some cuttings from stories that interested him." Leontine showed her a few more. Several mentioned Nuada, including clearing his name of corruption charges. "He thought that this corruption was real and that someone in the Griffins covered it up."

"Did he say why?"

"He left notes..." Leontine dug another sheet of paper from the heap. Instead of a neatly written account of a case, this one was incomplete and incoherent in places. Among the more legible parts, Twylan read the words "coverup," "FN seen with MS," and "FN vs. HK— why did H back down?"

Twylan grabbed the newspaper cuttings and read them more closely. They talked about allegations of corrupt business practices. An unprecedented investigation by senior Silver Griffins had cleared Finn Nuada, but Valnay clearly hadn't been convinced. He'd seen existing ties between Nuada and the Griffins and suspected that corruption had got the businessman out of trouble.

It would have been bad enough, but Twylan recognized the initials connected to the case. MS for Margaret Sunder, HK for Harold Kowal. Surely neither of them could be corrupt? They were still senior Silver Griffins.

"What's the matter?" Leontine asked.

"I don't know," Twylan whispered. "I have a bad feeling about this."

CHAPTER FOURTEEN

"I'm just saying that it's in the wrong place," Ashley explained as the Herons walked into the Natural History Museum. "The things Dylan helped dig up are human history, not natural history."

"There isn't a human history museum in Los Angeles," Dylan said.

"There are plenty. There's one about the Old West and one about—"

"Fine, there are lots, but the Tolderai site didn't fit with any of them. There isn't a right place for it, so they found a place here."

"I still don't like it." Ashley folded her arms. "It could be confusing."

"It's only temporary," Lucy pointed out. "Try not to talk about the Tolderai while we're here. Remember, the archaeologists have no idea what they really found."

Or what they missed out on, she added in her head. Dylan's and Charlie's intervention, alongside Heather and her people, had stopped mundane archaeologists from unearthing some truly dangerous magical artifacts. It would have blown their minds to know what they'd missed at the ancient tribal village, but it was better to leave those minds intact. Wands and scrying bowls were for magicals, not inquisitive academics.

The Herons weren't the only ones who'd come to the museum for the opening of the new exhibition. Lots of kids had volunteered on the dig, thanks to a special educational program, and plenty of them had dragged their parents along. Some of the archaeologists had brought friends and family too, so there was quite a crowd in the exhibition hall by the time Professor Angie Werner stepped up onto a portable podium. She cleared her throat and smiled brightly.

"Thank you all for coming," she said. "Particular thanks to the museum staff who have made us so welcome here. They've made a fantastic effort on the displays, elevating our humble analysis to a spellbinding story. You can't see them yet..." She gestured around the room at the sheets and curtains covering all the exhibits. "...but when you do, you'll see how brilliantly they've laid out the context and meaning of our finds.

"Before I officially open this exhibit, I should say a few words about the circumstances surrounding this dig. We were very lucky that the company working on the site came to us when they found what looked like remains and were so cooperative. Their further sponsorship has proved that the private and public sectors really can work fruitfully together and that forward progress need not trample on the past."

There was polite applause. Near the front of the room, a man in a suit waved and beamed with pride.

"I know what you all really want to know about," the professor continued, "and that's the mysteriously disappearing grave goods. I wish that I had an answer to what happened there, a neat story we could tie to it, but I can't. Given the state of the site, we can safely exclude theft by modern looters. So were the objects never there, just a glitch in our equipment? Were they traces in the dirt, and we lost the remaining evidence as we dug? Did aliens take them away?"

More laughter.

"Or witches," Dylan whispered to his mom, who smiled at him.

"Ssh."

"We may never know," the professor continued. "Perhaps that's for the best. After all, a good mystery gives life flavor.

"On that note, it's time for me to end the mystery of our exhibits." At her nod, museum staff whipped away the sheets and curtains, unveiling the displays. "Please, enjoy this opportunity to see a unique part of Los Angeles' past. Thank you all for your help in bringing this puzzling place to light."

There was a final round of applause, and the crowd broke up, heading off to look at the exhibits.

Dylan's friends Sofia and Lance rushed over, both of them grinning.

"This is so cool," Lance said. "Knowing something the grown-ups don't!"

"Shut up, dummy." Sofia kicked him in the shin. "We're

not supposed to know either." She looked up at Lucy. "I mean, um, hi Mrs. Heron, we were just talking about, um, a thing from school that..."

"I know," Lucy said. "But ssh. You don't want to take the mystery out of the professor's life accidentally, do you?"

They shook their heads and grinned.

"I'm going to go say thank you to the professor. Why don't you guys show Ashley and Eddie the artifacts you found?"

The kids hurried off, leaving Lucy and Charlie amid the milling crowd.

"They're not going to blow this, are they?" Charlie whispered. "I'd hate for your colleagues to have to come clear up secrets our kids let out. That would make for a really awkward weekend."

"They'll be fine," Lucy said. "Have a little faith in your parenting."

She took Charlie's hand and led him across the room to where the professor had finished talking with a group of journalists.

"Professor Werner?" Lucy smiled. "You probably don't remember, but we're Dylan Heron's parents. We wanted to say thank you for making him part of your dig."

"It was my pleasure," the professor replied. "Dylan was very diligent and insightful. He'll make a fine archaeologist one day if that's a path he chooses to go down."

"It's certainly the one he's after now, but he's twelve years old so a lot could change."

The professor laughed. "Well, I wanted to be Indiana Jones when I was twelve, and this is about as close as you can get, so fingers crossed for Dylan."

Across the hall, Lance was pointing at arrowheads in a display case.

"...and that one, and that one, and that one," he said. "Maybe that one too."

"How can you tell they're all ones you found?" Ashley said. "They all look very similar."

"I remember the details like it was yesterday," Lance said. "The feel of each one in my hand, the tiny details of each edge, the spirit of them..."

Sofia made a snorting sound. "He's being silly again. You see those little numbers?" She pointed at labels next to the artifacts. "They tell you which ones are which. We each got a report at the end of the dig with a list of what we found, in case we want to check it out in a museum when we're older, and our brains are all rotten."

"Take all the drama out of it, why don't you?" Lance flung his hands in the air. "At least I know which ones are mine, and it'll be good practice for when I have to learn lines for TV shows."

At the next cabinet over, Dylan was showing Eddie one of the last things they'd found on the dig. It was a long piece of tree bark rolled out like thick paper. On it were the faint remnants of a picture, once brightly colored but now faded by time and stained with dirt. Next to it was a photographed version which enhanced some of the colors, helping to make the picture clearer.

"It shows people hunting in the hills," Dylan explained. "The archaeologists think it might have been a gift for a chieftain or a shared piece to celebrate the tribe's achievements. They say that the style is very unusual for the region." He lowered his voice to a whisper. "That's probably because of the Oriceran influence on the Tolderai tribe."

One day, he was going to become a magical archaeologist and write about these things properly. He would reconstruct the past for an excited audience. For now, he had to make do with explaining his theories to his little brother.

"Treasure map." Eddie pressing his nose up against the case. His breath clouded the glass, and his sticky fingers left smears to either side.

"I guess it does look a bit like a map," Dylan said. "But that's not how people navigated then. This is only a picture."

"No, map," Eddie insisted. "Hills and river and trees and cave makes map."

"Cave? What cave?"

"Look." Eddie reached up and pressed a finger on the glass, just over a dark point on the photo. "Cave."

Dylan took a step back and looked at the whole thing again. If he ignored the people and the animals they were hunting, the background did read a lot like a map. A cave or tunnel mouth would explain that dark patch at the back, which the professor had dismissed as a symptom of aging on the bark. In fact, one of the hunters' arrows was pointing at the cave mouth, and that hunter was the only one of the group looking straight out of the picture, catching the viewer's eye.

"It is a map," Dylan whispered. "It's supposed to lead us to something hidden." He looked around. "Ashley! Come here!"

His sister walked over. She was holding a tablet, on

which she had been reading about the science of archaeological dating.

"These labels are too simple," she said. "They don't tell you anything about how the geophysics works, or the chemical analysis, or any of it. It's like they're not even trying to explain the science."

"It's a history exhibition."

"There's science too."

"Never mind that. Does that thing have a camera?"

"Yes."

"Is it one of your enhanced cameras?"

"Of course."

"Could you take some photos for me?"

Dylan wiped Eddie's breath and sticky smears off the case, then set Ashley to photographing the artifact. She took a range of images: ordinary, enhanced, infrared, ultraviolet, magical traces, and others Dylan didn't pretend to understand.

"That's all I have," she said at last.

"It's brilliant." Dylan looked over her shoulder at the images. "There are things here that I couldn't see before, things that Professor Angie has no idea about."

"What is it?" Ashley asked.

"This," Dylan said, "is our next Mini Griffins adventure."

CHAPTER FIFTEEN

"Did you find anything that wasn't an arrowhead?" Lucy asked as Lance pointed out his finds behind the glass of the display case.

"Oh, sure," he said. "Let me show you this..."

"Sorry, sweetheart, my phone's going." Lucy turned away and pulled out her mobile. Jackie's name flashed on the display, so she answered. "What's up?"

"Just got a pigeon. We're needed."

"Is it urgent? I'm at a thing for Dylan. I don't want to disappoint him."

"Sorry, but duty calls. I'll text you the address."

Lucy put her phone away and hurried over to her family, who were peering at a picture on a strip of bark. Ashley's complaints about potential confusion at the museum seemed entirely forgotten.

"Sorry, sweetheart." Lucy ruffled Dylan's hair, "but I've got to go."

"That's okay, Mom." Dylan hugged her. "You go save the world."

"Do you need the car?" Charlie fished for his keys.

"There's a Starbucks at the junction. I'll catch a lift from there."

Lucy kissed each of them on the cheek, then hurried away, out through the museum's busy Saturday afternoon crowd and down the street. At the corner of Exposition and Figueroa, she hurried into the Starbucks and straight to the back, forcing herself to pass the counter without stopping for a cup of tea.

Outside the toilets, she tapped her wand against the wall. A hidden door opened and she stepped in, hidden from view by a cloud of protective magic, then ran down the stairs two at a time.

"Hold up!" she shouted, hearing a train about to leave the subway station. "Silver Griffin incoming!"

She sprinted across the platform and through the doors a moment before they shut. Then the train carriage rocked as it pulled out of the station and away.

The carriage was full of all sorts of magicals, out enjoying their weekends. Dwarves and elves, Willens and gnomes, witches and wizards, the sheer variety was part of what Lucy loved about the world she lived in. Not that the mundane world didn't have its moments, but the magical was something more.

Fortunately, the train was fast, and she soon reached her destination. She leaped out and raced up the steps, out through another Starbucks, this one quieter than the one by the museum. She dashed down the street, following instructions on her phone to a tall white building.

Jackie was waiting outside, one eye on the street, the other on the building's lobby.

"What's the crisis?" Lucy asked.

"Magical fight. I cast a quick containment spell on the lobby, but I thought I'd better wait for you before going in."

Lucy glanced at the sign on the building. "Some sort of research lab?"

"Apparently, they develop new sorts of lights." Jackie laughed at Lucy's disappointed expression. "You were expecting something more exciting?"

"I suppose somebody has to research lights, I just... It's a lab, you know. If I'm going to fight around science, I want bubbling vats and cloning tubes and a mad assistant named Igor waving a lightning rod at the sky."

"Not every science company comes out of a Marvel comic."

"I'd rather have DC anyway." Lucy slid her wand from her back pocket. "Shall we?"

They walked into the building through a pair of sliding glass doors and an invisible barrier that felt like static across Lucy's skin. Behind the front desk, a receptionist lay snoring.

"Sleep spell?" Lucy asked.

"Either that or the world's worst-timed power nap."

"Did someone here call it in?"

"No, one of our magical detectors picked up signs of a spell fight, and the pigeon got sent out."

"So there could be anything going on in there?"

"Exciting, isn't it?"

Crashing and sizzling sounds drew them down a set of stairs into a cavernous underground laboratory. A whole range of equipment lined workbenches down the near side of the room. Apart from the microscopes, Lucy didn't recognize any of it. On the far side, someone had over-thrown the workbenches, and the equipment lay smashed on the floor.

Flashes of light and sizzles of evaporating magic burst from that side of the room. At one end were three magicals in lab coats, two dwarves and a gnome. They were flinging spells at a single figure down the other end of the room, a human-looking man in a black suit and wraparound shades. He must have been flinging unhealthy amounts of magic around because his skin seemed to be glowing from the effort. Or perhaps that was part of his nature, as he clearly wasn't only a wizard. He wasn't using a wand.

"Silver Griffins!" Jackie held up her ID amulet. "Everybody freeze."

One of the dwarves held up his hands, releasing the rune-encrusted disk he'd been using to cast spells. He immediately regretted it as a bolt of magical light from the other end of the room hit him in the chest, knocking him flying against the wall.

"Stop this right now!" Lucy said in her best "mom" voice. "One more spell and you're all heading for Trevilsom."

"We should do what the Scottish lady asked," the gnome said to the remaining dwarf.

"And let this asshole take us down?" The dwarf flung a shadow spell at their opponent, but a blast of light obliterated it. "Not likely."

"I'm English, not Scottish," Lucy said. "You buggers are all under arrest."

She waved her wand and chanted a spell. Chains shot out, wrapped around the gnome, and knocked him to the floor, bound and ready for transport. At the same moment, Jackie cast a freeze spell. The dwarf tried to dodge, but he was too slow. The spell caught him in the leg, and a wave of frost raced up his body, freezing him in place.

"We're the victims here," the gnome protested. "We were trying to work when he broke in."

The two witches turned their attention to the glowing man down the room.

"All right, sunshine." Lucy waved her wand. "No more funny business. Put your hands in the air, or we'll make you wish you'd never got of bed this morning."

There was a flash of dazzling magic, but Lucy flung up a counterspell, dispersing the light halfway across the room. Another bright bolt hurtled at Jackie, who dove out of the way. The magic hit a machine against one wall, which exploded into shining pieces.

"I don't think he's coming quietly," Jackie said.

"Then he'll have to come noisily," Lucy said. "I'm not wasting any more of my Saturday than I have to."

She started striding down the lab, but a series of magical bolts forced her to take cover behind one of the machines. She flung a spell blindly over the workbench, then rushed down to the next spot able to hide her, moving from cover to cover while Jackie kept their opponent busy.

"What's this all about?" Lucy called. "If these lads did something bad to you, we can get you justice. That's what we do."

"Why would we have done anything bad?" the gnome wailed.

"I don't know. Curiosity, profit, mad science. These things happen."

"I just want to make light bulbs!"

"That's what they all say."

Lucy peered out around the end of a workbench. She was close to the glowing magical. Perhaps she could hit him with a spell faster than he could counter it. She raised her wand and chanted to summon the magic.

"Form to contain in bonds of chain."

Chains shot from the wand again, rattling as they went. The magical turned too late. The chains wrapped around his legs, and he crashed to the floor.

"Got him!" Lucy emerged from cover and walked toward the floored magical. "Now, about that cell in Trevilsom..."

The magical glowed brighter. His suit smoked and burned away. The chains turned red, then orange, then yellow, then melted into a puddle on the floor. A bitter, burnt smell made Lucy gag.

"Refrigero!"

Her spell hit the magical, but instead of freezing him in place it evaporated, vanishing in a cloud of steam. He raised his hand.

"Crescent plantae." Lucy waved her wand.

This time, the magic filled the ground around the magical's feet. Plants burst forth, growing quickly under the influence of her magic and his bright, nourishing light. But as they reached out to entangle the magical, he stepped forward, and the tendrils touching him burned away.

There was a flash from the palm of his hand. Lucy staggered back, temporarily blinded, a pain like hot needles appearing behind her eyes.

"He's making a run for it," Jackie shouted as footsteps raced across the lab.

Lucy turned and waved her wand, but she had no idea what she was aiming at, and she didn't want to hit Jackie.

There was a *thud*, then a *crash*.

"Got you, you glowing asshole," Jackie shouted. There was another *thud*, a sizzle, and then she shouted again. "Ow, my eyes!"

Lucy blinked hard. She could see again, though black spots were dancing across her vision. She turned, saw Jackie lying in a heap of tangled wires and broken equipment, and saw the magical rising out of the heap and heading for the door.

"Occludo," she called.

The spell hit the door, but it was too late. The magical ran through a split second before it slammed shut. Lucy raced over, wrenched the door open, and ran after him, following the sound of footsteps up the stairs. They wound around and around, ascending to the very top of the building. When she emerged into daylight and looked around the rooftop, he was nowhere in sight.

When Lucy returned to the basement lab, Jackie was on her feet and preparing the other magicals for a portal ride to Silver Griffins HQ.

"It's not fair," the gnome said. "We were defending ourselves."

"If that story holds up, we'll let you go," Jackie said. "There are questions to answer first."

The air glowed, and a portal appeared, an opening leading straight to the Griffins' transport room. Jackie pushed the captives through, then closed the gap.

"What a little whiner," she said. "You'd never think we'd saved him from a magical beating."

"We did save him by attacking him with spells," Lucy said.

"Eh." Jackie shrugged. "He was asking for it." She looked around the lab. "We should probably tidy this up, right?"

"I'm afraid so," Lucy said. "Though I doubt we can fix this equipment."

With some careful wand work, they got the workbenches upright, and the debris gathered in a single heap, along with the slag from the melted chains. It would be up to the building's owners to work out the next steps.

"That lad who got away," Lucy said, "did he remind you of anyone?"

Jackie shrugged. "Should he?"

"Glowing skin, smart suit, light-based magic..."

"Holy..." Jackie laughed. "You're right. There was something Finn Nuada about him. You think they're connected?"

"I don't know, but if I see him again, I'm going to have some very pointed questions."

CHAPTER SIXTEEN

Lucy and Jackie stepped out into the sunshine. It was a busy Los Angeles afternoon, with mundane Angelenos going back and forth about their business, oblivious to the strange goings-on behind the walls and wards of the magical world. Lucy felt proud. She and Jackie had kept the magic hidden once again, had helped to keep the world safe, stable, and secure.

"Great feeling, isn't it?" Jackie said. "Seeing all these people go past, knowing that we have this secret they have no idea about."

"That's not quite how I was feeling," Lucy said. "Honestly, I sometimes feel a bit sorry for other people, that they're missing out on the brilliance of magic."

"It's all right to enjoy what we have."

"There's a difference between enjoying it and feeling smug or superior about it."

"Feeling smug is one of the things I enjoy." Jackie gave a mocking grin. "Sometimes I think you're too good for the world, Lucy Heron."

Lucy laughed. "You wouldn't say that if you saw the mess on my side of the bedroom right now."

Jackie gave an exaggerated shudder. "Urgh, discarded clothes. I've ended relationships for less." She glanced at the time on her phone. "You want a lift somewhere? I have a date this evening, but I still have an hour or so to spare."

"Thanks, that would be great. Can you drop me at home? Charlie and I have a date night tonight, and it would be nice to get ready at my pace instead of rushing around while the kids are eating dinner."

They strolled down the street to Jackie's car. As they were about to get in, a pigeon landed on the roof.

"Oh, come on," Jackie said. "Haven't we dealt with enough today?"

The pigeon didn't offer an opinion on their workload, just held out its leg with the message attached.

"You grab it," Jackie said. "You can read while I drive."

Lucy grabbed the pigeon, which squawked in protest, and climbed into the passenger seat. While Jackie started the car, Lucy unfastened the message from the pigeon's leg and started reading.

"Hey, stop that!" Jackie said as the bird pecked at the dashboard.

"We're going to get closer to home, at least," Lucy said. "Magical disturbance in Elysian Park."

"Again?" Jackie shook her head. "That place is like a magnet for magical weirdness."

"Probably explains why we both live nearby."

The message, having been read, disintegrated into a pile of wiggling worms. Lucy started trying to brush them from her lap.

"Don't you dare spread worms around my car," Jackie said. "Let the bird clean them up."

"Fine. It's not like I haven't dealt with worse messes from the kids."

By the time they pulled onto the side of the road on Elysian Park Drive, the pigeon had finished gobbling up its worms and was back on the dashboard, watching the world roll past. It stayed there when Lucy opened the door, its head shifting from side to side as it peered out at the palm trees.

"Out," Jackie said firmly. "I won't have some bird staying in here, making a mess of my interior."

"Coo?" the pigeon said, not even looking at her.

"I said get out!" Jackie banged on the dashboard. The pigeon leaped up with a squawk and took off into the blue sky, leaving behind a couple of stray feathers. "I'll clean that up later. Now, where's the disturbance?"

Lucy pointed across the park, to where half a dozen humans stood, slack-jawed, staring at nothing in particular. Next to them stood Jim Lamont, one of the most junior Griffins, dressed in a baggy t-shirt and board shorts.

"You're a long way from the beach, Jim," Lucy said as they approached.

"Just got back." Jim brushed a fine film of salt from his forearm. "Pigeon caught me at the convenience store before I'd even had a chance to get home and put my board away."

"Looks like you got here in time."

Jim nodded. "I've rounded up all the mundane folks who saw anything and cast a couple of small enchantments to ward off new arrivals, but the main event's still going on." He pointed with his wand into an area of trees and bushes. The plants were swaying too fast and in the wrong directions to be in response to what little wind was blowing. "Couple of magicals throwing down in there, a witch and a wizard, I think. The magic's not too flashy, but it's escalating."

"You hold these people here. We'll go settle things down."

Lucy and Jackie drew their wands and headed down the trail between the trees.

The first thing Lucy noticed was that the place was more overgrown than usual. More plants had sprung up, expanding the area and making it more tangled. While the tops of palms and other familiar L.A. trees emerged from the upper reaches, the lower layers were all sorts of plants, from dense thorn bushes to miniatures firs to oversized Venus fly traps.

"Plant magic," Jackie said. "I bet you a donut this involves your Tolderai friends."

"I'm not even taking that bet." Lucy heard familiar voices up ahead. "No one else in L.A. could create a place like this."

No one except perhaps Dylan, who had once accidentally turned his schoolyard into a jungle, but she knew her son wasn't here. He wouldn't miss out on his big day at the museum to go for a walk in the local park.

In the center of the plants was a space that might have been a clearing but was fast becoming as overgrown as the rest. Tall grass and flowers were tossed around by billowing swirls of magic and by the branches and creepers reaching in from the surrounding wood. The whole area was a flurry of moving greens and yellows, with a magical standing at each end, directing the magic against each other with their wands.

Mackam looked the same as ever, a lean, wiry man in worn clothes, his braided gray beard giving him the appearance of a mad prophet. Though one hand rested on the long knife on his belt, he hadn't drawn it, keeping the fight purely to magic.

Carol Winters, on the other hand, was a witch transformed. Normally calm and gentle, her face was a vision of fury, her loose green dress billowing around her. She levitated two feet up in the air, dark hair flying, thorns flaring from her skin.

Carol flicked her arm and thorns flew from it. A spray of them shot across the clearing, straight at Mackam. He twitched his wand, and the grass in front of him surged up, formed a barrier, and absorbed the impact. Another wand movement and creepers stretched out of the trees to either side of Carol, grasping at her arms and legs. At the last minute, they seemed to lose their sense of direction and tied themselves in knots, creating a platform on which Carol settled in a crouch.

"I'm done with your insults, old man," she said. "Done with you putting me down. Done with being the butt of your crude humor and your foul moods."

"I'm done with the likes of you," Mackam snarled as he sent sharp-edged leaves flying at her. "With all we've worked for being endangered by your lust for attention. Risking all we protect for a few pathetic pictures."

"I'll give you pathetic." The leaves turned fall brown and crumbled to dust around Carol. As the dust hit the ground, the grass shot up, surging like a wave toward Mackam.

"Silver Griffins." Jackie held up her identity amulet. "Stop, both of you."

They ignored her, too caught up in their private conflict to care.

"Guys, please," Lucy called. "There's no need for this. Whatever's going on, you can settle it peacefully."

Branches swung down, knocking both Lucy and Jackie aside, then lunged at Carol.

"That's it, no more Ms. Nice Witch." Jackie got back to her feet and raised her wand. Lucy joined her.

"Renuo!" they chanted in unison.

Counterspells shot from both their wands, stopping the movement of branches and making the grass fall flat. The knotted creepers under Carol untangled, and she fell to the ground. Both she and Mackam turned their attention and anger toward the Silver Griffins, but a flurry of spells was already coming at them. Lucy and Jackie hadn't already spent most of their energy in a magical duel. The Griffins sliced down overgrown plants and dismissed exotic growths as the Tolderai tried to weaponize them.

"Form to contain in bonds of chain," Lucy chanted. Chains shot from her wand to entangle first Carol, then Mackam. Both magicals fell to the ground, cursing and writhing. Jackie and Lucy grabbed their wands.

The plants had gone still, but the unnaturally overgrown copse still loomed around them.

"Seriously?" Lucy said, glaring at the captives. "After all

these years of secrecy, after we helped keep you hidden, now you act like this? What do you think Heather will have to say about it?"

"We're about to find out." Carol looked over Lucy's shoulder.

Heather emerged from the greenery. Standing amid the trees in her solid boots and checkered shirt, with her muscled arms tensed, she looked more than ever like a lumberjack. She stared around her at the lush magical growth, then down at the two members of her tribe.

"Idiots." She spat on the ground by Mackam's feet. "You, of all people, should know better."

"She's endangering us," Mackam snarled. "She won't listen. Someone needs to teach the little girl a lesson."

"You're the one who needs a lesson if you think this is acceptable. And you..."

"I'm sorry," Carol said, her normal soft voice returning. "It was inexcusable."

"I should have them cart you two of to Trevilsom, but the tribe deals with its messes." She turned to Lucy. "I'll make sure they're no more trouble and that this gets cleared up."

"Hang on a second," Jackie said. "They've caused a major magical disruption. Our colleague had to 'never was' a bunch of mundanes to cover it up. What makes you think that you get to keep these two out of jail?"

Heather turned to Jackie, her face stony, her muscles tensed. For a long moment, Lucy thought that she would have a whole new fight to settle. Then, to her surprise, Heather gave a small nod.

"I'm sorry," she said through gritted teeth. "That was presumptuous. L.A. is your ground, as much as the woods are ours. I will accept your decision."

"Damn right you will." Jackie glanced at her colleague. "Lucy, convince me."

"The Tolderai are good people," Lucy said. "Although it looks like they're going through some difficult times. I trust Heather, and I think it would be a shame to waste Carol's and Mackam's potential by locking them up if we don't need to."

"The code says we should send them to Trevilsom."

"It does."

Jackie stared at Heather for a long time.

"Fine," she said at last. "The magical code's there to do good for people, not the other way around. You can deal with this within your tribe this time, but if it happens again, they're off to Trevilsom."

"That's fair."

"You three clear this up right now." Jackie waved her wand at the surrounding greenery.

"Of course."

"We'll be waiting outside."

Jackie and Lucy walked out of the overgrown area, leaving the Tolderai to tidy up their mess. Nearby, Jim was inserting suggestions into the minds of the mundane witnesses, then sending them on their way.

"Thanks, Jackie," Lucy said. "I know Heather's not the easiest person to deal with."

"No problem." Jackie shrugged. "What can I say? I love a woman with big boots."

"Did you just—"

"Boots with a 't.' Honestly, your filthy mind." Jackie grinned. "Now come on, we both need to get home in time for date nights."

CHAPTER SEVENTEEN

"Howdy, ma'am," Ellis said as he sat. Around him, the coffee shop was late Saturday afternoon levels of busy. The establishment was full of shoppers resting after a busy day of bargain hunting, couples meeting up for an evening out, and plenty of people who were only there to get out of the house. They read books or magazines or the screens of their phones while they took their time over large cups of coffee.

"I've told you before, Ellis, you don't need to call me ma'am." Margaret Sunder gave a slender smile across her coffee cup. "You don't work for me any more. You can call me Margaret."

"Sorry, ma'am, but it just don't seem right." Ellis grinned. "Habit's the hardest chain to break."

"You sound like a fortune cookie. Please don't tell me this is what Los Angeles has done to that fine mind of yours."

"Don't reckon I've gone full native yet, but if you see me

with a yoga mat, maybe it's time to knock some sense back into me."

"Didn't your charming young lady mention the other night that she does yoga?"

"Yes, ma'am, and I'm grateful for all the happiness it brings her and her friends, but I ain't saluting the sun any time soon." He took a sip of his coffee and looked around at the bustling shop. "I've got to say; I didn't figure you for a Starbucks fan."

"What did you expect?"

"I don't know, something more..." Ellis trailed off, realizing that there was no good choice for his next words.

"Refined?" Sunder asked. "Classy?"

"I, uh, I didn't mean that..."

She laughed, a sound that Ellis had seldom heard in the decade they'd known each other.

"You can stop sweating, Ellis. I'm not going to take offense. I know there are better places around here, ones with a more distinctive style or staff who are more passionate about getting their coffee right.

"I feel a certain loyalty to these people, given where we put our underground stations. Something is comforting about finding the same place in a different city. The same chairs, the same menu, the same sort of staff in the same outfits. You know where you stand."

"I guess that's one way to look at it."

"You've not found that? I thought with all the travels I've sent you on that you would've craved an anchor in the familiar."

"Travel was never a burden for me. I liked going to new places, finding new things. I looked for coffee shops that weren't like those I knew, for restaurants with weird local menus. I didn't want an anchor holding me down. I wanted a brisk wind carrying me forward."

"And now?"

"Guess an anchor found me." Ellis grinned. "Or maybe I found a harbor pretty enough to make it worth anchoring myself."

"I fear this metaphor may be straining beneath the storm wind of reality."

"Reckon you might be right, ma'am."

"What did I tell you about that word?"

"I don't rightly remember. It was a whole two minutes ago."

They sat and chatted for a while longer while the people changed around them. Families came and went, couples met up and departed, friends gathered in excited clusters while the staff labored at their steaming machines. The rich, uplifting smell of coffee was everywhere.

"I have to admit, this isn't only a social meeting," Sunder said. "I wanted to ask you a favor if that's all right."

"Of course." Ellis set aside his cup. "I owe you my whole career. If I can help, I will."

Sunder slid a piece of paper across the table. Ellis unfolded it and read the name and address of a business. Underneath was a list of keywords.

"They're a magical business," Sunder said. "One that I have some concerns about."

"And these words?"

"I would like to see whatever documents the company has relating to those words. I was hoping you could help."

"A break-in?"

Sunder nodded. "If that's what it takes."

Ellis tapped the paper against the table. It wasn't as if he hadn't done this sort of work before and done it for Sunder. It was something he was good at. It was part of what had made him such an invaluable roving agent. It was hard for a fugitive to stay hidden when the agent on their trail could get into almost anywhere and get out again without leaving a trace.

Still, something about this felt odd.

"Hope you don't mind my asking, but ain't there no one in your division who you can use for this?"

"There are people I could ask, but there are issues as well. This company is well connected, and if the wrong person finds out that I'm investigating them, it could cause trouble. The whole investigation could unravel. I need someone who has the skills to do this discreetly and who I can trust absolutely. I can't think of anyone better than you."

"Shouldn't this have come through Applegate? He's my boss now."

"Roger is a good man, but he's not the most delicate of hands. I'd rather not involve him this time." Sunder tilted her head. "Of course, if you'd rather not do this, then I understand. I can try to find an alternative arrangement or perhaps deal with it myself. It's been a few years, but I think I still have the skills."

"No need for that, ma'am." Ellis folded the paper shut and slid it into his pocket. "I've got this. It might just take me a little while, between other commitments and finding the right time to keep it discreet, but I'll get it done."

"Thank you, Ellis. I knew I could count on you." Sunder

glanced at her watch, a delicate silver device. "I should get going. One of the local senators invited me to a fundraiser this evening, and I don't want to leave Harold Kowal upholding the good name of the Griffins all by himself." She stood. "It was very good to see you. We should do this again soon."

"I'd like that. You take care, ma'am."

"Margaret."

"You take care, Margaret."

She patted him on the shoulder, then headed out.

Ellis sat for a moment toying with his half-empty coffee cup, very aware of the piece of paper sitting in his pocket. Then his phone buzzed.

"Hey, honey," said Sarah as he answered the phone. "I'm ready earlier than expected. Are you in town already?"

"Starbucks on Wilshire."

"Great, I'll come find you there. I assume you don't need time to change."

After hanging up, Ellis played a game on his phone, trying to distract himself while he waited. When Sarah arrived ten minutes later, she found him staring out the window, gazing into the distance. She kissed him hello, and he blinked at her in surprise.

"I'm not that shocking, am I?" she asked with a playful smile.

"Don't reckon you've ever been shocking in your life."

"Sounds like it could be a compliment, so I'll accept it." She took the seat across from him, where Sunder had been. "Are you okay? You seem distracted."

"Nothing important."

"Are you sure? Whatever it is, you can talk to me. You know that, right?"

"I guess. I just..." Ellis laughed at himself. "There are certain things I ain't used to being able to talk about with anyone. But then, I want to be open with you about everything."

"You do?"

"Of course. I love you." He reached across the table and took her hand. "This one, it's got to be kept absolutely secret, you understand?"

"Of course. Anything you tell me goes no further. I promise. Now, what's got your face so crumpled up with worry?"

Ellis explained the favor that Sunder had asked him, how similar it was to his previous work, but how it also felt out of place.

"Am I worrying over nothing?" he asked. "I've done work like this before, and it's been fine."

"I think you should trust your instincts. They've gotten you this far, haven't they?"

"I guess. But my instincts are pulling me in two different directions here."

"Well, for what it's worth, I think this sounds shady. I mean, why did she meet you here instead of briefing you at the Silver Griffins' offices?"

"Keeping it on the quiet, I guess. She did say that she didn't want to run it through Applegate."

"That doesn't seem at all suspicious to you?"

"Maybe." Ellis shrugged. "It's like meeting here. It could be perfectly innocent, but..."

"You don't have to do it. She's not your boss anymore."

"She's still important to me. I owe her."

"Pineapple smoothies are important to me. That doesn't mean I'd burgle an office for one."

"Did pineapple smoothies ever save your life?"

"Yes, from scurvy. Vitamins and minerals save our lives every day."

Ellis laughed. "Have I told you lately that you're the cutest?"

"You have, but you can tell me again."

"You're the cutest."

"So are you."

He got out of his seat and held out a hand.

"You wanna go get one of those fancy cocktails you love?"

"Ooh, yes! Something with pineapple. But only one, then dinner."

"To fend off the scurvy?"

"To stop me getting too drunk before we go out dancing!"

"We're going dancing?"

She took his hand and stood. They smiled at each other, only an inch between them. An inch and all the love in the world.

"I'd like to go dancing," she said. "Would you?"

"I'd like to go dancing with you."

"Well then." She kissed him briefly, then dragged him toward the door. "Drinks, dinner, dancing, in that sequence. Doctor's orders."

"What's this prescription supposed to cure?"

"The problem weighing on your mind. It'll feel a lot lighter by the end."

Ellis figured that she was right. Time and distraction would alleviate the burden of his uneasy conscience. That in turn would make it easier to do what he had to do. For all his qualms, he owed Margaret Sunder too much not to do like she'd asked.

There was burglary in Ellis' future. First, there were drinks, dinner, and dancing.

CHAPTER EIGHTEEN

It was a beautiful evening in the underground forest. Although when Twylan thought about it, every evening was a beautiful evening in the forest. That was how the forest was supposed to be.

It wasn't a necessity for the forest to have an evening or at least one that was recognizably like an evening on the surface. Given that it was lit entirely by magical light, the cave could have been kept in a state of bright daylight twenty-four hours a day or followed any other rhythm the Tolderai came up with. They could have lit it with night-club-style strobes, and it would still have been functional.

However, keeping to the patterns of nature suited the Tolderai, and it suited the plants they were growing, giving them the sorts of rhythms they would have had on the surface. This encouraged the cycles of life, growth, and death on which they'd founded the forest.

It was also pleasing to experience. Twylan enjoyed seeing the light around her fade to a golden sunset glow, then into a twilight gray. It never descended into pitch darkness, retaining at least the pale shine of a brightly moonlit night so that work could continue on the forest if anyone was in the mood for it.

Tonight, many of the Underfoot Brigade were in that mood. They came here more and more, using the forest as a way to get outside without actually getting outside. If they went out in the parks of L.A., they had to do so in disguise, hiding Leontine's wings, Twylan's eyes, and all the other features that made them unique. Down here, they could run freely through the woods. They could be themselves.

Sunset was approaching as Twylan planted lilies around the base of a tree. It felt good to get her hands into the soft dirt while the warm light flowed across her. She smiled as she patted the earth down around one plant, then reached for another. Leontine, Kix, and Siltor were all working nearby. Mackam was there to oversee them, the rest of the Tolderai being busy elsewhere.

"Have you planted other forests?" Twylan asked. "Up on the surface, I mean?"

"No need to plant forests up there," Mackam said. "Nurture them, protect them, but not plant them. Forests plant themselves."

"Even now, with so many chopped down?"

Mackam grimaced. "All right, maybe plant some now. The problem is, with those planted forests, they end up being neat rows of trees, regular and unnatural, waiting for some logger to chop them down. It's not right."

"Maybe you can plant more like these forests up there?"

"That's the plan, in the end. If we're not too late." Mackam bent to look at Twylan's work, and the tinfoil under his t-shirt crinkled noisily. "This is good. You've a gift, girl. Shouldn't be wasted on the Griffins and their detective work."

"I like that work."

Mackam shook his head. "What a waste."

There was a flicker, the lights of the cave briefly stuttering on and off. Mackam looked up, eyes narrowed.

"That should not happen," he said quietly.

Like a sprinter from the starting blocks, he took off at an extraordinary pace, dashing through the trees. Twylan and the other Underfoots ran after him. Though decades younger, they couldn't keep up with the Tolderai.

At the edge of the forest, Mackam leaped onto the wall and scrambled up, clinging to the intertwined network of roots and branches. He ascended until he was hanging almost horizontal from the underside of the ceiling, his feet hooked into branches, one hand holding him in place while he ran the other over one of the magical lights.

"What if he falls?" Kix asked fearfully.

"Then I'll catch him," Twylan replied, readying magic in her hands.

If there was ever a risk that Mackam might fall, he covered it well. He hung unwaveringly from the ceiling, fiddling with the light until it came out in his hand. Across the ceiling, other lights flickered and erratically throbbed while he worked.

"Here, gifted girl," he shouted. "Catch."

The light dropped from his hand, still glowing, and fell through the forest canopy. Twylan reached out with her magic, slowed the light's descent, and drew it straight into her hands.

"Work out what's wrong," Mackam shouted. "I'm going to try to fix the rest."

All across the cave, the light faltered for a moment, plunging them into complete darkness. Twylan imagined with dread how much harder it would be to find handholds on the ceiling in the complete absence of light. Then the sunset glow returned, and she saw Mackam scamper, spider-like, across the ceiling.

Deciding that there was nothing more she could do to stop or to help him, she sat with the light in her lap and examined it.

Like so much else in the cave, it seemed to have been grown. The cluster of glowing flowers together made something like a regular light bulb. When she peeled back the outer petals, she found a delicate tracery within, like fragile green veins that held in a swirling, shining mass of magic and pollen. It had a powerful magical aura, but one that was reassuring rather than overwhelming.

Siltor waved a hand across the light. "It's not an illusion."

"We could tell," said Leontine. "On account of how it was really lighting up the whole cave, and it didn't vanish when she held it."

"Actually, illusions can play on your sense of touch as well, and they can even produce light that will illuminate other things around them. How else do you think they trick your eyes?"

"Through magic."

"Magic that uses light."

There was another flicker from the lights, including the one in Twylan's lap. She felt a shift in the magic. It was as if it was shifting in line with some external force, its vibration like static on an old-fashioned radio.

"Something else is causing this," she said. "But what?"

She closed her eyes and ignored the conversation of the other Underfoots, focusing all her attention onto a single sense—that of magic. She felt its strands flowing around her, sensed the rhythms and the changes, the spells at work in the cave. She knew the aftereffects of others cast there earlier in the day and the hints of other magic flowing under it all.

On the ceiling, Mackam kept scrambling from light to light, trying to get them back to stability. He was a glowing beacon of magic amid the foggier, more uncertain images around her. Those images shifted as a pulse of magic, faint but still significant, ran through the cave, and the lights flickered again.

She opened her eyes.

"There's something out there," she said. "I'm going to look for it."

"We'll come with you," Leontine said, and the others nodded.

"Mackam!" Twylan called. "I'm going to look for the source of the problem."

"Good girl," he shouted back. "I'll be here stopping these things from busting apart."

Twylan closed her eyes again for a moment and looked at the patterns in the magic of the world all around them. Now she had a sense of the magic that was interfering, it was easier to find, not just one signal but three or four. She picked one and headed out of the cave, keeping that magic in her head, watching for it as she strode down the tunnels with the others in tow.

"Where are we going?" Siltor asked.

"Tracking the magic," Twylan said as they reached a junction. The magic was stronger on the left, so that was the way they went. She still had the Tolderai's organic light in her hand, but she summoned others as well so that the way remained lit even when that one faltered or flickered, as happened more often the further they went.

"What should we look out for?" Leontine asked, flexing his wings as he often did before charging into trouble.

"I'm not sure yet," Twylan replied. "Let's keep going."

The twists and turns of the tunnels carried them upward, closer to the surface, but otherwise kept them close to the cave's location. Bends eventually turned back on themselves, repeated left forks evened out into a spiral until they came into a concrete tunnel and another junction. The pull of interfering magic was powerful in both directions.

Twylan sat on the floor, the flower light in her lap, and tried to work out how she should progress.

"Leontine, Siltor, you go left," she said. "Kix, go right. All of you, just go a little way, see what you can find, then come back to me. Understand?"

"Got it."

They hurried off, Twylan's lights floating around them, while she sat and cradled the glowing flower ball.

"What is wrong with you?" she whispered to it. "You seem fine in yourself, so are you just too delicate for this world? Can you not cope with other magic around?"

After a few minutes, the others returned.

"We found a dead end," Leontine said. "It looks like someone built down from whatever's above, and their basement plowed through the old tunnels."

"Could you tell what was inside?" Twylan asked.

"Magical machinery of some sort. It was noisy."

"What about you?" Twylan looked at Kix.

"One of those old transit tunnels. There are a bunch of magicals in there casting a ritual. I think they're trying to improve their acting abilities."

"Their acting abilities?"

"There were a lot of video cameras lying around. I suspect they're all YouTubers and TikTokers, or whatever video influencing platform's popular this month."

"Two completely different things and both are contributing to the interference." Twylan stroked the flower bulb. It was flickering more often now and more intensely. The proximity of the sources of interference was making the situation worse. "I suppose the city has more and more magic, and it's used more intensely. It's getting in the way of the Tolderai magic, causing it to fail."

"So what do we do?" Kix asked.

"We could go beat up some influencers," Leontine said. "Anyone who gets paid for posing in the right pair of sneakers deserves it."

"I'm not sure that's a solution."

"It'll make me feel better."

"We're not beating anyone up," Twylan said. "We go back, we tell Mackam, and we make sure Heather knows. This could be affecting the other caves too. The Tolderai will need to work out a plan for how to solve it."

CHAPTER NINETEEN

"Should we have picked somewhere fancier?" Charlie asked, looking around the Mexican restaurant. The place was cheerful, with warmly colored walls, wooden furniture, and a mass of happy customers. "I mean, it's not every week we get a date night out without the kids. Maybe we should make more of the occasion."

"I'm here with you," Lucy said. "And with this mojito. That's good enough for me."

Charlie grinned. "You have a point. It's about the company, isn't it?"

"And about where we could get a table for Saturday night."

"Well, here's to excellent company and to the babysitter. May she have a peaceful evening."

They *clinked* their glasses and drank. The mojito was crisp and refreshing, just what Lucy needed after a long day of dealing with the difficulties of the magical world.

"I don't think peaceful is going to be the order of the

day," she said. "Eddie was reading a book about kangaroos before we left."

"Oh, dear. Poor Emily."

Charlie imagined their gray-haired sitter chasing Eddie the kangaroo around the house, trying to persuade him to stop bouncing off the furniture and to return to bed. The image amused part of him, but another part was appalled.

"Should we go back?"

"And miss out on this?" Lucy held up her menu. "Not likely. He'll tire himself out in the end, and it's not as if Emily hasn't coped with these things before. After all, she raised magical kids of her own."

"Yeah, but there's raising a couple of junior witches and wizards as they struggle to master their spells, then there's trying to herd Eddie as he changes through whichever dozen animals are on his mind this week."

"Relax." Lucy squeezed her husband's hand. "Enjoy yourself. If Eddie's going to jump on the dining table and break it in two, he'll have done that by now."

"You think he might—"

"I'm winding you up. Now settle in your seat and decide what you want to eat."

"Oh, I already decided that. I'm having enchiladas."

"Then stop fussing and give me time to decide."

The waiter appeared a few moments later, and they placed their order, then sat back, enjoying their drinks.

"You still look tense," Lucy said. "Please tell me you're not worried about Eddie."

"No." Charlie shook his head. "Well, mostly not."

"Then what is it?"

He looked at his drink, frowning as he sifted through

the thoughts clogging up his brain. "I think it's a work thing."

"You think it is?"

"You know how it goes. Sometimes it's hard to work out which thing's really bothering you, as opposed to all the things you're getting bothered by because of that thing. Does that make sense?"

"Near enough. So what's this work thing? Keiran finally slacked off so badly that he's in trouble? Gail got a job elsewhere, and now you're stuck with all the real work?"

"Those guys." Charlie shook his head. "Honestly, I barely think of them when I'm not in the office these days. No, I was thinking about my other work."

Lucy couldn't help smiling. Since she'd encouraged Charlie to chase his dream and set up in business making magical changes to reduce the pollution from cars, she'd enjoyed seeing how it enlivened him, how it added to his passion for life. Although it had taken time away from her and the kids, it had been totally worth it for the quality of time they got when they were together. But "work" had still been the software job that took up his regular office hours. This was the first time she'd heard him refer to the side business as if it was his default job. It was clearly turning into a serious thing.

"What's the matter?" She squeezed his hand. "Is this a conversation we need more mojitos for?"

"Not need, but I wouldn't say no." Charlie polished off the contents of his glass, then held the empty up for a passing waiter, a pair of fingers extended beside it.

"Of course, sir," the waiter said. "On its way."

Charlie sat back and used a straw to push the ice

around the inside of his glass like it might reveal some hidden cache of booze.

"I guess this was the right place," he said.

"So, work..."

"Oh, yes! So, we're picking up more business, which is great, but it's causing a couple of problems."

"Problems like..."

"Well, first up, there's time. It's okay for Ringo. He's a freelancer. He can take on less work to fit this in. He's even started doing his bounty hunting at night, and apparently that works really well because people are less likely to be in a state to resist him."

"Seems fair. I'm a lot less combat-ready in my PJs."

"Right, but I can't switch to a night shift, and I have to do my set hours regardless. That means that we can't fit in all the jobs we're being offered or that we have to put them onto a long waiting list. That puts some people off, so we might lose their work, and it's not great for our reputation."

"Exclusivity isn't a selling point?"

"Not for this."

Now it was Lucy's turn to sit back thoughtfully. She knew what she wanted to suggest, but was it too soon? The business had only been going for a few months. Its long-term potential was unproven, whereas Charlie's office job had been supporting them for years. Still, dreams were dreams, and they deserved to be chased.

"You could give up the day job," she said. "I earn enough for us to get by, and hopefully, you'll soon earn more from your business than you ever did fixing other people's code."

Charlie smiled. "That's really sweet of you, and I might

take you up on it someday, but I'm not there yet. The thought's a little too scary. Besides, we need to solve the other problem first."

"The other problem?"

"When I said we had a couple of problems, this is the big one. We don't have anywhere suitable to work."

"Then what have you been doing up until now, if not working?" Lucy pressed her hands to her cheeks in mock horror. "Are you and Ringo just driving around L.A. all day, drinking beer and beeping the horn to scare little old ladies?"

"Very funny. We've been working in clients' garages, or occasionally at home, like that paint job the other day. We can't do all our work in the driveway because of the magical components, and not every client has enough space for us to work in. We've had to put some jobs onto a backup list because we don't have anywhere to do them."

"Could you convert our garage into a workspace?"

"Have you seen how much junk there is in our garage? The old furniture, the toys the kids don't use anymore, those bikes we keep saying we'll ride again someday. Plus, there are your supplies for work."

"We could clear some of that out. Not the work stuff, admittedly."

"Even if that made enough space, imagine the practicalities. If we're in there working every day, then sooner or later, Al from next door will take an interest. You know Al —the emphasis is very much on sooner. He loves a project and he understands practical work. He'll start sniffing around, he'll spot the holes in the answers we give, and eventually, he'll work out something he shouldn't.

"Even if we didn't have our very own Al, the issue of neighbors would be a problem. If we keep doing work there, people will notice and comment and maybe spot a pattern they shouldn't. It's not the place for it."

"Have you got enough money in the business now to rent a workspace?"

"Maybe, but it would need to be the right sort of workspace, and we'd have to inform the landlord about what we're doing, so we run into a lot of the same problems again."

The waiter returned, bringing their food.

"Quesadillas for you, madam, and enchiladas for you, sir. Oh, and the extra mojitos. Enjoy!"

The moment he was gone, they tucked into their food. It really had been a long day for Lucy, with the trip to the museum and two magical disturbances on the trot. The mojito she'd already drunk only added to her sense that she needed refueling. As she ate, a thought came to mind, and she slowed down on her chewing to mull it over.

"I think I might know somewhere you could work," she said. "Somewhere that's suitable for vehicles, where they won't ask awkward questions about magic, and where you can even borrow the tools you need when yours aren't suitable."

"Really?" Charlie set aside the joys of cheese and guacamole while he considered a real working future. "Where?"

"You know Gruffbar the dwarf?"

"That lawyer you've talked about? I thought he was a bad guy."

"He is, most of the time."

"Isn't he up against Max in a trial right now?"

"If he is, you can bet that Max is on the right side. That's not the point. Gruffbar's office is above an auto shop run by a lad called Gunther. Gunther's got some ogre in his ancestry, and he clearly knows about and accepts magicals because he's fine with Gruffbar and his clients."

"You think this Gunther has other magicals working in his shop?"

"Almost certainly. Maybe he'd be up for having two more."

"Why would he let us set up shop there? Surely he needs the space for his work? And we'd be competition."

"It's a big shop, and you wouldn't really be competition because you're offering a different sort of service from him. You might even be able to help each other. As well as paying rent, you could send your customers his way for other work, and maybe some of his clients would be interested in what you do."

"Hm." Charlie stroked his chin in thought, then realized that his fingers were greasy with melted cheese and hurriedly wiped the strands off his face. "It might work. Could you put me in contact with this Gunther?"

"I'll give Gruffbar a call." Lucy raised her glass. "Another toast to expanding your business. And to getting good things out of bad contacts."

CHAPTER TWENTY

The fundraiser was taking place in the ballroom of a grand hotel, one that Finn and his entourage had stayed in while they were scouting out L.A. prior to the move. That made things easier for Halldora. She'd been able to get most of her security checks done in a single day and had arrived secure in the knowledge that her boss would be safe here. Or at least that if he weren't safe, it wouldn't be because of any failing on her part. Ultimately, wasn't that what drove everything in the world of business? Responsibility and the unquenchable desire to avoid it.

Technically, she wasn't on duty tonight. Finn wanted her free for him to introduce to people, which she thought was a damn fool idea. She didn't like people. She certainly didn't like the sort of people she met at these events. She liked them least of all when Elethin was there, and Halldora was subjected to the sickening response every man in the place would have to the elf, with her ethereal beauty and her blatantly low-cut dresses.

That combination turned Halldora into the worst sort

of company, which was fine, because even if she was officially off duty, to her, that just meant she had an excuse to roam where she wanted and to provide a proper level of security for her commander and his people. Still, orders were orders, and Finn had ordered her to have a drink, so she sipped a Scotch as she circulated, dressed in a tuxedo with a classic black bow tie.

There was a noise from the stage at one end of the room, a wail of feedback as some idiot failed to manage the audio equipment. When it had settled down, their host took to the stage to deliver his speech. Halldora didn't listen. She knew what a politician's words were worth, and she could provide her own farts. Instead, she took the chance to ascend the stairs in the entranceway and assess the crowd.

There must have been four hundred of L.A.'s best and brightest in the room, or at least the city's wealthiest and most listened to. She didn't recognize all of them, although she made a mental note to get the guest list and start files for future reference. Still, from what she could see, around a quarter were magicals of one kind or another, whether passing like her and Elethin, heavily disguised like the obvious Arpak in the far corner, or the sort who seemed human to a mundane eye.

At least another quarter, the senator included, knew about magicals. That sort of information was more available higher up the social food chain. As for the rest, some must have picked up a hint that there was more to the city than most knew. Those were ones she had to look out for, the humans prying at the lid of a box they had discovered, trying to find the treasure within.

"...but of course, tonight isn't about me," the senator declared, having talked about himself for ten straight minutes. "So please, drink deeply, then dig even deeper into your wallets and give what you can to the disaster relief fund."

Applause rippled politely across the hall while Halldora made her way back to the Nuada Industries group. She hoped that no one tried to talk to her, as she'd realized that she had no idea what disaster the relief fund was for, and the senator's self-serving speech hadn't helped. Was it an earthquake somewhere or some outbreak of disease? It didn't matter. Once she got close to her commander and his ridiculous elf, no one would want to talk to her.

"Halldora, we've been looking for you!" Elethin exclaimed. She managed to make the words sound like an accusation as if Halldora hadn't been where she should, even though her orders were to mingle. The elf wore a diaphanous gold dress and a diamond necklace, with her hair carefully piled up to conceal the tips of her ears. She looked like something out of one of those ridiculous perfume adverts in which impossibly elegant women muttered meaningless phrases over a montage of abstract imagery.

Finn turned, and Halldora's resentments went onto the back burner. The commander was more compelling than ever, dressed in a white tuxedo with a gold cummerbund that—this annoyed Halldora more than it should—perfectly matched Elethin's dress. Finn smiled, and the whole world seemed to smile around him. He might have muted the glow from his magic, but the glow of his personality was inescapable.

"Senator Jones, this is Halldora Helmsguard, my head of security. Halldora, this is Senator Jones."

Halldora fixed her face into something approximating a smile.

"Pleased to meet you, Ms. Helmsguard." The senator reached down to shake her hand, and she caught that little spark of excitement in his eye, the thrill of a mundane man who thought he was in on a secret. "Is that name..."

"Icelandic, yes," Halldora said. She wanted to scream at him, "yes, of course, it's dwarvish, you ignorant stain on the inside of a good suit," but she was a professional, and screaming at important contacts was frowned upon. Besides, she was about to make the senator's life uncomfortable in a far more lasting way.

"I was wondering if you could spare a few minutes to talk privately with Halldora, Senator?" Finn was still smiling brightly. "Just to cover a few issues around policing near our new facilities."

"Of course." The senator smiled so wide it must have ached. "Anything for an upstanding member of our community like you, Finn."

Anything for a massive donor like you, more like, Halldora thought, but again she stifled it. There was a reason why Elethin did the PR work, not her.

"Why don't we go take a seat, Halldora?" The senator gestured at one of the booths at the side of the room. They'd been set up like diner fixtures, in keeping with the evening's 1950s Americana theme, and probably with soundproofing, so that all these important people could have the private conversations that fundraising events were really about.

Halldora followed Senator Jones to a booth and took a seat across from him. His bodyguards waited outside, hands loose at their sides, ready for any sort of trouble. Halldora noticed how the one on the left kept his head slightly turned so she was in his peripheral vision, and the jacket carefully settled for easier access to the holster under his arm. She'd get his name later. It was always good to keep an eye out for skilled recruits.

"So, policing, huh?" The senator's eyes sparkled like the bubbles in his champagne, a gleam that spoke of wealth, privilege, and things that could easily evaporate away. "You been having trouble around those new facilities of yours? Protesters, perhaps, or squatters? I'm sure I can get them moved along for a friend like Mr. Nuada."

Halldora took an envelope from her pocket and slid it across the table.

"Another donation?" The senator grinned. "For the relief fund, or me?"

It wasn't the man's greed that sickened Halldora. It wasn't even his directness; she liked directness. It was his sheer unflinching lack of class. Was he really nothing more than a wallet in a sharp suit?

If this had been a movie, she would have made implications, danced around the subject, and said things that people could interpret one way, but she clearly meant in another. Her words, set out on paper, would simply seem like a discussion of the fundraiser. Still, this wasn't a movie, and Senator Jones hadn't earned that level of effort.

"For you," she said. "Open it."

The senator's grin somehow grew even wider. Then it fell as he opened the envelope and saw the photos inside.

"Are these..."

"You?" Halldora asked. "Yes. But most definitely not your wife."

"This is..."

"An intrusion? An outrage? Don't try to play the offended party with me, Senator, because I won't give a crap. I have the originals and proof that they're real. With them, I could screw you as thoroughly as you've been screwing your top donor's wife."

For a moment, the senator went pale. Still, he was a professional, as Halldora was, and that finally gave her something to admire about him. He fixed his smile back in place and slid the photos back to her.

"You don't want the souvenir?" she asked.

"So this is how your boss works, huh?"

"Of course not. This is just me."

"Bullshit."

"Do you see my boss here?"

"So he has deniability."

"Think what you like."

"What does he want?"

"What I want, Senator, is for you to find distractions for the various regulators sniffing around our facilities. There will be no investigations into the pollution we produce, both magical and mundane. There will be no inquiries into any alleged mistreatment of our magical workers. And if any of our staff get ideas about unionizing again, they'll get no support from you or your office."

"I can't go anti-union, not with my support base."

Halldora pulled out another envelope. "I have photos of you with other parts of your support base. Would you like to see? I'm sure I missed a few, but it's an impressive collection."

"Screw you, and screw your boss." The senator was still smiling brightly, but his voice was icy cold.

"Not my boss, just me. Remember that, if any of this ever comes to light, or else..." She pulled out a third envelope. "This is the one with the whips." She slid all three envelopes back into her pocket. "We've paid you well, senator. We've paid your charity well and linked it to your influence. This is to make sure you understand who's in charge. Now, are you going to do like I asked?"

"Of course," the senator said. "What choice do I have?" He reached across the table and shook Halldora's hand. To her surprise, it wasn't some sort of crushing, alpha male handshake, a petty bit of punishment for what she had done. Instead, it was firm and respectful. "You're damn good at this, Ms. Helmsguard. If you ever find yourself in need of employment, and it's not because I've crushed you myself, come find me."

He headed off, his bodyguards following him. A few minutes later, Finn and Elethin slid into the booth.

"Well?" Finn asked.

"It's all good, sir," Halldora said. "He'll call off the dogs."

"Excellent. Thank you, Halldora."

"My pleasure, sir."

"Which ones did you show him?" Elethin asked a little too eagerly.

"Only envelope number one. He declined the rest. Apparently, the senator is only a philanderer and a kinkster, not a self-loving voyeur."

"And deniability?" Finn asked.

"I was very clear. You know nothing about this."

"You're my rock, Halldora. Both of you are. It's by standing on you that I reach higher." He took Elethin's hand. "Now, I need to take you out on the dance floor to give the tabloids something striking to share." He raised an eyebrow at Halldora. "Maybe you could find someone to dance with you."

"Thanks, sir, but no thanks." She waved her empty Scotch glass at a passing waiter. "I have better plans."

"Very well." Finn smiled at Elethin. "Come on then, my favorite arm candy, the dance floor awaits."

CHAPTER TWENTY-ONE

It was early on Sunday morning, and Elysian Park was quiet apart from the chattering of birds and an occasional jogger clumping along the dirt trails. Dylan stood at Angels Point, a tablet in his hand, comparing the landscape around him with the Tolderai bark pictures. Ashley was huddled around another screen with two of her Mini Griffin operatives, Mia and Tommy, trying to make sense of the same set of images.

"You really think there's treasure here?" Tommy asked excitedly.

Dylan tended to forget what younger children were really like because Ashley was so much more mature and sensible than her eight years should have allowed. Ten-year-old Tommy's grinning and rushing around the hillside had already reminded him what other kids were like, even magical ones.

"There's something," Ashley said. "Or at least there was, and if it's still there, I want to find it."

"Don't you think that the Tolderai will have found it by

now?" Mia asked. At twelve years old, she was closer to Dylan in outlook, and he appreciated having her on the case. It was always good to have company his age.

"They didn't have the picture or the map hidden in it," Dylan said. "It's been buried for centuries. Unless someone made another copy, we might be the first ones to hold a clue to the treasure since they abandoned that old settlement."

"Wow." Mia gazed across the landscape. "We could soon hold artifacts centuries old. Maybe even things that will go into a museum."

Dylan smiled. He didn't often meet kids with his same enthusiasm for history and for sharing it.

"Seriously," Tommy said, "treasure, here? It's all so ordinary!"

"Statistically, you're incorrect," Ashley said. "There are a disproportionate number of Silver Griffin call-outs to incidents in this area. In fact, I feel a little foolish for not spotting the pattern sooner. Magic attracts magic, and perhaps something here has been drawing other forces on a subliminal level."

"Subliminal, sure." Tommy lifted the front wheel of his bike and spun it so the shiny stickers on the spokes caught the sunlight. "Will there be gold, like in the pirate films?"

"There's only one way to ascertain that." Ashley slid the tablet into her backpack and picked up her bike. "This way."

They cycled a short way across the hillside, all the while watching for unusual activity or signs of a lost ancient civilization. Dylan knew that being sensible, it was unlikely they'd see anything out in the open, given how many times he'd been here with his family and how they'd not stumbled on any ruins. Still, he couldn't help feeling a little of the excitement that drove Tommy to pedal at a furious pace, racing ahead of the rest.

"Stop there!" Ashley called.

Tommy slammed on his brakes and stopped in a dip between two rises. Bushes sprang up on either slope, and a few trees hid them from general view. Once they'd all caught up with Tommy, Ashley got off her bike and took the tablet out again.

"We've come this way," she said, showing them the map she'd put together by combining clues from the Tolderai art, historic maps of the area, and modern online information. "That ridge matches the one that the goats were on in the picture. This one mirrors the route through the hills, with some adjustments for perspective and modern understanding. Which means that the entrance should be somewhere around here."

"Brilliant!" Tommy exclaimed. "I'm going to go look in the bushes."

He dropped his bike and ran off into the undergrowth.

Ashley shook her head and turned to Dylan. "You're our historian. What will the entrance look like now?"

"That depends on how it was left. I'm assuming that they hid it somehow, so there could be rocks blocking the entrance, or they might even have filled it with dirt. If that happened, we'll need to use detection spells then dig our way in. Since the Tolderai use so much nature magic, they might also have hidden it with plants, so we should look for a concealed entrance behind old trees."

"Could it be hidden magically?" Mia asked. "I mean by a spell, instead of using magic to cover it with dirt."

"Could be. We should look for that too." Dylan got a thoughtful look on his face. "Wow, that's a whole part of magical archeology I hadn't considered: finding and recording residual magic, like finding layers of dirt and recording them for information instead of just throwing them away."

"Do you know anyone who works like that?"

He shook his head. "Do you?"

"No." Mia smiled. "Let's go make a new sort of archeology."

With wands in hands, the kids spread out across the area, peering around trees and into dips in the ground, casting detection spells wherever they went. Rustles and creaks accompanied the search, and excited exclamations as Tommy kept plowing through the undergrowth.

After ten minutes of searching, something responded to one of Dylan's spells. There was magic around a particularly old and twisted tree, its bark gnarled and knotted, its trunk broad and squat. He stopped in front of it and looked up into the branches, then down at the roots. What was the spell doing?

"What are you looking at?" Tommy asked, appearing next to him.

"A magical tree."

"Cool. Like Treebeard?"

"Probably not. It hasn't tried to talk to me yet, or to crush you underfoot."

"I'd crush so many things if I was an Ent." Tommy stamped with one foot then the other and pitched his voice low for a monstrous roar. "Stop killing my forest, puny humans!"

Dylan walked slowly up to the tree and peered at its surface, then closed his eyes and focused on the magic. It was ancient and complicated, built to endure. That probably meant that the tree was far older than it should be, preserved by the spell. That also meant there was a good chance this was the hiding place. But how could he disentangle the spell, to understand how it worked?

Tommy, still in Ent game mode, ran in a circle around the tree, his wand outstretched and leaving a trail of leaves as he tapped into the one nature spell he knew.

"The forest shall march on Isengard!" he shouted.

Drawn by Tommy's noise, the girls approached.

"What's happening?" Ashley asked.

"This is the place," Dylan said. "The tree is full of ancient magic. I'm trying to work out what to do about it."

Ashley set her backpack down and pulled out a handful of silver strings. Each one was a robot, and as she tapped them together, they connected into something more complex, a stand with a cluster of sensors at the top and the robots' combined processing power behind it. She aimed the sensors at the tree and pulled out her tablet to see the results.

"This might take a little while," she said, "but I have all sorts of sensors. They should give us clues about how the tree works."

Mia walked a little way around the tree, then stopped.

"Tommy," she called, "was there anything strange around this side when you went past?"

"No, why?"

"Because there's a door now."

They all hurried around to see. Sure enough, an irregularly shaped door had opened in the trunk of the tree, bark hanging inward to reveal an opening onto spiral stairs made out of living roots.

"That's so cool!" Tommy said. "How did you do it?"

"I didn't," Mia admitted. "At least, I don't think I did."

Dylan touched the tree trunk, feeling the shape of the magic flowing through it. Then he looked at Tommy's wand, which was still spraying leaves into the air, and he laughed.

"Tommy opened it."

"I did? I mean, yeah, I did!" Tommy smiled proudly. "But, uh, how?"

"The magic was set so that someone could unlock it by casting nature magic in a circle around the tree. It's something that any Tolderai could do but that few other magicals would think of."

"Cool! Let's go get the treasure."

Tommy headed for the door, but Mia held him back.

"I think Dylan should go first," she said. "He has the strongest magic, he understands old things, and he's less likely than you to run straight into a trap."

"Hey, that's not fair!" Tommy scowled, then shrugged. "Okay, it is a bit fair. If I'd been Indiana Jones, I would have set off every trap in the place."

Dylan approached the shadowy doorway and raised his wand. "Lumen."

Glowing orbs appeared in the air around him.

"I'll stay here." Ashley reached up to lay a string robot

over his shoulder. "I can keep an eye on the bikes, and this will send me a video feed of what you see."

Dylan drew a deep breath. This was scary and exciting, both a thing he'd dreamed about and a step into the unknown.

"You got this." Mia squeezed his robot-free shoulder. "We'll be right behind you."

He nodded, then stepped through the doorway and into the tree. The root steps were uneven, and even going carefully, he nearly lost his footing twice as he descended them. They burrowed down into the hill, spiraling around and around, until they opened into a natural cave, long and rock-lined, disappearing into the darkness.

Dylan directed the lights ahead to show them the cave. But the glowing orbs had barely gone five feet before they stopped. Thinking that something was wrong with his magic, Dylan tried to move them again, but they wouldn't advance. He walked up to where the lights had stopped and reached out.

The air in front of him was as solid as stone and as smooth as ice. He ran his fingers across the surface, all the way to the cave wall. There, a line had been carved in the stone, with magical runes etched around it. The runes were cold to the touch and pulsed with power.

"How do we get through?" Mia asked, tapping on the magical field.

"I don't know," Dylan admitted.

"But the treasure!" Tommy wailed.

"We'll get to it. We just need time to work out how."

Ashley's voice emerged from the robot string on Dylan's shoulder.

"Sorry, guys, but Dad just called. We have to get home for lunch."

"But the treasure!" Tommy wailed even louder.

"We'll take photos of this," Dylan said, "go away and study it. If there's treasure through there, we'll get it another day."

CHAPTER TWENTY-TWO

Lucy pulled up her Rivian outside the Starbucks and Jackie climbed in, carrying a pair of cups.

"Tea for you, coffee for me." Jackie buckled herself in and they set off. "If I'm going to have what remains of my weekend ruined, I'm at least going to be caffeinated for it, so I've got the energy to be properly mad."

"Apparently some criminals work Sundays," Lucy said. "Shocking, I know."

"Only the inconsiderate ones."

"I don't think that consideration for others ranks high on a criminal CV. At least the traffic isn't so bad today."

"That's cold comfort for hauling me out of bed this early."

"It's one in the afternoon."

"Exactly."

"Oh, how did your date go?"

"It reminded me why I have a no accountants rule."

"Was she really that bad?"

"He this time. Not bad, only uninspiring. The kind of

guy whose life consists of work and the gym. Those things are fine, but there's only so much conversation you can get out of spreadsheets and deadlifts."

"So no second date?"

"Well, maybe. He was as good looking as the photos on the app, which is rare, and all that gym time's done wonders for his body."

"Jackie!"

"What? I've got to keep myself entertained while I'm waiting for Ms. or Mr. Right."

"What if you're too busy being entertained to see Ms. Right going past?"

"Then at least I'm having fun."

It was obvious when they reached the house the call was for. Police cars were parked outside, and there was yellow crime scene tape enclosing the front yard.

"I haven't done one of these in a while," Lucy said as she pulled up. "It always feels weird, intruding on other people's investigations. Like we don't belong."

"I like it. We're adding an air of mystery. Imagine the conspiracy stories some beat cops must invent about us."

"What if someone works out the truth?"

"When they could believe that we're from the *X-Files* instead? Not likely."

Holding their precious cardboard cups of caffeine, they walked up to a beat officer standing by the yellow tape.

"Good afternoon," Lucy said brightly and held out a business card that introduced her as an employee of Griffin Consulting. "We're the specialists Captain Phillips called about."

"Oh, right, sure." The cop shook her head. "Captain started calling in specialists from Scotland?"

"Actually, I'm English."

"Sure, whatever. In you go. Detectives are in the kitchen."

Lucy walked up the path and into the house, gathering her thoughts as she went. Not every part of L.A. had someone in its police command who knew about the existence of magic, let alone someone smart enough to realize when magic was part of an otherwise ordinary crime. That meant she got rusty at how best to work around cops, with all the complications involved.

The kitchen was a mess. Crockery lay shattered across the floor, and water had run out through it from the sink, although someone had now turned off the tap. A chef's knife stood upright with its tip plunged half an inch deep into the sideboard. Either the victim or the attacker had kicked over the trash can. The messiest part was undoubtedly the body.

The man had been in his late forties, going gray and expanding around the waist. He wore suit trousers, Simpsons socks, and the charred remnants of a white shirt. Whatever his attacker had used, it had melted holes through that shirt and into the flesh beneath, leaving charred circles across his skin.

In the center of his chest, a more intense attack had burned through his body, searing itself shut so that only the slightest hint of blood oozed out around the edges. His eyes were wide open, the pupils tiny and the whites bloodshot. All around him was a stink of magic.

Two detectives were crouching by the body.

"So you're the specialists, huh?" The first detective shrugged then stepped away, gesturing toward the body. "Take a look. See if you can make more sense of this than us."

The other detective nodded at Lucy as she crouched next to him. For a brief moment, something flashed in his eyes, and Lucy felt magic. So that was how this one had come to the Griffins' attention: a wizard on the case.

"Victim is a James Hooper," the detective said. "Forty-eight years old, works for the Patent and Trademark Office. Found this morning by a friend after he didn't turn up for golf. Looks like the attacker used some sort of heated implement."

By heated implement, the detective clearly meant heat spell. The precision of the circles and the lingering trace of magic around them made that clear.

"Maybe not heat," Lucy said. "Maybe light."

"What makes you say that?"

"The eyes. I've seen this sort of effect from certain sorts of bright light technology."

"So the light blinded him when it hit his eyes but converted to heat when it hit other parts of his body?"

"Yep. The attacker probably achieved different effects using different settings." Settings or spells, she didn't need to say.

"That explains the cameras," the other detective said.

"Cameras?" Jackie asked.

"Hooper got a home security system installed recently. Seems he was nervous about something. Around ten-thirty last night, the feed from the cameras went white one by one. Could be someone was shining bright lights at all of them." The mundane detective shook her head. "This is some proper supervillain bullshit. Frank, if it turns out that your consultants here work for Lex Luthor, we're going to have words."

The other detective laughed and rose to his full height. "I figured we could do with their scientific knowledge."

"Whatever. I'm going to see if the uniforms found anything in the back yard."

"Think you might find a cigarette while you're out there?"

"I said I'd quit slowly. A day like this isn't the time to rush it."

Once she was gone, there were only magicals left in the room. The remaining detective lowered his voice.

"Thanks for coming, guys. This one is... Well, I don't think it's only the obvious part, magic as a weapon."

"What do you mean?" Lucy asked.

"Hooper dealt with magical patents as well as mundane ones. He sometimes got called in as an expert by companies wanting to make sure they got the paperwork right or when lawyers needed a specialist witness. If you're developing magical tech in LA, you've probably encountered him and his team."

"You think that provides a motive for murder?"

"Maybe. There's a lot of money riding on this stuff. But then I—" He stopped mid-sentence as his partner strode back in, her phone in her hand and a lit cigarette between her lips. "What's up, Jill?"

"Brainwave," she said. "This is why I smoke. Those quiet moments give me time to compute."

"There are other ways to—"

"Save it, preacher man, and look at this." She showed them all an image on her phone, another body with a charred wound, this time a single one through the chest. When she flicked to another image, it showed bloodshot eyes and shrunken pupils. "I picked this one up while you were on leave last month, almost forgot about it because that idiot in the morgue called it an electrical accident. But look, it's the same weapon, right?"

They all looked from the photo to the body, then back again.

"Who was this?" Lucy pointed at the phone screen.

"An executive at a tech company, Leading Lighting maybe, something like that."

"Leader Luminosity?"

"Yeah, that sounds about right." The detective took a last drag on her cigarette, then flicked it out the window. "Smart guy. He'd started as a technician, actually understood his company's tech, which is more than you can say for half these guys. I thought that seemed strange, guy like that managing to electrocute himself."

"Could one of you send me these photos?" Lucy asked.

The detective looked at her partner, eyebrow raised. "Is that allowed?"

"I'll arrange it," he said. "Do you guys need to see anything else?"

Lucy shook her head. In an ideal world, she would have gotten her wand out and done a thorough sweep for residual magic, but she couldn't do that with all these mundane cops around. It looked like she'd be back after dark once they were gone. There went even more of her weekend.

"We'll go run some tests," she said. "See if we can find the tech that did this. If we make any progress, we'll let you know, and if not..."

"I know how it goes." The detective wizard gave them a knowing nod. "See you around."

As the Silver Griffins headed out into the street, Jackie was on her phone, using a Griffins app to call up recent investigative reports.

"It's not only two of these cases," she said quietly. "There are two more, at least. The cops haven't joined the dots yet."

"Let's hope they never do. I don't want to have to 'never was' half of L.A.'s finest."

Lucy's tea had started to go cold, forgotten in the excitement around the body, but she took a big gulp of it anyway. Like the detective with her cigarettes, Lucy found that a moment with tea could often help her think.

"Light magic," she said. "One lad winds up dead at Leader Luminosity, and another in the patent office. What are the odds he had a connection to Max's court case?"

"You think Leader's up to no good?" Jackie asked.

"No." Lucy drew a deep breath. "I think it's Nuada Industries."

They reached Lucy's SUV and stood, staring across the hood at each other. Jackie took a swig from her coffee and grimaced.

"It fits," she said. "Nuada and his minions rely on light magic. We already had that run-in with a light-powered magical at the lab, and now we're finding bodies dropped by light."

"We have to tell Applegate. This could be huge."

"No." Jackie shook her head. "It's too huge. Nuada's powerful, rich, influential. Even senior Silver Griffins have been telling us to cooperate with him. If we turn up with nothing but suspicions, they'll tell us to drop it, or worse yet, word will get back to him. We need solid proof before we even tell anyone about this."

Lucy frowned. She didn't like this. Their work was supposed to be above politics and vested interests. Sure, they kept the secrets of the magical world from outsiders, but within their community, they tried to be honest and open. Thinking about this case twisted her insides in knots. Still, Jackie was right, and there was more at stake here than Lucy's comfort.

"All right," she said. "We'll do some digging around on the quiet, try to prove what we know. But it's only a secret for as long as it needs to be."

CHAPTER TWENTY-THREE

"Shall I drop you at home?" Lucy asked as they drove away from the crime scene.

"If that's okay," Jackie said. "Then I can get back to the important Sunday business of doing nothing."

Lucy's phone buzzed. It had slipped from its usual resting place, and the screen was at an awkward angle. She didn't want to crane her neck that way while at the wheel but didn't want to miss it if there was yet another emergency. The weekend seemed to be full of them.

"Can you check that?" she asked.

Jackie picked up the phone and tapped the screen.

"Text from Heather Fields checking if you're on your way."

"Oh, bollocks!" Lucy slapped herself on the forehead. "I completely forgot to put that in my diary."

"What is it?"

"It's a phone app you use to keep track of your appointments."

"Very funny."

"Sorry, couldn't resist. Truth is, I'm supposed to be meeting Heather for coffee, and I completely forgot."

"When are you supposed to be there?"

"Ten minutes ago."

"Doh." Jackie glanced at the screen again. "This is your Tolderai friend Heather, the one who's always wearing lumberjack shirts?"

"That's her. Don't worry, I'll drop you at home, then give her a call and apologize."

"No, that's okay, you head straight for wherever you're meeting her."

"You're sure?"

"I'm sure. I have things I need to do out and about."

"Thanks, Jackie. I didn't want to be late. I think something's not right with the Tolderai, especially after what we saw yesterday, and I'm a little worried about Heather."

"She seems like someone who's got her stuff sorted."

"She's very capable, but everybody has days when there's too much to deal with."

"True. You want me to message her and tell her you're running late?"

"You have her number?"

"I have your phone, dummy, and I bet I can guess the unlock code."

"Oh really?"

"Let's see..." Jackie started typing. "Charlie's birthday? No. Eddie's birthday? No. Okay, you haven't gone for the most obvious ones." Jackie looked up at the ceiling, then laughed. "Of course, the date you and Charlie met."

"It might not be."

"Yeah, right." Jackie put the phone down. "That one, I don't know. Well played."

They found a parking space off South Vermont Avenue and walked up to Alchemist Coffee Project. Heather nodded at them from a table in the window.

"You want to come in and say hello?" Lucy asked.

"It would be rude not to, after nearly arresting two of her friends."

The interior of the coffee shop was very young tech user, combining whitewashed walls, wood, and chrome. Heather sat with a black coffee and a half-eaten grilled Caprese sandwich.

"Hi, Lu," she said. "Jackie. Good to see you."

"I was with Lucy, so I figured I'd say hi."

"Hi back. You want to stick around?"

Jackie shrugged. "Is the food any good?"

"Hard to tell from one sandwich, but I've got no complaints."

"Then I'll risk it. Work called us out before I had breakfast." Jackie turned to Lucy. "Tea, right? Another black coffee for you, Heather?"

"Thanks."

While Jackie headed for the counter, Lucy sat across from Heather.

"I'm sorry," Lucy said. "I intended for us to have a chance to talk alone. I'm sure Jackie won't be here too long."

"It's fine. I asked her to stay."

"I guess."

"She didn't have to let me take care of Carol and

Mackam yesterday, but she did. Plus you trust her. That tells me she's someone I can trust."

"Okay." Lucy looked around the coffee shop and smiled. "Nice place, right?"

"You don't have to make me relax, Lu. I'm ready to talk."

"I..." Though she'd been exposed to Heather's bluntness before, Lucy didn't quite know how to handle it. The fact that her friend so seldom smiled didn't help. How was she supposed to judge whether Heather was happy or sad, comfortable or tense? How would she know when to stop asking questions? Better to start bland and see how the conversation went. "How are things?"

Heather drew a deep breath. She didn't usually couple her bluntness with openness, and Lucy half expected her to clam up.

"Everything's too much," Heather said. "That's why I agreed to talk. I don't like it, but what I'm failing at is affecting other people, including you, and that's when I need to do something about it."

"Failing?"

"The Tolderai. I'm failing the Tolderai." Heather's hand clenched around her knee.

At that moment, Jackie returned, carrying three cups on a tray.

"Here." She passed the others their drinks. "I have kimchi avocado toast on the way. I'm telling you both in advance as a warning. I'm hungry, I'm grumpy, and I will gut you if you mock my food choice."

Lucy glanced between her friends. Heather was clearly troubled, and Jackie wasn't exactly oozing sensitivity, but if it bothered the Tolderai chief, she didn't show it. Of course, she wasn't showing a lot, so that might not help.

"You were saying, Heather?" Lucy asked uncertainly.

"I'm not giving my tribe the time they need from me as chief, and that's why things are falling apart. That's why we had the nonsense you saw yesterday."

"You found time to give them a verbal shoeing afterward, right?" Jackie asked, drawing a frown from Lucy.

"Of course."

"Good."

There was a moment of quiet, all three women sipping their coffees. A waiter set a plate down in front of Jackie, then returned to the counter. Jackie set to devouring the food.

"So what's filling your time?" Lucy asked.

"Teaching the Underfoot Brigade." Heather set her cup down. "I enjoy teaching them. Really enjoy teaching them. I'm glad you pointed me in that direction, Lu. It uses up a lot of time and energy though. Even when I'm not teaching or planning, I'm thinking about the classroom. I don't have the attention and energy I want for other things."

"I'm sorry it's affecting you like that. The kids are getting so much out of it, but if you don't have the time, maybe you need to take a step back?"

"No." Heather practically stabbed the air with the word. "No, I... They need this. I can't give it up."

"And the Tolderai need you too?"

"Yes."

"And presumably your employers."

"I don't have employers."

Now it was Lucy's turn to frown as she took that one in and tried to work out its implications.

"You must have a day job," she said. "A way to pay the bills."

"I told you, the Underfoots are taking up my time."

Lucy rubbed her eyes. She knew plenty of magicals who lived double lives, maintaining a voluntary magical job alongside the mundane one that paid the bills. Similarly, there were people she'd met through the PTA who did lots of mundane charitable work alongside their jobs or alongside full-time parenting. This was the first person she'd met who had given up regular life for the sake of two voluntary jobs: teaching the tunnel kids and running her tribe.

"Heather, how are you paying the bills?"

"Savings."

Lucy looked at her, aghast. The thought of giving up long-term security for the sake of something like this terrified her. Sure, she'd suggested that Charlie give up his day job, but that was because she had a good job too. Even then, she'd felt a twinge of uncertainty. For Heather to let her safety net fall away was barely comprehensible to her.

"What happens when the money runs out?"

Heather shrugged. "Then I deal with that problem."

"No offense, but that's one of the dumbest things I've ever heard," Jackie said. "And I've listened to a three-year-old explain the plots of superhero cartoons."

Lucy glared at her friend. If she'd known that it would be like this, she never would have brought Jackie in.

"I agree," Heather said. "It's dumb. But I'm committed."

Lucy blinked in surprise. Maybe Jackie's approach

wasn't so bad. Had she misjudged what sort of treatment Heather needed?

"Could you cut back on the commitments?" she asked.

"Who else is going to teach the Underfoots?"

"All right, so there's no one for that. Could someone else lead the Tolderai?"

Heather snorted. "Carol's a soft-hearted artist who spends her days painting watercolors. Nathaniel's a postdoc who thinks like an academic and talks like a nervous student. Mackam wears tin foil to stop the government from listening to his heartbeat. Which of them has the strength to hold the tribe together?"

"None of them," Lucy admitted.

"Without a strong hand, and with public attention on them, they'd all wind up in Trevilsom," Heather said. "All our good work would fall apart. Nature would lose its protectors. I can't allow that."

"No time for a regular job then," Jackie said.

"No time."

"I bet knowing that adds to the sense of pressure?"

Heather nodded reluctantly. "It's hard not to think about it. My bank balance is..." She looked down into her coffee dregs. "...dwindling."

"I'm so sorry," Lucy said. "Is there anything we can do?"

Heather shook her head.

"This is my problem to deal with. I needed you to know because there might be consequences. I wanted to ask you to be gentle with my people. They'll need more attention than I can give once I find a job."

"You've started job hunting?"

Heather sighed. "I don't have much choice."

So that was how far the bank account had dwindled. At least Lucy could help a little.

"Let me get this," she said, gesturing at the plates and coffee cups. She took out her wallet.

"No," Heather said. "I will pay my way. I paid for this already."

"Same here," Jackie said. "You'll have to be faster off the mark if you want to play mom to either of us."

"I'm not playing mom, I'm—" Lucy looked at her friends' expressions, and her eyes narrowed. "You're teasing me."

Jackie nodded. Heather almost laughed.

"But I really have paid my bill," she added.

Lucy put the wallet away. "Well, if there's anything else I can do to help, you let me know, understand?"

"Thank you." Heather gave a small smile. "Thank you for listening, Lu. And, this is hard for me to say, but if you have any ideas, please let me know. I need some way to square this circle."

Lucy glanced at the time.

"I should probably go," she said. "I made promises to the kids about some Lego building. You still want a lift, Jackie?"

"I'll stick around, get another coffee." Jackie waved Lucy away. "Go, do mom things. We'll be fine."

"Goodbye, Lu," Heather said.

As she walked out of the coffee shop, Lucy looked back over her shoulder. Heather and Jackie didn't seem to be talking, but they both looked quite content, sitting together with their coffee cups. That, at last, was how a weekend should be.

CHAPTER TWENTY-FOUR

Ellis crept through the darkness of the night toward an anonymous office block. For once, he wasn't wearing his suit, with the red tie and sneakers. Instead, he was all in dark gray, woolen hat covering his blond hair, down through the loose unbranded sportswear, to a functional pair of sneakers.

He walked up to the building quietly, looking around as he went, careful in case anyone was watching, but this was the precious time between when most bars closed and the first morning workers emerged, a period that was longer on a Sunday night like this. In short, it was the perfect time for a break-in.

He pulled out his phone and tapped on his spell readout app. Today, he was working with a complex mix of magic and technology, the two playing off each other, and this was his best tool for it. On the screen were readings from a spell he had cast, which detected security cameras in the local area.

He tapped his wand against the screen, and the spell

went into feedback mode, sending a magic jolt to the cameras. There was *hissing* in the air as every one of them blanked out. He didn't want to permanently break them, as that was more likely to raise questions so the spell would wear off in two hours. Conveniently, that also gave him an excuse to cut his burglary short.

With the watchful eyes of the information age cut off, Ellis approached the ground floor of the building. There were glass walls all around the lobby, which contained two rings of leather sofas and some abstract oil paintings. A security guard was on duty, but he was sitting behind his desk, reading a battered paperback.

"Dormio," Ellis whispered and waved his wand.

The guard yawned, stretched, and fell asleep at his desk.

"Liquescimus." Ellis tapped the glass in front of him. The wall melted, and Ellis stepped through, then poured the glass back into place with a wave of his wand.

He hurried across the lobby, vaulted the waist-high security barrier next to reception, and strode to the elevators. Thirty seconds later, he was riding to the eighteenth floor.

He stepped out into the reception of the company Sunder had sent him to—Living Sun Tech Ltd., a solar energy company. Past the reception desk, with its sign-in sheet and a flower vase emptied for the weekend, was another glass wall with an electronically locked door.

"Recludo." It was an old spell, using an old word, but wizards and witches had adapted it down the years to deal with all manner of modern locks. At a touch of Ellis's wand, the lock *clicked*. A gentle nudge opened the door, and he walked into an open-plan office lit by the sickly green glow of emergency lights.

Now came the question of where to start. Again, years of experience guided him. The best information came from the offices of senior executives and the desks of their assistants. Find a corner office with plenty of windows, and he would be almost certain of finding what Sunder had asked for. In a place like this, finding corner offices was the easiest thing in the world.

He started with the assistant's desk. A quick unlock spell got him into the drawers, which seemed at first glance to hold nothing but blank stationery and chewing gum. A closer look revealed a password on the last page of a notepad, where the assistant probably thought it was safe. The password got him into her computer faster than messing around with spells would have done. He plugged a thumb drive into the computer and activated the software stored on it, which would seek out and copy data related to his search terms off the computer and the parts of the network it had access to.

While that ran, he unlocked the filing cabinet that stood in a corner behind the assistant's seat. It was a surprisingly old-fashioned touch, which probably meant it contained something of interest.

Sure enough, in the second drawer down, Ellis found folders full of documents relating to the terms Sunder had given him, which appeared to be names for specific new technologies, as well as the chemical and engineering processes behind them. Ellis took out his phone and started photographing the pages.

A sound made him look up. Footsteps. Someone was on

this floor. He carefully slid the drawer shut and switched off the monitor, leaving the thumb drive to do its work. He crept through the door into the executive office and quietly closed the door behind him, then hid in a corner against the wall.

Through the glass of the door, he saw a security guard amble down the office, waving a flashlight from side to side, illuminating pieces of furniture apparently at random. The light wasn't really necessary. If anything, it would ruin its bearer's night vision and make it harder to spot things in the shadows. Still, if the light fell on Ellis, there would be no denying he was there.

He pressed himself further back, silently cursing the fashion for glass walls and open-plan offices, which left a burglar like him so exposed. The beam of the flashlight danced toward him, drifted across the assistant's desk, across the filing cabinet, across the floor toward Ellis's feet...

Then turned away. He breathed a sigh of relief as the security guard walked on.

Ellis approached the executive's desk. No computer— the guy probably had a laptop which he'd taken home to work over the weekend—and only one drawer. Ellis unlocked it just in case. The paperwork there definitely wasn't meant to be seen by anyone else. It contained confidential HR reports and secret internal emails the guy had probably printed out for proof in case of some trouble later.

There were also a couple of memos relating to the technology Ellis was after, so he snapped photos of those. He considered taking pictures of the other documents, which could have provided Sunder with useful leverage if she needed it. However, this whole situation still made him uneasy. Those documents lay outside the parameters of the specific mission she'd given him, so he put them back in order and locked the drawer without making copies.

He eased the door open and listened. The footsteps were gone, but he should be more careful, just in case. The guard might have sat to take a rest. He might come back around. The ghost of him couldn't freeze Ellis in place, or he would never finish his mission and get out, so there was a delicate balance to achieve. He let the silence wash over him a little longer, then crept out and returned to the assistant's computer.

He turned the monitor on and a glaring blast of artificial light hit him. The time at the bottom of the screen told him that he didn't have much longer before the security cameras came back on. That was the problem with an information raid: as soon as he started reading through documents, it was easy for time to get lost.

The thumb drive was almost done with its work. Two minutes left.

One minute.

Half a minute.

Footsteps again. Ellis switched off the monitor and crouched behind the desk. Once again, the security guard ambled down the office. Once more, his flashlight shifted across the floor, the desks, the walls. It hit the filing cabinet behind Ellis, slid across the desk in front of him, down to the floor, then jolted back up.

"Hey, you!" The security guard drew a taser. "I see you there. Come out with your hands up."

"Okay." Ellis rose into the spotlight's glare. He held his hands out in front of him. "It's a fair cop."

The guard walked toward him.

"Whatever you're up to buddy, I'm sure the police will be real interested." The guard put away his taser so he could reach for a radio.

Ellis flicked his wrist. His wand leaped from its quick draw holster into his hand. "Never was, never will be."

The guard stopped slack-jawed, radio in hand, unaware of the wider world. The spell had wiped the past few minutes from his brain and Ellis with them.

Ellis switched the monitor back on. His software had finished. He pulled out the thumb drive, shut down the computer, locked the desk, and hurried out past the security guard.

If there were more guards around, he shouldn't use the elevator. Instead, he rushed down eighteen floors of stairs, uncomfortably aware of the security cameras waiting to switch back on. If he ran that spell again, could he be sure of getting them all from in here? He wasn't sure, and he didn't want to take the risk.

At the bottom of the stairs, he paused to catch his breath and ease the door open. The only sound from the lobby was gentle snoring, which meant no one had found the sleeping guard.

Ellis walked past the elevators and looked around, making sure no one was there to see him, before hopping over the security barrier again. The external glass wall melted at a touch of his magic, then reformed after he stepped out into the cool night air.

Gray was seeping into the sky at the east end of the

street, a new day coming for Los Angeles. Ellis walked toward it. He pulled off his hat and stuffed it in his pocket, then unzipped his hoodie, revealing a green t-shirt for some sports club that he'd picked up in a thrift store. He tied the hoodie around his waist and set off at a run, one more early morning jogger among the enthusiasts who had emerged to beat the heat of the sun.

As he ran, the thumb drive bounced in his pocket. It felt heavier than it should, weighed down with the burden of illicit information, but it would soon be off his hands. As soon as he got home, he would message Sunder to let her know he had it.

Or maybe not straight away. He'd told her it might take a while, and he had other work to do. If that gave him time to ponder what all this was about, what was the harm in that?

Ellis picked up his pace and ran toward the dawn.

CHAPTER TWENTY-FIVE

There was one upside about having been called out several times over the weekend. Lucy didn't have to go anywhere near work on Monday. Instead, she lay on the sofa with her sketchpad in her lap and a cup of tea on the coffee table.

Eddie was playing on the carpet, rattling through a box of Legos as he tried to find the perfect piece for construction. He'd only recently started getting into Lego, but Lucy heartily approved. While it was fun to watch his imaginative games with his superhero toys, it was even more satisfying to see him get creative.

It was good to exercise her creativity too. She did a quick sketch of the ornaments on the shelf, then started drawing Eddie. She couldn't draw him from life, he moved around too much, but she'd spent so much time watching her adorable little son that she'd etched his face across her brain. Any time she wasn't sure about a detail, she could look up.

"Eddie?" she said.

He looked up, holding two fistfuls of Lego.

"Yes, Mommy?"

She drew a quick couple of lines, catching the shape of his jaw where it ran toward his neck.

"Nothing, sweetheart. You keep going with whatever you're building."

"It's a elephant."

Eddie held his construction up proudly. Very little of it was gray, and Lucy wasn't completely sure which end was which, but it certainly had the air of a large mammal. There were at least four legs, a trunk at one end and a tail at the other, though she wasn't completely sure which was which.

"That's lovely, sweetheart," she said. "Are you going to give it ears?"

That way she might be able to tell which end was the head.

"Ears." Eddie turned the elephant in his hands, contemplating that possibility. The tail fell off, or possibly the trunk did, but it didn't seem to bother him. "Yes, ears."

He rummaged in his box of Lego while Lucy continued to draw. After a while, the rattling stopped, and there was a contemplative pause.

"Mommy?"

"Yes, sweetheart?" Lucy smiled at him. A moment like this usually meant a request for a snack. She wondered if she would be able to get some fruit into him or if it would have to be cookies.

"Play outside?"

Lucy considered that one. At least she didn't have to dissuade him from consuming something sugary.

"Lego isn't really an outdoor toy, sweetheart. You could lose the pieces."

"Not Lego. Play outside."

"You want to play something else out there? Sure." Lucy picked up her tea. "Let's go."

They walked through the kitchen, out into the yard. It was a bright, sunny day, golden light streaming down onto the lawn. Lucy settled into one of the plastic chairs on the patio and watched as Eddie charged off around the garden, filled with joy and excitement. She almost hoped that he would interrupt her drawing and ask her to play with him. She liked the idea of joining in on those high spirits.

With a smile, she started sketching again, her focus on the paper instead of the yard. The sunshine warmed her skin, and she stretched her legs out, basking like a lizard.

A *thud* made her look up. An elephant had appeared in the middle of the yard, pressing against the lemon tree.

"Eddie!" She leaped to her feet and looked around. "You can't change into something that big. The neighbors will see you!"

Eddie raised his trunk and trumpeted.

"No, absolutely not! Change back this instant."

The elephant sank to its knees and looked at her plaintively. Its ears flapped against the sides of its head.

"I don't care how much you're enjoying this body. You change back right now."

The elephant sighed and closed its eyes. The air around it shimmered, and for a moment, its body flickered, but it didn't change. Another deep breath, another flicker. Then it opened its eyes and looked at Lucy with alarm. Its trunk reached out to her.

"Oh, sweetheart, are you stuck?" She laid a hand on the elephant's head. "We'll work this out together, okay? But we do need to work it out quickly. Now, what were you—"

"Hey, Lucy!" Footsteps approached down the side of the house. "You out here?"

"Sorry, Al," Lucy called to her neighbor. "Now's not a good time. Could you come back later?"

"It's the craziest thing," Al said, undeterred. "I swear I just saw the weirdest thing over the fence. It looked like—"

He fell silent as he stepped into the garden and stood gaping at Eddie the elephant.

"I've got a really good explanation for this," Lucy said.

"Uh-huh," Al said. "And that is?"

"Um... Well... Oh, shoot, I give up." Lucy pulled her wand out of her pocket. "Never was, never will be."

Al's mouth fell even more open as he stared vacantly into space.

Lucy turned back to Eddie. "Right, we need to sort this out before he recovers. So, why don't you try turning into a different animal instead of a boy? Maybe you can get back one step at a time."

The elephant nodded. The air around it shimmered, and a moment later, a giraffe replaced it.

"No!" Lucy exclaimed as the giraffe raised its towering neck. "A smaller animal, not one that can be seen all over Echo Park!"

The giraffe shimmered and turned into a gorilla, which beat its chest in excitement.

"Well, that's progress, at least." Lucy glanced from the gorilla to the back door of the house. Eddie could fit through there in this body, right? "Go inside, Eddie, before someone else sees you. I'll be there in a minute."

While Eddie maneuvered his muscular bulk through the doorway, Lucy took Al by the shoulder and led him around the house to his back yard. Gardening tools lay next to one of the flower beds, so she knelt him down there and placed a trowel in his hand.

"You've been here the whole time," she said. "Understand?"

Al nodded vacantly.

"Great. If you start to worry about where an hour went, you'll realize that you were enjoying the garden in the sunshine, and it was too lovely for words, okay?"

He nodded again.

"Great. Got to go. I have a gorilla to shrink."

She hurried back into her house. Eddie the gorilla was sitting on the sofa, which was buckling under his weight, stroking Buddy with one giant finger. If the dog was at all perturbed by the giant ape, he had overcome his qualms for the sake of attention.

"Okay, Eddie, let's get you down to something more normal, shall we?"

The gorilla nodded at her, then pointed out the window. A couple was walking past the front yard, a dog on a leash in front of them. Lucy grabbed the curtains and yanked them shut before the couple could catch sight of what was happening in her living room.

"Can you keep scaling down?" Lucy asked. "How about you turn from the gorilla into a sheep? You love sheep."

The air around the gorilla shimmered, and the fluffiest

sheep Lucy had ever seen replaced it. To her relief, the sofa no longer buckled under Eddie's weight.

"What next?" she asked. "How do we keep going down?"

Eddie apparently had his own ideas. The air shimmered, and a golden retriever appeared. It leaped off the sofa and started sniffing at Buddy, who sniffed back and yapped excitedly.

"You're not finished yet," Lucy said. "Keep going."

Another shimmer and the dog turned into a cat, which climbed back onto the sofa and curled up, ready for a nap.

"Not yet," Lucy said. "I know magic's tiring, but there's one more step to go. You can do it."

The cat yawned and stretched, and for a moment, Lucy thought that Eddie was going to ignore her request. The air shimmered one more time, and at last, he was a little boy again, curled up on the sofa.

"Cookie?" he asked sleepily.

"Maybe later. You have a nap first. Then we'll think about how to avoid this happening again."

When Dylan and Ashley got home from school, they found their brother and their mom in the secret base under the house. Eddie was drawing pictures in wax crayons, using lots of blocky shapes and straight lines. Lucy had a tape measure out and was taking notes of the lengths of walls and corridors.

"Mom, what are you doing?" Dylan asked. She had a purposeful demeanor that made him nervous, especially because she was in the special space the three kids had created together.

"Eddie needs a new room," she said. "Somewhere big enough that he can change into whatever animal he wants."

"Isn't the training room big enough?" Ashley asked.

"Not for an elephant, or a giraffe, both of which Al saw in the back yard this afternoon."

The kids looked at each other.

"Oh," they said in unison.

"Oh indeed. What's through here?" Lucy knocked on a wall.

"Not enough space," Ashley said. "Al's basement's that way."

Ashley opened a filing cabinet in a corner and pulled out a roll of blueprints. She spread them across the floor, revealing a plan of the whole tunnel complex and surrounding area.

"If we dig a tunnel this way, we can build a large enough chamber. We might need to line it with something though, so that the vibrations from elephant footsteps or lion roars don't disturb the neighbors."

"Roar!" Eddie exclaimed, and the air around him shimmered.

"Please, sweetheart, not now," Lucy said. "At least let us plan this first."

The shimmering subsided. Eddie, still in small boy form, came to look at where Ashley was drawing on the plans.

"It'll take a lot of work," she said. "But it will be an interesting challenge for my new generation of robots."

"And I can use my magic again," Dylan added. "Especially for getting rid of the soil. Precision digging will be really useful practice for when I'm an archaeologist."

"Mole dig." Eddie waved his hands around.

"That's the spirit." Lucy smiled. "Tell you what, why don't I fetch milk and cookies while you plan this out together?" She ruffled Eddie's hair. "Soon, you'll have the best transformation room a little boy ever had."

"Probably the only one a little boy ever had," Ashley said.

"And therefore definitely the best. Especially since you guys are building it." Lucy headed for the exit tunnel. "You keep planning. I'll be back as quick as I can."

CHAPTER TWENTY-SIX

"Have you all got your prisms?" Heather asked, looking across the underground classroom.

"Yes, Ms. Fields." The Underfoot Brigade held up their prisms.

"Have you all got your flashlights or light spells ready?"

"Yes, Ms. Fields."

"All right then." Heather waved her wand and the lights dimmed. "Now, set the prism on the paper and shine your light through it. What do you see?"

At their desk near the front of the room, Twylan and Kix shone a beam of light into the triangular column of clear plastic. On its other side, a rainbow of colored light fell across a sheet of white paper. Twylan smiled. She'd read ahead on the science they were studying and knew that this would happen, but it was still lovely to see, the clarity of the colors shining into the world.

"That's so cool," Kix murmured.

"Who can tell me what we see here?" Heather asked.

Several hands went up. Twylan's wasn't one of them.

She wanted to show off her knowledge, but she was starting to understand how important it was to give the others their chance. It was enough for her to know that she knew.

"Yes, Siltor." Heather pointed at the elf at the back of the room.

Before he could answer, the potted tree in the corner of the room started violently shaking. The whole class turned to stare as there was a creaking sound. The slender trunk swelled and buckled, and the bark split. Carol Winters stepped out of the gap, one hand clutched to her chest and a look of panic on her face.

"Heather, you have to come quick," she said. "It's Mackam. I think he's going to do something terrible."

Heather tossed a textbook to Kix.

"Page two-four-seven. Read it out to the class. Then I want everyone to write about what it means in their own words. I'll be back as soon as I can."

She followed Carol back into the gap in the swollen tree.

"Where are you going?" Kix asked as Twylan hurried after them.

"To help."

Twylan stepped into the tree, and the bark snapped shut at her heels. She had never traveled through the Tolderai's tree teleportation network before, hadn't even been sure that it would work for her, but she didn't want to be left behind, worrying about what was happening to her teacher.

Traveling through the trees was like being swallowed by a beast made of the living forest. Heartwood muscles tightened around her, then loosened, propelling her through a solid mass of rippling sinews. Sap flowed around her, into her mouth and nose, and when she gasped, there was no air, just sticky, green-tasting liquid flowing down her throat. In the packed, throbbing darkness, she had the terrifying realization that she didn't know how to get out, that she might die here.

Then a crack of light appeared ahead, there was a wave of cool, fresh air, and Twylan fell out of a tree onto the mossy ground of a Tolderai forest. She coughed up sap until her throat ached, then stumbled to her feet, dizzy but elated. She had done it. She had traveled by tree.

Carol stared at her.

"You shouldn't have done that," she said. "It could have killed you."

"But it didn't," Heather said with a note of pride. "Well done."

The Tolderai strode away across the forest cave, and Twylan followed, to where Leontine stood by the exit, his wings spread and shoulders tensed as if he was trying to make himself look big.

"Tell Heather what happened," Carol said. There was a hard edge to her voice that took Twylan by surprise.

"We were talking about the trouble with the lights," Leontine said. "He asked again what we found when we went to look for the cause, so I told him."

Heather's jaw twitched.

"There was a reason I asked you not to share that," she said.

"He was here when it first happened. He fixed the lights. He deserved to know."

"What did he do with that knowledge?"

Leontine's defiant demeanor faltered. He looked at his feet, then toward the tunnel mouth.

"He said he was going to teach them all a lesson. Something about removing a blight. Then he ran off that way."

"This, Leontine." Heather prodded him in the chest with one finger. "This is why I didn't tell him yet. Because I need to find a solution first. Because this isn't going to be fixed by Mackam's temper."

"He deserves the truth."

"You say truth like it's a good thing."

"Isn't it?"

"Too much truth can destroy us. Like bright light, it burns, and if you're not ready for the heat, you won't survive."

"I haven't killed him. I've just—"

"Sent him out on a rampage?" Heather shook her head. "I don't have time for this. Come with me, all of you."

Heather ran out of the forest cave. They all followed, racing along the root-lined tunnels, then into the concrete ones, and up, following a route that was familiar to Twylan. A route toward the causes of magical interference.

"How can you be sure he went this way?" Twylan asked.

"He's Tolderai, and I'm his chief," Heather replied. "I know. Besides..." A scream sounded from up ahead. "When Mackam loses his temper, it's hard to miss."

They emerged into the concrete chamber where Twylan had seen influencers working on their magic. The influencers were back, but their careful posing had completely fallen apart. Some pressed up against the walls in panic. Others were running around in circles and screaming, while phones and cameras lay scattered and shattered on the ground.

The cause of their panic was a vast willow tree that had sprung up in the middle of the chamber. Its roots and branches writhed like the tentacles of a giant squid, grabbing at people, chasing others as they fled, or pinning them against the walls with rippling strips of wood. At the ends of the chamber, viciously barbed thorn bushes blocked any hope of escape. Some of the magical influencers were trying to use spells to fight their way out, but their power was nothing next to the plants.

"Oh my God," Carol said. "This is worse than that time in Toledo."

Twylan drew her wand and rushed in, deflecting roots and branches, setting protective fields around the most vulnerable victims, trying to get the injured ones clear. A thick branch rose creaking above her, then slammed down. She raised her protection just in time. The limb shattered against Twylan's protective field, disintegrating into fragments, but hundreds more were still writhing, grabbing, slamming people against the walls with sickening *thuds*.

Carol laid her hand on Heather's shoulder, and Heather raised her arms to either side. She drew a deep breath and let the power of her people flow through her, ancient power from before anyone built these tunnels, before people raised cities, before humanity stepped off the plains and started to farm the land. Her eyes went green, and tears of sap ran down her cheeks. Then she reached out, stroking the air.

The tree stopped moving. Its branches and roots shifted, turning their attention to her. Those within reach brushed her skin. The plant, which had raged and destroyed only moments before, now touched Heather as gently as a mother holding a newborn baby.

"Time to let go," she whispered.

The leaves on the tree turned brown, then fell. Its branches shriveled and died. Roots retreated. Bark peeled from the trunk and tumbled to the ground as the tree's body caved in, then collapsed. At last, there were only fallen branches and dust, while the bushes at the tunnel exits withered to pale skeletons and crumbled away.

The terrified influencers stared at Heather. One of them reached with trembling fingers for a phone.

"No," Heather snapped, and the influencer's hand withdrew. "Carol, you stay here and tend to their injuries. Leontine, you help her. You made this mess. You can face its consequences."

Even Leontine didn't dare to resist the bludgeoning force of Heather's will.

The chief of the Tolderai turned and strode back the way they had come, each footfall hammering at the ground. Twylan hurried after her.

"That was amazing," Twylan said. "That tree, was it an embodiment of Mackam's anger?"

"Yes."

"You calmed it away."

"No. I took it into me." Heather's voice was a growl like a wild beast. "Now he's going to find out how it feels."

They followed the tunnel past the junction they'd come in by and headed the opposite way. There were crashes from up ahead and cries of alarm.

Heather and Twylan stepped through the shattered

concrete that had been a dead-end wall into a workshop. Like the influencers' chamber, plants had seized it. Roots had burst in, shattering the concrete walls and smashing the machines that lined them. Workbenches and tools lay scattered all around. Three gnomes, a wizard, and a Willen were all pinned to the ceiling by vines that tightened with each passing second, squeezing the air out of their lungs.

In the middle of the room stood Mackam, wand in one hand and knife in the other.

"You'll make fine compost." He waved the blade at his captives. "Oh yes. You upset the forest, but now you'll help it to grow. Roots will creep through your veins. They'll drink your goodness amid the silence of your noisy, filthy machines."

"Mackam," Heather said, her voice full of menace. "Let them go. Now."

"Their careless magic was hurting the forest. We can't allow that, Heather. You know this."

"As your chief, I'm ordering you. Let them go."

"Some chief." Mackam turned to her, and the light of a cracked florescent tube gleamed from the tip of his blade. "Too weak to fight back against outsiders. Too busy to lead the way."

"I'll show you who's weak." Heather held out her hands, and thorns sprang from them like wooden claws.

"Wait, stop!" Twylan stood between them. "Please, Heather, it doesn't have to be like this. That's not your anger you're feeling. Let it go." She turned to Mackam. "Please, do you think this will fix anything? That all the noise and magic of other people will go away?"

"More might come, but I'll cut them off as well." He

swiped at the air. "I'll cut and cut and cut until they don't dare come near."

"That's not how the world works. It's too crowded, too busy, too full of people and animals and plants. You can't win by constantly fighting. You have to find ways to work with others, to live with their magic, or you'll be fighting your whole life."

"I like to fight."

"More than you like to sit at peace with the trees?"

Mackam narrowed his eyes, snorted, then slid the knife into the sheath on his belt. "Smart girl. What's your solution?"

"I don't know yet, but we won't find it here. Now let them go. Please."

Mackam waved a hand. The plants released their captives, who fell to the floor. Roots and vines retreated through the shattered walls. All the plant life flowed away, leaving broken remains.

Twylan turned to Heather, nervous at how her teacher would respond. After all, she was chief, and this hadn't been her way of resolving things.

"Is this okay?" Twylan asked timidly.

"It's better than okay. And you..." She turned her attention to Mackam's victims, who lay shaking with relief. "Find a way to limit the magical pollution from this place. You don't want us to have to come back."

CHAPTER TWENTY-SEVEN

After the mayhem in the tunnels, it was with a sense of calm and relief that Twylan headed to the Silver Griffins' office the next morning. She loved the Underfoot Brigade, and she really enjoyed spending time around the Tolderai, but being with the Griffins gave her a sense that she could be something more than she had once thought, that she didn't have to live her life in the dark.

Except that now, things were more complicated. Having seen the notes left by Leontine's Uncle Valnay, doubts were creeping in. What if something bad had happened back in the day, something involving Finn Nuada? Was it really possible that someone in this organization would cover it up?

She couldn't imagine that. Not given the people she'd met. It had to be a misunderstanding. She just needed to ask someone about it.

She pressed her wand against the security box in reception, and the light went green.

"Careful on your way in," the receptionist said. "We had an accident with a piece of over-empowered messenger paper. The pigeons are clearing it up, but watch where you put your feet."

Twylan opened the door and walked in. Sure enough, the floor was crawling with worms. They were wriggling under the desks, down the corridors, even heading into the ventilation system. Almost the entire office's supply of messenger pigeons had been released to deal with them, and they were hopping eagerly about, gulping up juicy worms left, right, and center. Between the wiggling bodies and the fluttering wings, it felt less like an office than a pet store.

Twylan carefully made her way over to Lucy's and Jackie's desks. Neither witch was around unless they had turned into the pigeons occupying their seats, devouring pink piles of worms.

"This was Ground Zero." Sam, Roger Applegate's assistant, was wearing rubber gloves and scooping handfuls of worms into a bin. "Apparently, someone got a decimal point wrong when setting the enchantment on a batch of messenger paper. The first message sent with it was to Agent Heron, and when she read it..." Sam's arms went wide, miming an explosion of worms across the room.

"Oh, dear. Are Jackie and Lucy busy cleaning the worms off?"

"No, they had to go deal with the incident in the message. They left the rest of us to clear up instead." Sam smiled. "Although in fairness, they're now chasing a gang of trolls around the backstage parts of Disneyland, so maybe they didn't get the better option."

Twylan swept worms off a chair, ready to sit and wait, then thought better of it. "Would you like a hand?"

"If you're sure. I can go find you some rubber gloves."

"That's okay. I've been planting trees in my spare time. I'm used to dirt and worms."

Together, they roamed the office, gathering worms and dumping them into trash cans. Whenever one was full, Sam would carry it down to the pigeon loft, ready to provide future meals. After half an hour, they could walk around the office without constantly treading on worms. Another half an hour and it was almost back to normal, although the pigeons were still fishing loose worms from nooks and crannies.

"Thanks," Sam said. "You're an absolute legend."

Twylan blushed. "Happy to help."

"Go get yourself a coffee and chill out for a bit. If Agent Kowal turns up, I'll tell her you're here."

"Thanks."

Twylan headed for the break room and the delights of the Silver Griffins' coffee machine. It was far fancier than anything the Underfoot Brigade had, and she took the opportunity to treat herself to a cappuccino, complete with chocolate sprinkles.

Rather than head back to the pigeon-filled office floor, she sat on a sofa in the break room. When she'd first started visiting the Griffins, this had seemed like the least interesting part of the office. She couldn't see new tech here, learn new spells, or get a better understanding of the

Griffins' procedures. Over time, she'd come to appreciate the benefits of the break room. This was where people relaxed, which made it a good place to hear about the unofficial side of the job, the little niggles, the small triumphs, the office politics, the in-jokes, and stories about past adventures. Even to see who came in and out and learn the faces of the people she hoped to become colleagues with.

After a few minutes, Harold Kowal walked in, smartly dressed and smiling.

"Hello, young lady," he said. "How are you on this fine day?"

"I'm very well, thank you, Director Kowal. How are you?"

"I won't be running any marathons." He patted his hip and chuckled. "Other than that, I'd say all is well. And by this time in life, you learn to live with the phrase 'other than that.'"

Twylan watched as he fiddled with the coffee machine. She gripped her cup tight, nervous at the thought of what she wanted to say. No one else was around, which made this the perfect opportunity to ask the director about what she had seen in Valnay's notes. But what if the words came out wrong? What if it sounded like she was accusing Kowal of corruption?

She couldn't let that put her off. If she wanted to become a Silver Griffin, she had to commit herself to find the truth of the magical world, even when it wasn't comfortable.

Especially when it wasn't comfortable.

"Could I ask you something, Director Kowal?" she

asked.

"Of course, my girl." Kowal set his cup of coffee down on a table near her, then eased himself into a seat, facing the sofa. "Is it something procedural?"

"Something historical about an old Silver Griffins investigation."

"Ah, one of my favorite topics! Do you want to hear about the French mountain troll disaster? That was one of my finest moments if I do say so myself."

"Actually, it's about Finn Nuada."

"Head of Nuada Industries." Kowal looked away while he sipped his coffee. "Certainly an illustrious figure within our peculiar community and one who has often shown his support to the Silver Griffins."

"Wasn't he investigated once?"

The coffee cup stopped halfway to Kowal's lips.

"Where did you hear that?"

"I found an old newspaper cutting. It stuck in my memory because Mr. Nuada doesn't look any older now than he did then."

Kowal chuckled. "That's Finn for you. I believe that he's made up almost entirely of pure light, as are the rest of his kin. His body doesn't age at the same rate as us poor, sagging mortals."

"Were you involved in the investigation?"

"I was, for my sins."

"It was something to do with corrupt use of magic?"

"Essentially, yes. Another party accused Finn of using several magics that he shouldn't have had access to and applying his powers to twist governments and competitors to his whims. Essentially, to grab control of the market's hidden hand using magical power."

"You found him innocent."

"Oh, yes. The other party had blown things entirely out of proportion."

"Did you always think that?"

"Well, no, I was quite a vociferous critic at the start." He looked away. "Others made me see reason."

"So you don't think he did anything wrong?"

Kowal chuckled again, but the sound seemed hollow this time like he was forcing it out.

"My dear girl, we all do wrong from time to time. That doesn't make us creatures of evil. Sometimes it's better to correct someone's course than to sink their ship."

"You corrected Finn?"

"Yes, absolutely."

Kowal still wasn't looking her in the eye. Whether he was uncomfortable with what he was saying or with what he wasn't, something was clearly amiss. Before Twylan could decide whether she even knew how to dig into this further, Kowal pushed himself to his feet.

"It's been splendid seeing you," he said, "but I'm afraid that I have a meeting. No rest for the wicked, even when we're supposedly retired."

With another chuckle, he headed out of the room.

Twylan sat and drank her coffee, contemplating the conversation. It wasn't like she had anything else to do until Jackie turned up. A few Griffins went in and out, making coffee or using the snack machine, but for the most part, she was left on her own.

Then Margaret Sunder entered. She walked straight

over to where Twylan sat, pulled up a chair, and sat with arms folded, staring at her.

"I hear that you've been asking questions about Finn Nuada," she said.

Twylan nodded and pulled her arms in close. Sunder's tone had the sharp edge of outraged authority.

"This office's relationship with Nuada Industries is an important one. They provide us with essential equipment, as well as information and funding. Do you understand?"

Twylan nodded.

"I need to hear an answer," Sunder said.

"Yes, I think I understand."

"Good. Now understand this. Such relationships are delicate. They rely on the goodwill and good intentions of both sides. Nuada supports us, and we support Nuada."

"Nuada the man or Nuada the business?"

"I'll pretend I didn't hear such an obviously stupid question from a girl who thinks she's smart enough to work here. We support Nuada, Nuada supports us, and we need to maintain the atmosphere of goodwill that lets that continue. This means not reopening old wounds."

"I was just asking about an investigation."

"One that we resolved decades ago."

"What if the investigators missed something back then?"

"I assure you, *we* did not miss anything. This case is in the past, and that is where it should be left." Sunder stood, looking down at Twylan. "To be a Silver Griffin requires a certain strength of character and an ability to focus on what's important. We don't hire people who will waste their time on wild goose chases. Am I clear?"

"I...I think so." Twylan swallowed, fighting back the sick

feeling rising inside her. Something was very badly wrong here, and it was putting her dream of becoming a Silver Griffin in jeopardy.

Sunder leaned closer. "Don't wreck your career before it's even started, Twylan. That would be a tragic waste."

CHAPTER TWENTY-EIGHT

Ringo pulled the van to a stop in front of a large, blocky building with shutters raised on the front. Inside, mechanics were working on a variety of cars and vans. The floor was grease-stained; tools and engine parts lay all around.

"Pretty sure we have the right place." Charlie glanced one last time at the address they had. "Do we just go inside?"

"Why not, man?" Ringo adjusted his wraparound shades, unbuckled his seatbelt, and climbed out of the van. "We've got to give it a go."

As they walked into the auto shop, most of the mechanics turned to look at them. None were obvious, outright magicals, although Charlie suspected that most were only passing for human. All wore stained and well-worn overalls with well-appointed tool belts.

"Is Gunther around?" he asked.

A huge man in oil-stained overalls emerged from the

back of the shop., wiping his calloused slabs of hands on a rag.

"I'm Gunther," he said, his voice low and booming. "You the guys Gruffbar sent?"

"That's right." Charlie held out his hand. "I'm Charlie Heron, and this is Ringo Fuller. We're the practical side of Green Machine Conversions."

Gunther shook Charlie's hand with a grip that made him wince.

"I made you a space." Gunther pointed to one side of the shop, where there was enough room for a couple of vehicles. There was an empty tool rack on the wall and a heap of worn tires in the corner. Charlie assumed the tires weren't for them unless they were some sort of weird welcoming present.

"I'll bring the van in." Ringo headed off, spinning his keys around one finger.

"Nice place you've got." Charlie looked around. "Been here long?"

"Years."

"You fix hybrids as well as gas-powered cars?"

"Sure."

It was so tempting to make the next question about whether Gunther used whole sentences, but that was no way to start a working relationship.

"If we have a client who needs other work, do we call one of your guys over?" he asked. "Or do you want to check each job yourself?"

"Whoever's near. I don't hire idiots."

"And if you have a magical client who's interested in making their car greener..."

"I'll send them to you. But I don't got a lot of clients like that. Mostly, my people like their cars noisy and dirty."

Charlie had some responses to that, but again, they wouldn't help with a working relationship. He could try to win Gunther and his crew around to greener living later. For now, he should focus on getting started. Ringo had driven in and was opening up the van.

"I should go unload," Charlie said. "We've got a client coming in shortly."

"Do your thing. I'll do mine." Gunther lumbered off.

Charlie stood at the back of the van while Ringo handed tools, components, and paint cans to him. None of it was obviously magical or out of place in a workspace like this. At least it wouldn't be until they started using it.

As they finished unloading, their client turned up, a middle-aged wizard with an old hatchback.

"Take good care of her," he said as he handed the keys to Ringo. "We've been together a long time."

"No problem. Come back at the end of the day, and she should be ready for you."

Once the client was gone, Charlie pulled out his wand, ready to levitate the car.

"Whoa there!" one of the mechanics called. "You can't do that."

"I thought this was a magic-friendly workplace," Charlie said. "I mean, Gunther is—"

"Boss!" the mechanic bellowed.

Gunther emerged from under a van and strode over. A heap of loose bolts shook as he walked past.

"What?" he asked.

"These clowns was gonna cast a spell."

Gunther raised an eyebrow. "That true?"

"Well, yes," Charlie said. "Our whole business is about magical cars. You knew that when we took the space."

"You said you use magical components. You didn't say nothing about casting spells in the middle of the day."

"I'm sorry, I thought... I mean, you have Gruffbar the dwarf working out of your spare office. You must have magical things going on around here all the time."

"Yeah, well, that's not how we work on the floor."

"It's how we work," Ringo said.

"You wanna work around here; you'll find another way."

"Why?" Ringo persisted.

"Because this is my place and that's how we works. Got a problem with that?"

"Yeah, I have. It's a dumb way of working, not using powers when you could. They let you get stuff done faster and better. Hell, they're what our whole business model's based on, man."

"That so, man?" Gunther stepped up to Ringo. He took the edge of the bounty hunter's shades between a pair of thick fingers and lifted them off his face so that the two men looked each other directly in the eye. "Then you'll have to work slower and worse or learn to use your tools."

He tossed the shades aside, and they clattered on the floor.

"I've beaten guys senseless for less than that," Ringo said.

"You think you can beat me?"

"Yeah, I do."

"You wanna try?"

"Guys, guys, guys!" Charlie pushed in between them.

"We're off to a rocky start here, but there's no need to go nuts. Gunther, we'll hold off on the magic as much as we can. Ringo, this is still better than working on my driveway. Now come on, we've got an order to fulfil."

Gunther strode away, leaving Ringo to retrieve his shades. He put them back on, completing the outfit with a sneer.

"What an asshole," he said.

"You might not get on, but can you keep that to yourself?" Charlie said. "This place is valuable to us."

"Fine." Ringo grabbed a jack and slid it under the car. "But you're dealing with the bits that are awkward because of no spells."

With some extra effort, they got under the car, assessed its condition, and started dismantling the components they would need to adjust. Coating the car with magical spray paint, though an easier way to reduce fumes, was also more expensive, and there were no guarantees that the car would come out the color it had started. On one occasion, they'd accidentally coated one in chameleon paint that magically shifted with its background, which was awkward for driving around L.A. As a result, mechanical solutions were the default solutions, following the original technology whenever they could.

After a while, Charlie looked up from his work to see one of the mechanics staring at him. She had red hair and freckles that crowded together as she frowned.

"What you doing?" she asked.

Always happy to enthuse about their technology, Charlie held up the exhaust and started explaining the spells and filters that they would add to it.

"Stupid way of doing it," she interjected.

"What?"

"I said that's stupid."

"No, see, altering the exhaust is the easiest way to—"

"Not that. The rune. You want chill, not freeze. It'll put less wear on the pipe."

"I..." Charlie stared at his handiwork, then smiled. "Actually, yeah, that's a good idea. Don't know why I didn't think of it."

"Because you're a freaking amateur." The red-haired mechanic shook her head and walked away.

With practice, Charlie and Ringo were getting better at their work. By the middle of the afternoon, they'd made all the changes they needed to. All that remained was to run tests and do the fine-tuning.

"Let's get her down," Ringo said.

He drew his wand and lifted the car off the jacks, which Charlie hurriedly pulled away.

"Hey, what did I say!" Gunther strode up to them. "No spells."

"It's just a quick one, to get the car down off the blocks. Not like we kept it levitated for hours like we usually do."

"Are you trying to be a dick, or is it just an accident?"

"Hey, man, we're paying for this space. I reckon that earns us a little respect."

"Like hell it does."

"Guys, please." Once again, Charlie stepped between the two men. "There's no need to get worked up. The car's back down now. Everything's sorted, okay?"

"No, it ain't okay. If you're gonna work here, you need to follow the rules."

"The stupid, wasteful rules?"

"Ringo!" Charlie snapped. "Just keep quiet for a minute. Gunther, why have you even got this rule? If you used magic, you could get so much more done, even if you had to close the shutters to do it."

Gunther glared at him for a minute, but then something shifted in the big man's face. He looked around, grabbed the other two by a shoulder each, and dragged them to the corner, next to the heap of worn-out tires.

"These guys," he said in a low voice, nodding toward his employees. "They're all from magical backgrounds, but they ain't what you'd call magically gifted. Most they can do is levitate a pen, maybe summon enough fire to light a cigarette every few hours. They work here instead of in some magical place so's they're not reminded of that shit all the time. I don't use magic. They don't use magic, so why keep reminding them that they can't?"

"So they're, like, magically impotent?" Ringo asked.

Charlie pressed a hand to his forehead. "Excuse my colleague. Apparently, his mouth is working far harder than his brain today."

"I'm just telling the truth."

"Maybe try saying something helpful instead."

Gunther looked like he was about ready to punch Ringo's lights out, but he still kept his voice quiet. "I let you work here because Gruffbar persuaded me," he said. "Maybe he's got a point. If these guys can tap into what magic they've got, we could achieve more. But that ain't gonna happen through yous two showing off in the corner. Got it?"

"Got it," Charlie said. "We'll be extra careful. For what

it's worth, one of your employees has already shown that she might be ready to tackle magi-tech."

"I still think it's a stupid—"

"Ringo!" Charlie snapped. "I keep telling Lucy that's she's wrong about you being a useless jackass. Please don't prove her right." He sighed. "Look, Gunther, we're pretty much done for the day. Let us pack up and get this car back to the customer. Then we'll get out of your way. We can come back another day, get a fresh start."

"Maybe," Gunther said. "I need to think it over."

"Thanks for giving us that much, at least. Come on, Ringo, let's finish up and go for a drink. You can give me all the truth you want, as long as it comes with a chaser."

CHAPTER TWENTY-NINE

Lucy picked a worm out of her pen pot.

"How are you still here?" she asked. "It's been nearly two days."

The worm gave a wriggle that could as easily have been a shrug as a nod. A passing pigeon, seeing an opportunity, landed on the desk and looked hopefully at Lucy.

"Sure, why not."

She dropped the worm in front of the bird, which set to eating it, while she got back to her work. The file she had open was an old case report from the New York Silver Griffins. It covered a series of murders in that city, which they'd eventually connected to the magical mob. Bright lights and burn marks had featured prominently. There had also been some extortion and blackmail involved, though no one had ever worked out how the pieces fit together.

Critically, the people involved had been competitors of one of Finn Nuada's previous companies, a connection she might've missed if she'd simply searched for Nuada Industries. Nuada seemed snake-like in more than just his toxicity. He was also a man who liked to shed skins.

She reached the end of the file, a PDF scanned in during a recent archiving operation, and went back to the beginning. The document was dated 1987. Another she'd looked at was from the mid-nineties, and there was at least one of interest from the 1960s. Nuada and his light-powered minions, or someone a lot like them, had been up to shady business for decades. The problem was proving a connection.

Sam walked over, wearing a troubled look. "The boss wants to see you."

"Is something the matter?" Lucy asked.

"No, I..." Sam hesitated. "He just got a call from someone senior. I'm not sure who, but you know how his tone changes. It's left him rattled. Tread carefully in there."

"Thanks for the heads-up." Lucy grabbed the tub of home-baked cookies she'd brought in that morning. "I'll try to soften him up first."

She walked into Applegate's office and, at a wave of his hand, closed the door behind her.

"Biscuit, sir?"

"Oh, thank you, Agent Heron." Applegate took one of the cookies and nibbled on the edge while drumming the fingers of his other hand on the desk. "Mm, that's good."

"A little bit of cinnamon. It makes all the difference."

"Take a seat." Applegate set down the cookie and looked at her solemnly. "Agent Heron, have you been looking into old case files?"

"Yes, sir. Trying to connect the dots on some recent magical murders."

"In this research, have you been deliberately seeking out information about Finn Nuada?"

"Yes, sir. I have reason to believe that—"

"Let me stop you right there." Applegate held up a hand. "Do you have any proof that Finn Nuada is involved in a current magical crime?"

"No, sir, but—"

"Do you have any evidence proving that an employee of his is involved in such a crime?"

"Not yet, but—"

"No buts, Agent Heron. No ifs. Unless you have direct proof that Finn Nuada is involved in a contemporary case, you are going to drop this right now, and you will tell Agent Kowal to do the same."

"What makes you think that Jackie is involved?"

Applegate raised an eyebrow. "I may be older than you, Agent, but not all of my brain cells have died."

Lucy didn't have an answer to that, so she sat back and waited. Clearly, Nuada had found a way to get his hooks into Applegate, whether directly or through someone else in the department. It was frustrating, but what was the point in arguing back when he had shown his attitude this strongly?

"Finn Nuada is a good friend to this department," Applegate said. "And to the current political administration. But he has enemies, and we will not do their dirty work by digging up the corpses of long-dead scandals. Do you understand, Agent Heron?"

Lucy understood, all right. These weren't the sorts of words that Applegate himself would come up with. They had been fed to him, setting him up with the excuses he would need, and he was uncomfortable regurgitating them. He was equally incapable of defying his instructions.

"Will that be everything, sir?" she asked.

"Yes, Agent Heron, that's all."

"Very good, sir."

She headed for the door.

"Lucy," he called. She turned in the doorway. "They really are very good cookies."

"Thank you," she said. "Sir."

Out in the main office, Lucy flung the cookie tub down on her desk and scowled at her screen. She was supposed to be reading more reports, but apparently, that wasn't allowed. What could she do that would help with this case?

"How was he?" Sam asked her.

"Weird," Lucy said. "Frustrating."

"I don't know if this helps, but just before the call, he was talking to Jenkins, asking him to dig out some old tech." Sam took a cookie from the tub. "They were talking about light."

"Light?"

"Uh-huh."

Lucy grinned. "Thanks, Sam. You're a legend."

Lucy set off down the office at just short of a run. Maybe Applegate wasn't so badly twisted around after all. He had known about her investigation, he had seen the call from above coming, and he had set up some help for her just in time. Was this really what it took to run a branch of the Griffins, playing superiors and employees against each other? For all her management training, Lucy wasn't sure that was something she ever wanted.

She dashed down the stairs and stopped at the sturdy

door of the Special Equipment and Weapons lab. It took a few seconds for the hefty slab of steel to draw back, then she hurried through, around the corner, and onto the echoing firing range.

Jenkins and Nigel were standing at a trestle table, on which they'd lined up a row of devices.

"Ah, Agent 485," Jenkins grinned. "I heard that you might be on your way."

"Is this all new?" Lucy looked over the objects on the table. There was a chunky bracelet made of silver and mirrors and engraved with magical runes, a set of black baseball-sized orbs on a belt, something like a broad-barreled pistol in matte black, and a set of handcuffs, unusual only in the runes engraved around their locks.

"No, this is all material we've worked on in the past," Jenkins said. "We've hauled it out of storage and dusted it off for you today. Well, you and Agent Kowal. Is she coming?"

"I can take things to her," Lucy said.

"Oh." Nigel sagged a little. "Well, um, do you want to see..."

"Of course she does." Jenkins slapped the bracelet onto Nigel and thrust him away. "Go take your position."

With weary resignation, Nigel went to stand halfway down the firing range. Jenkins pulled a large tube with a handle from under the table and rested it on his shoulder.

"This one is a light cannon," he said. "Not for you, but the perfect test. Ready, Nigel?"

"Um, I..."

"Fire!"

A beam of light blazed from the cannon, struck Nigel, and scattered like strands of light reflecting off a disco ball.

"The bracelet's got a reflector field," Jenkins explained. "It will deflect ninety-seven-point-one-eight percent of light-based attacks, leaving the wearer completely unharmed. Isn't that right, Nigel?"

"I think so, yes. It didn't hurt this time."

"Splendid. Now, Agent Heron, I'm sure that, after seeing the cannon, you'll want a firearm of your own, and this is the answer."

Jenkins picked up the pistol. It was so dark that it seemed to swallow the light around it.

"I don't really like guns," Lucy said. "I've never been terribly good with them. Can we maybe leave that one out?"

"Are you sure?"

"I'm sure."

"You wouldn't like me to give it a few test shots to see your options?" Jenkins waved the pistol at Nigel, who flinched.

"No, thank you," Lucy said. Seeing Jenkins' disappointment, she added, "But I'll let Jackie know that it's available."

"Good enough. Now, how do you feel about grenades?"

"Probably not. I don't want to hurt a whole load of people at once."

"These won't hurt anyone." Jenkins held up the strip of black orbs. "They're shadow grenades. They cast a temporary magical field that absorbs all light in the area, no matter its source, plunging you into total darkness. Completely negates light-based weapons and will confuse and debilitate light-powered magicals."

"Okay, maybe that's worth taking." Lucy accepted the proffered grenades. "What do I do? Pull out this pin and throw?"

"Exactly! There's a small dial on the side if you want to adjust the time on the delay until detonation."

"Thanks, these could be really useful." Lucy remembered the charred body in the kitchen. Anything that could protect people from that had to be worth carrying.

"Last but not least, absorbing manacles." Jenkins held up one of the sets of handcuffs. "I don't know how many people you're facing, so I fished out every set I could find. They'll soak up almost any kind of magic or energy the captive can summon. It stops them melting the cuffs with heat, or blinding their jailer with bright light, or even using an unlock spell."

"That's brilliant." Lucy snatched the manacles from his hand, then scooped up the rest from the table. Annoyingly, she'd left her backpack at her desk, and she didn't have enough hands to carry all these goodies. "Do you have something I can transport them in?"

"Here." Jenkins pulled out a rainbow-colored backpack. "I won it in a raffle at Pride. Might as well put it to good use."

Nigel had returned to the table. He removed the reflecting bracelet and put it in the backpack, alongside the heap of manacles and the belt of grenades.

"I feel like James Bond," Lucy said as she zipped the bag shut. "I got the kit from Q, and now I'm heading out to risk my life on the mission."

"In that case, who's Miss Moneypenny?"

Lucy considered that for only the briefest moment. "Given the options around this office, I'd rather not know."

"Well, do be careful out there, Bond."

"Thanks, Q." Lucy adjusted the backpack and headed out through the blast door. She didn't have a plan yet, but she had the weapons, she had the suspect, and she wasn't going to let the bad guys win.

In her head, the *007* music played.

CHAPTER THIRTY

Lucy had just got back to her desk when her cell phone rang. Of all the people she might have heard from, she hadn't expected this one.

"Hi, Gruffbar," she said. "Is there a problem with Charlie and the garage?"

"Maybe, but that's not why I called. Can we meet?"

His tone sounded grim. Lucy couldn't work out what he thought he might get out of her, the criminal lawyer calling a representative of the authorities, but it seemed serious. Given his involvement in the Nuada trial, she shouldn't arrange a meeting with him now. He was on the opposite side of the Griffins and their powerful patron. Still, that was exactly why she needed to talk.

"There's a new exhibit at the art museum," she said. "I thought I might check it out this afternoon, see what all the fuss was about."

"Understood." Gruffbar hung up.

Lucy put her cookie tub into her backpack, then picked up both that and the rainbow backpack and headed for the door. Trying not to catch anyone's eye for fear that they would see her tension and doubt, she made her way across the office, through reception, and out through the Griffith Observatory to the magical subway. Normandy was at the station as usual, sweeping dust from his immaculately kept platform.

"Good afternoon, Agent Heron," the smartly uniformed gnome said.

"Afternoon, Normandy. How are you doing?"

"Not bad, not bad at all. I like your new bag."

Lucy glanced at the rainbow backpack. "It certainly stands out."

She got onto the next train and rode a few rattling stops down into L.A., then climbed the spiral of metal stairs to the secret magical door in the back of a Starbucks. The whole way, she thought about the mess into which she was getting tangled. Friends of the Griffins up to no good, her superiors telling her to back off a case, and an old opponent calling her for help. For years, the lines had seemed clear-cut, good guys on one side and bad guys on the other, but now they were tangled together in a terrible knot.

Walking from the Starbucks toward the Los Angeles County Museum of Art reminded her that things had never been that clear cut. When the Knights of the Hinterland had come to town, apparently set on magical theft, they had ended up as friends. Sometimes, good people got on the wrong side of an argument. Sometimes, bad people got on the right side. The truth wasn't anyone's to control.

Inside the gallery, she made for the hall displaying the new exhibit. Her spirits lifted at being there, walking past paintings and sculptures, admiring the beauty that human inspiration could create. She found a bench facing one of the new pieces and sat, admiring its swirls of color. This was more like it. No politics, no dubious motives, just her and the things she loved.

The bench creaked as Gruffbar sat. Neither of them looked at each other. This wasn't a meeting, just two art fans who happened to be in the gallery at the same time. No one could fault her for that.

"Nice bag," Gruffbar said.

"It's a bit too conspicuous," Lucy replied. "Especially given what's inside. I'm afraid I might have to stop using it."

"What is inside?"

"Best if you don't know."

"Now that's lawyer talk."

"What do you think of this one?" Lucy nodded at the painting.

"Nice choice of colors, but the brushwork's too loose for my tastes. I like to see control. That's real mastery of the craft."

"Mastery is good, but without inspiration, it leads to cold, mechanical results."

"I like cold and mechanical. Reminds me of the mines."

"Great. Now we can honestly say we talked about art. Why don't you tell me why I'm here?"

"Nuada Industries. How much do you know about them?"

Lucy froze. She didn't know whether to be excited that Gruffbar might give her a new angle or flinch in dread at this situation getting even messier. Ultimately though, she wasn't someone to hide from what was hard.

"I know that they're trying to sue your client out of

existence," she said. "And I know that they're up to no good elsewhere. Which means that, for once, I think you might be on the right side."

"You know I've worked for friends of yours, right?"

"Still, I default to suspicious where you're concerned. I'm sure you understand why."

"You're a master of your craft. I can accept that."

A couple of tourists came close and paused for a while, looking at the painting. Lucy and Gruffbar sat in silence, gazing at the art until they were alone again.

"I guess there's something to be said for a looser approach," Gruffbar said, "as long as it's purposeful."

"Much as I enjoy a good art conversation, I've got work to do and my kids waiting for me at home, so let's get a move on, eh?"

"All right. It's about the court case."

"You know I can't tell you anything, even if I knew it."

"Then let me tell you some things." Gruffbar stroked his beard while he gathered his thoughts. "First, I think my client might be in the right. I didn't expect that when I took on the case, but everything I've seen points that way. Which means that Finn Nuada lied under oath and that his people are perverting justice to get their way."

"I thought that was the sort of thing you approved of."

"Not when it's turned against me. I'm consistent that way. Second thing is that Nuada is adding to the lies, bringing in documents that didn't exist a few weeks ago, adding surprise witnesses to the pile. He's not just covering up for some past screw-up. He's building a lie to sink my client under.

"Which brings me to the third and most bitterly ironic thing. While I'm facing him in court, I can't lie."

"I thought that no one could lie in court. You all take oaths."

Gruffbar snorted. "People lie in court all the time. Part of being a lawyer is learning which lies you can get away with. 'I believe my client' is fine, 'I saw the judge robbing a bank' might cause problems. But facing Finn, I can't even tell the first sort of lie."

"He's casting a spell in court?"

"No, that wouldn't be allowed. But I think he's got some sort of background magic, something linked to that glowing light of his. It makes it impossible to say anything other than the truth."

"If you thought that was going to get you my sympathy, you really haven't considered who you're dealing with. I like seeing someone keep you honest, even if that someone is a scumbag."

"You shouldn't. Lies matter. They give us comfort. They give us defenses. They let us keep our private lives private. Without them, we're all shields down, exposed to the world. Yes, they're often used to shitty ends, but people can use the truth that way too, and that's what Finn's doing.

"Think what it means that he can stop people lying when he's meeting all these big, important people, and only one side has to tell the truth. He can dominate any negotiation, reveal the truth of a dark secret, dig out the emotional wounds we all try to hide. He can twist people around, and half of them will tell themselves that they always wanted to be honest with him, that he's a good buddy who's done them a favor by making them open up.

"Truth doesn't equal beauty. It doesn't equal justice. It's a weapon, and Finn Nuada is taking an atom bomb to a fistfight."

Lucy gritted her teeth. Gruffbar was right, and she hated that he was right. Hated it because it showed that Nuada was winning. Hated it more because it meant that she and Gruffbar were on the same side.

"It's a bloody awful situation," she admitted. "But just because you've got to tell the truth, that doesn't justify me telling you anything that could help you in court. That is what you're after, right, information you can use against him?"

"Come on, Agent Heron, this guy is abusing magic in a courtroom. Doesn't that mean you have to shut him down?"

"I can't argue that forcing people to tell the truth under oath is abuse, especially not if it's part of his nature. Maybe, possibly, if it was a spell he'd chosen to cast, but not this."

"What if I told you he was having witnesses killed?"

A chill ran down Lucy's spine as she realized where this was going.

"Go on," she whispered.

"James Hooper, a patent consultant. He was involved in lodging the intellectual property I'm defending. He wound up dead at the weekend. You think that's coincidence?"

"No, not given the way he died."

This time it was Gruffbar's turn to pause and absorb what she had said.

"You're on the case?" he asked.

"Uh-huh. He was killed using light."

"Of course he was. Nuada."

"More likely one of his minions, while he made sure he had an alibi. There was an executive at your client's firm too."

"Thompson?"

"That's the one."

"I thought that was an accident."

"So did the coroner. So did we, until now."

Gruffbar laughed. "This is great. If you've got this much piled up, you'll be storming Nuada's office any day now, right? I keep delaying, and you take care of the case for me."

"I wish." Lucy sighed. "Nuada's too well connected. People high up in the Griffins are protecting him. I thought it was because they weren't willing to see the truth about him, but maybe he's used his powers to get a hold on them."

"By my beard, this is worse than I thought. Can't you do anything?"

Lucy clutched the rainbow backpack close. Nuada's people were out there, taking down anyone who seemed like a threat to him. Blackmail, bankruptcy, murder, nothing was off the table. What happened when they decided that she or Jackie knew too much? Or when they wanted to take over more of L.A.'s green industries, like the part Charlie worked in? What happened when people like that were allowed to run free in her city?

"I can't do anything yet," she said. "But I'm working on it."

"And my client? Are you going to let this guy destroy him?"

Lucy drew a deep breath. She felt like she was about to cross a line. Still, Finn Nuada had wiped that line out himself, left it so that nothing separated her interests and Gruffbar's. Maybe, just maybe, Nuada had scuffed out the rules that had kept him safe.

Maybe she was kidding herself so she would feel okay doing what she wanted to. In the end, she might never know the truth. All she could do was what seemed right.

"I can't help you openly," she said. "But give me long enough, and maybe some information will fall into your inbox. Keep delaying until then."

She stood, a backpack over each shoulder.

"The judge won't give me much longer," Gruffbar said. "I've already pushed my luck on postponements."

"Then keep pushing, and I'll bring you what I can."

"Is that a promise, Agent Heron?"

"No promises, Gruffbar. Just the truth."

CHAPTER THIRTY-ONE

Dylan ran his hand over the magical field that blocked his way. It was the third afternoon in a row that he'd come down here, to the ancient secret Tolderai tunnel, along with Ashley, Mia, and Tommy. They'd thrown stones and spells at the field, tried to push through it with Ashley's robots, even spent an hour reciting as many likely magical passwords as they could think of, all without luck. The tunnel remained as firmly closed off as when they'd first found it.

"What about a battering ram?" Tommy asked. "I watched this film where they used one to break into a castle, and it was totally awesome. It, like, smashed right through the gates."

"Do you have a battering ram?" Dylan asked.

"No, but I bet Ashley could make one. Right, Ashley?"

"That's hardly a practical solution." Ashley looked up from rearranging her string robots. "It would be impossible to get any sort of working battering ram down the stairs. Even if we assembled it in here, there wouldn't be space to swing it for a good strike. Even if we somehow managed that, the force exerted wouldn't be superior to what we can apply through less cumbersome devices."

"So no?"

"No."

Tommy tapped on the magic field. "How about a bomb?"

"You want to blow this place up?"

"Just blow a hole through the magic."

"There are so many reasons why that is a bad idea. I don't even know where to start."

"I guess bombs are hard to get hold of, huh?"

"That's one problem, yes."

While Tommy discussed the challenges of bomb-making with Ashley, Mia came to stand with Dylan at the barrier.

"Do you understand it any better?" she asked.

"A little," Dylan said. "The magic is bound into the runes, and they're grounded in earth and stone, like roots reaching into the ground. It's a different approach to the natural world from what I've seen the Tolderai use before. Maybe they had different approaches back then or lost the knowledge, or I haven't been in the right place to see this before. I'm really looking forward to asking my mom's friend Heather about it."

"If you know the Tolderai, why don't we ask them to open it up?"

"Because it's our treasure hunt."

"You want to keep their treasure from them?" Mia frowned.

"No. It's not about what we find at the end, whether

that's a golden wand or a handful of dirt. It's about getting there and improving ourselves along the way."

"I like that."

"Thanks."

"Although it is the moral of half the Saturday morning cartoons I've ever seen."

"We're twelve years old. We can come up with the original insights later. For now, I want to get down this tunnel."

Mia ran her hand down the field until she was crouching at its base.

"Have you noticed how the field is weaker down here?" she asked.

"Really?"

Dylan crouched beside her and ran his fingers over the barrier. She was right. It wasn't a serious weakness, but it was there, like a thinner spot in the barrier.

"I think the ground has shifted." She pointed at a crack in the rock, which ran through one of the carved runes. "It hasn't broken the enchantments, but it's introduced an imperfection."

Magic flowed from her hand, pressing against the weak point in the barrier. Light glowed, and there was a crackling sound, but the wall held firm. After a minute, she gave up and sat back on her heels.

"It's no good," she said. "The magic is too strong. If only the imperfection was bigger, we might be able to wedge our magic into the gap and pry the barrier open. Even here, the barrier's too strong."

"Let me try." Dylan pressed his hand against the barrier and pushed with all of his magical strength. The field bulged, giving a little under the pressure.

"Wow," Mia said. "I've never seen anyone with that much power before."

"You should see my mom," Dylan said through gritted teeth. "It's no good, though. It won't break."

"Something has." Mia pointed at the ground. "Look, the crack's gotten wider."

"Not. Enough." Dylan kept straining, but the barrier wouldn't give way.

"Maybe not with only you..." Mia turned to the others. "Ashley, could your robots pry open a crack in the rock?"

"Maybe." Ashley hurried over with a handful of twitching silvery strings. She laid some of them down where Mia was pointing, pulled out her tablet, and started typing instructions. The robots braced against each other, then gripped the sides of the crack, their precisely designed bodies clinging to the tiniest of holds. Miniature motors whirred as they pulled at the stone.

There was a *click*, only a tiny noise.

"It's working!" Mia said. "Look, the crack's spreading."

Sure enough, one of the runes had split in two. While its parts still touched, their magical glow was faltering.

Dylan gave a renewed push against the barrier. It buckled under the pressure of his magic, and he leaned in, pressing against a growing weak spot. As the barrier shifted, the broken rune flickered, and its magical glow vanished. There was another *click*, and the crack grew wider.

"A gap!" Mia exclaimed. "Look, there's a gap!"

"It's so small," Ashley said. "Can we get through?"

"I can." Before anyone could stop him, Tommy dived forward and wriggled through the gap to the other side.

"That was silly," Ashley said. "You could get trapped there."

"It was awesome! I'm the first one through."

"Use your magic," Dylan said. "Link it to mine, and we can pull at the barrier from both sides."

"How do I do that?"

Dylan chanted a spell, and Tommy mimicked it. Trailers of magic ran from their hands down to the gap, where they linked up, forming a single stream of magic. Then, at Dylan's signal, they both shifted the spell, pressing against the barrier. At the same time, Ashley typed more instructions into her tablet, and the robots shifted, giving themselves more leverage.

There was another *click*, then another, and finally a sharp *snap*. The crack spread through the rock halfway across the tunnel. The runes flickered, then went out, and the barrier disappeared.

Dylan and Tommy, with nothing left to strain against, both fell on their backs, flung over by the force of their magic.

"We did it!" all four kids cried out in unison.

They took a few minutes to check for bruises and gather up Ashley's robots, then they set off down the tunnel, magical lights floating ahead of them. The tunnels kept going down, twisting and turning as they went. Sometimes a smaller tunnel would branch off to one side, or there would be a carved room. It looked like people had lived here once, temporarily at least, as there were shelves and wooden bed frames, although the mattresses and sheets had largely rotted away.

"Do you think this was their home?" Mia asked.

"Maybe a place to hide," Dylan said. "Like a bomb shelter. Somewhere to go in emergencies."

"That makes sense. If you had powerful magical enemies, you'd want a powerfully protected place to hide."

At the end of the tunnel, it opened into a cave. Unlike the ones above, this seemed to be natural, found rather than made. Stalactites hung from the ceiling, and water coated the smooth but uneven walls in places, like a layer of sweat across the skin of a stone giant. A stream ran in from one side of the cave, parted around a small island, and came together before leaving in another tunnel. On the island was a rock pedestal three feet high, with something on top that glinted as it caught the light.

"The treasure," Tommy whispered.

Dylan led the way across the stream, using magic to create a bridge that would keep their feet dry. They gathered around the pedestal, staring at the artifact lying there.

It was a bulky bracelet, apparently carved from clear crystal. The material itself was inanimate, but the carvings were the shapes of living things: vines, roots, flowers, all kinds of plants from all over the world.

Carefully, Dylan picked up the bracelet. As he touched it, the crystal started to glow, and its light intensified as he clutched it in the palm of his hand.

"It's drawing on my power," he whispered, overawed by the beauty of the carvings and the clarity of the light that blazed from them. "I can almost hear it, like a voice in my head. It wants me to put it on."

"Careful," Tommy said. "It could be a trap. Maybe it's a cursed artifact, and it'll turn you evil."

"I don't think the Tolderai would have anything like that," Ashley said.

"They might have taken it off someone else."

"Then they would have destroyed it."

"Maybe they couldn't. Or maybe they secretly didn't want to. Or maybe they thought they could do something else with it. Or maybe—"

"What do you think?" Dylan asked Mia.

"Do you trust the Tolderai?"

"I think so."

"I trust you. Try it on."

Dylan slid the bracelet over his hand and down his wrist. Immediately, shapes made of light sprang out around it, like holograms hanging in the air. They were animals and plants, detailed and animated, like real living things carved out of light.

Dylan focused on one of them, a mouse nibbling on an ear of corn. The others blinked out, and that one expanded. At his direction, it rose above them, shining so bright that its light filled the whole cave.

"It's shaped from light itself," Dylan said.

"Make something we haven't seen yet," Tommy said. "Like a lion."

Dylan dismissed the mouse and called to mind a lion. In his mind's eye, the artifact showed him several different images. He picked one out, and it appeared in front of them, the king of the jungle carved out of light, flinging back his mane and opening his mouth in a silent roar.

"This is so cool," Tommy said. "How about a robot?"

"I think it only makes pictures from nature," Dylan said. "It's got a lot of them stored in here."

"Can you add more?"

"I don't know yet."

"Then do one that's in there, like an elephant or a rhino or—"

Mia placed a hand over Tommy's mouth.

"Or maybe we should go back to the surface," she said. "It's nearly dinner time. We can explore this properly another day." She grinned. "I want a go before we give it back to the Tolderai."

CHAPTER THIRTY-TWO

"For the record, sir, I don't think you should be here." Halldora shifted awkwardly in her seat. It wasn't only the limo's plush interior that made her feel uncomfortable. Challenging her commander didn't come naturally to her, even if it was a better alternative than letting him walk into a fight.

"I understand that Halldora," Finn Nuada said. "Tell me again, why is this situation still not resolved? Why hasn't work started on the foundations for the new factory?"

"Resistance from a magical community activist group, led by Ammalda Redear. They've heard rumors of magic pollution from our other plants and don't want it close to them."

"Why is this still a problem?"

"Redear refuses to be bribed and isn't susceptible to blackmail. When we sent our people to take her out, she was ready for us and heavily defended."

"Exactly. Ms. Redear is a tough, independent individual, one who refuses to bend to my will. I can't stand that sort of person. I can't have them standing in the way of progress. Most of all, I can't leave them around, a witness to their own attempted murder. That's a witness who could decide to cooperate with the Silver Griffins."

"I understand the need to eliminate Redear, sir, but I'm still not convinced of the wisdom of your direct involvement."

"Your security team failed to take Redear out. My kin failed to take her out. There's only one way we can escalate from there, and that's to do the job ourselves." Finn opened the door of the car. "Shall we?"

Halldora stepped out of the car and drew her silenced Glock 17. Most of her colleagues might rely on magic in a fight, but she preferred the certainty and stopping power of a well-designed firearm.

It was long past midnight, and the residential street was devoid of witnesses. Even if there had been people around, they wouldn't have seen Finn Nuada in his full glory. Instead, it was a muted version of the CEO who stepped out of the car with his radiance toned down until he barely glowed at all, just the faintest of glimmers around his skin.

Guards stepped out of two other cars. Some of them were ones Halldora had hired, wizards, dwarves, and elves who had served in the military and with private contractors, magicals who knew how to apply violence and who had no compunctions about doing it. The rest were her commander's kin, those pale figures in their dark suits, their glow muted to match their leader.

Halldora gave a signal with her hand, and the guards spread out, surrounding the house occupied by Ammalda Redear and her friends. It was a wide, two-floored building, nothing extraordinary in itself. It was the people inside who made it important.

Halldora crept up to the front door, gun raised, and tried the handle. It was locked. It would have been suspicious if it hadn't been.

Finn extended one finger. A fine, bright line of light shot from the tip. Where it touched the door, it burned through the wood. Within seconds, he had cut around the lock. Halldora pushed, and the door swung quietly open.

The two of them stepped into a hallway. By the faint light cast by Finn, Halldora made out a rug on the floor and doorways leading to other rooms. She crept along, Glock at the ready, Finn a few paces behind her, and into the kitchen. Cover the entry and exit points first, then move on to secure the other rooms.

Something moved in the dark. Finn raised his light level, illuminating the room.

Ammalda Redear sat at the kitchen table. She was tall for a Willen, her rodent nose stubbier than most. She wore a t-shirt with a slogan protesting against Nuada Industries. A shotgun lay on the table in front of her.

She wasn't alone. Half a dozen other magicals stepped out of the shadows. Those who weren't carrying wands or spell enhancers instead had guns. They were calm, but Halldora felt the hostility radiating from them.

"I figured you douchenozzles would turn up again sooner or later," Redear said, her whiskers twitching. "I was expecting more of you."

"The others are outside," Halldora said. "You're surrounded. Now would be a good time to give up."

Redear snorted, a particularly impressive sound from a Willen.

"Give up on everything we've fought for?" she asked. "Just roll over and tell people that it's all right, Finn Nuada's not such a bad guy, and the pollution will barely poison you at all?"

"It's never too late to compromise."

Another snort. "It's not about early or late. It's about doing the right thing, something you clearly don't understand. I don't think that's the sort of giving up you were after anyway, was it? We're too far gone now. If I surrender at this point, I don't get a payoff and a comfortable condo. I get a bullet in the brainpan and a resting place in your factory's foundations."

"If you pull a shotgun on us, we'll have to defend ourselves." Halldora kept her attention focused on Redear while watching her companions from the corners of her eyes. Too many of them for her tastes. Not that she hadn't survived these sorts of odds before, even excelled in them, but it could too easily go sideways, and right now, she couldn't even signal for the others to come in without kicking off a shootout.

"Maurice, call the Griffins," Redear said. "It's time to show the world what Nuada Industries are really about."

One of her companions pulled out a phone.

Finn's body pulsed. Halldora had a split second to react. Even with her eyes squeezed tight shut, she saw the blinding light that followed.

There were curses and cries of alarm, a crash as one of the group tried to find the door and instead walked into a wall. Halldora opened her eyes and aimed her Glock.

"Finish it," Finn said.

Two bullets straight to the head knocked Ammalda Redear back out of her chair and onto the floor. Two to the chest of the witch behind her, and she dropped. Two more for a dwarf, right between the eyes. The silencer reduced the gun's roar to a soft thud, no louder than the bodies hitting the ground.

A wizard had raised his wand and was wildly firing spells. He might be blind, but he had great hearing. As Halldora took a step to turn, he pointed the wand straight at her, and a bolt of magic flung the gun from her hand.

She drew a knife from her sleeve and slammed into him. Three swift thrusts and the wizard joined his companions on the floor.

One of the wizards had managed to find the door and staggered out, hands outstretched. There were soft *thuds* from outside, and he fell back in, riddled with bullet holes.

One left, an elf, and her sight was returning faster than the rest. She squinted and raised her hand to Halldora, who flung herself aside just in time to avoid a freezing blast. The elf's other hand held a Ruger LPC, and she opened fire, the sharp *bangs* filling the cramped kitchen. Either she was still half-blind, or she was a lousy shot. One round hit the floor at Halldora's feet, and two more smacked into the wall behind her.

Halldora charged the elf, bringing her knife around in a wide motion that slashed through the flesh of the elf's fore-arm. There was a cry of pain, and the gun fell to the floor. Then Halldora was in close, ramming the knife into the elf over and over. The elf brought her right hand around, and magic sparked between her fingers. She extended them, spreading out across Halldora's head, preparing to unleash some deadly magic. Then the light died in her eyes and the magic with it.

Halldora stepped back and let the body fall to the floor. The room was clear. She grabbed a tea towel off the counter, wiped her knife clean, and sheathed it.

"The elf's gunshots," she said. "People will have heard. We should get out of here."

She would have preferred to have time to tidy up, to check for any traces of magic, to dispose of the magical bodies, and leave a mundane-looking crime scene. There wasn't time for that. One way or another, the Griffins would be brought in on this one. At least all the killing had been knives and guns, which made a connection back to her people less likely.

She retrieved her gun from the floor, then followed her commander out the door. It would be a shame to get rid of the Glock, it was a good piece, but there was no point getting sentimental about these things. A gun attached to multiple homicides was a gun she needed to dispose of, along with any records that might connect it to her. There were plenty more handguns to be had.

Flanked by their guards, she and Finn returned to the cars. Everybody piled into their vehicles and drove away.

"Well done, Halldora," Finn said. "I knew I could count on you."

"Thank you, sir. You realize that some people will claim that this was us, just because of our conflict with Redear?"

"Of course. I trust you and Elethin to find a suitable scapegoat. She has such a way with words. I'm sure she can talk the authorities around to any case we build, or perhaps even talk someone into confessing for us. It's amazing what people will do for her."

"Yes, sir." Halldora scowled. The elf again. Halldora was the one who had succeeded here, but somehow praise fell on Elethin.

Finn watched her with a knowing smile.

"Don't worry, Halldora, I value you too. Your skills are invaluable in the right circumstances and in the wrong circumstances..." He shrugged. "Well, that's why I have her and why I know that you'll stay with me. Because you know your limits, don't you, Halldora?"

"Yes, sir," she said.

Outside the window, the city rolled past, the light from street lamps bleeding across the sidewalks as the Nuada convoy headed home.

CHAPTER THIRTY-THREE

The bark of the lemon tree in Lucy's back yard rippled, then peeled open, and Heather emerged. Her first few steps after the tree left sap-stained footprints on the lawn.

"You could have caught a taxi," Lucy said. "That's how most people travel in L.A."

"Today is about my tribe," Heather said. "I need to put myself in the right mindset, to remember what it is to be Tolderai. I have to make sure that I don't lose track of that."

Buddy trotted up and raised his snout to sniff at Heather. She crouched and let the dog lick her hand, then scratched him between the ears.

"You're a good boy, aren't you?" she said. "Such a good boy."

"This is cuter than I expected." Jackie appeared from the bottom of the yard, sticking her wand away. "I'd expect to find you in a rough and tumble with a bulldog, not getting soppy with this soft animal."

"I greet every one of nature's creatures in the way best suited to them."

"And what sort of greeting does that mean for me?"

Heather snorted, then she and Jackie both smiled.

"Did you set up the wards?" Lucy asked.

"All done." Jackie tapped the pocket holding her wand. "A shroud of silence around the whole yard. None of the neighbors will even notice how many guests you have; never mind be able to overhear the conversation."

"Thanks." Lucy looked at Heather. "Are you sure you don't want chairs or refreshments?"

Heather shook her head. "That's not the Tolderai way."

She sat on the grass at the top of the lawn, and Lucy and Jackie sat on either side of her.

"So now we wait for them to turn up?" Jackie asked.

"Now we wait."

It was ten minutes before the first of the Tolderai arrived. Nathaniel Oakmantle emerged awkwardly from the tree, one foot catching on the lip of the bark as he stepped out, then stood uncertainly in the middle of the lawn, his hand toying with his underdeveloped goatee.

"Where do I, um..."

"Just sit somewhere," Heather said. "There is no order among us, no rituals of precedence to follow."

"Should I, well, I don't know, like..."

"Sit."

He parked himself on the grass. A moment later, the tree rippled again, and another Tolderai emerged, then another, and another, witches and wizards who brought with them spring breezes and the scents of distant forests, one with an orchid in his buttonhole, another with snowflakes melting on his shoulders.

The last to arrive was Mackam. He looked around at

the assembled tribe, snorted, and flung himself down at the base of the tree. There was a crinkling of tinfoil as he crossed his arms.

"We're all here, then," he said. "Better get to it."

"Agreed." Heather looked across her tribe, back straight and head held high. "You must all realize why I've called you here. Our tribe has become troubled, unsettled, conflicted. We have found purpose in nurturing our hidden forests, and yet for the first time in decades, we are at risk of tearing ourselves apart."

"This is what happens when you let them see you." Mackam jabbed at the air with a bony finger. "Everything goes wrong. Others see us more and more. First this one." He pointed at Lucy. "Then all the Griffins. Then those underground kids. More and more people watching us, scrutinizing us. You've left us exposed, Heather, and this is the result."

Heather tensed as he talked, but her voice remained calm and firm.

"I agree that this has come from our exposure. You've understated its extent. Don't forget the art, which is out there in the world, acting as an ambassador we never asked for. I let someone sway me into having it put on display. Then I talked you all into accepting this, and now it has brought us more than recognition. In some circles, it is bringing the tribe fame.

"Don't forget, too, that part of our past ended up exposed to the mundane world. While we retrieved the magical items from the archaeological dig at one of our ancestral settlements, we couldn't hide the whole village from the world. Ordinary people are looking at the remains our ancestors left behind and asking what they mean. Although those people are unlikely ever to find us, the real, hidden us, they still add to our exposure."

"I'm sorry, Heather, but if you're hoping to make us feel better, this isn't the way to do it," Carol Winters said.

"I have no intention of making you feel better," Heather said. "I want you to appreciate the full discomfort of our situation before we discuss what to do about it."

Mackam nodded. "I can respect that. Reminds me why you're chief."

"Hold onto that thought. I'm about to say things that will make you question my leadership."

She already had their attention, but now it gained a new intensity, the Tolderai leaning in to hear what their leader was getting at.

"For a century and more, we've been resisting the modern world," Heather said. "We've found traditional jobs or ones that keep us away from most humans. We've shunned technology, even when it could help in growing plants. We've kept our old ways of living and of organizing ourselves as a new world has grown up around us."

"That's the Tolderai way, isn't it?" Nathaniel asked, his voice shaky. "Following the, um, old ways, holding to tradition and all that cool stuff. After all, the modern world is the one destroying the forests."

There were murmurs of agreement from around the seated group.

"The modern world has destroyed forests," Heather said. "But it's preserved some as well, and it's planted new ones, however flawed they might be. The modern world isn't good or bad, it's a mix, and we have to decide what we take from that mix."

"None of it," Mackam snapped. "The traditions are enough."

"So you don't want the tin foil for your vest? Or the phone you use to read about conspiracy theories? Because those are part of the modern world, just as much as pollution and deforestation."

Mackam glared. "Fine. Not all. But most. We need to shun most of it. It's a poison."

"Only if you take too much of it. You know that's nature's way." Heather sighed. "Look, all of our lives are already touched by the modern. We take on paid jobs so we can afford to eat and rent a roof over our heads. We watch the news to see what's happening to the forests. We live in this world, like it or not, and it's been a two-edged blade. Take the art display. It brought us unwanted attention, but it also brought us money, which can support the activities of the tribe."

"What activities?" Mackam snapped. "We've nothing we need to pay for."

"That's part of what I'm coming to."

Heather glanced at Jackie, who nodded and mouthed, "you've got this." It was a plan they'd developed together, one that went far beyond what Heather would have thought of or been comfortable with on her own, but it was a solution for her tribe's problems, and that was what she needed. Having Jackie's support and Lucy's, of course, made it easier to press ahead.

"I believe that it's time to reorganize how we run the tribe, to use the tools of the modern world."

"What, you're going to appoint a social media manager?" Mackam sneered.

"No, but I want us to form a legal company, one in which the tribe is all equal shareholders. The company will take in the revenues from the art we've allowed to be displayed and manage how we use that money. We'll also use the company to manage the election of positions in the tribe, like mine."

"We have a way of doing that already. We don't need a company."

"A company gives us structure, one that's suitable for the modern world. We took on the trappings of a tribe back when that was what humans did. But humans have changed since then. They've found better ways to organize themselves. We should use them."

"There's nothing better about this."

"Different, then. More suitable for our needs." Heather took a deep breath. "Needs that include paying some members of the tribe for their work."

"But why?" Carol asked. "Everything's working fine without pay."

"No, it isn't," Jackie said. Many of the Tolderai glared at her for intruding on their meeting, although a few listened with curiosity and interest instead. She didn't care how they looked at her, as long as she had their attention.

"Your chief has been working her butt off for you, unpaid, for years. Now she doesn't have time to do that and fulfil her other responsibilities, never mind to earn a living. She has no money supporting her. Don't you think her hard work deserves a reward, especially now the tribe's got money coming in?"

"Maybe not," Mackam said. "If she was doing the job right, we wouldn't be here now."

"That's the flip side of it. If your chief gets paid through the business, they'll have responsibilities written into their contract too. They'll be obliged to make the tribe their priority. Because they won't need to find another paid job, that will be easier to do."

Around the circle, heads nodded, acknowledging the wisdom of this, although some still looked uncertain.

"It won't only be about me," Heather added. "Or whoever's in the chief's seat. We can make other appointments and reward them. We can't pay for all our work on the forests, but we could reward someone for overseeing and planning it. Or perhaps we could try paying Carol to make art for a year, to see if we can make more money for the tribe that way, to publicize and fund environmental projects.

"The important thing is that we don't need to work the way we've been doing. If we form this company, we can structure our rewards and responsibilities to suit the modern world. We can accept the human world as it is like our ancestors did when they founded the tribe. By setting it all down in writing, we can reduce conflicts and misunderstandings. We can create harmony.

"What do you say?"

Around the circle, heads were nodding, but they all watched Mackam warily, waiting to hear what he thought.

"This company," he said. "It's our way into the world of the enemy, isn't it? To infiltrate this battleground of boardrooms and brand identities. To bring the beast down from within."

"It can be, yes," Heather said. "That's for the tribe, as shareholders, to decide."

Mackam grinned, a mischievous glint in his eye.

"All right, I like it." He rubbed his hands together. "Let's see what we can do to them."

CHAPTER THIRTY-FOUR

Dylan sat on his bike at the top of a ridge, with Mia on her bike next to him. He waved as two more cycles came up the trail toward them through the twilight descending over Elysian Park.

"Hey guys!" he called.

With a final burst of speed, Lance reached the top of the trail, huffing and panting for all he was worth. Sofia arrived thirty seconds later, looking a lot calmer and breathing a lot less heavily.

Mia looked at Lance in alarm. "Are you all right? You sound exhausted!"

"He's fine." Sofia rolled her eyes. "This is the problem with being in drama club. He can't resist making a scene out of everything."

"That's an outrageous slander!" Lance slammed his fist into the palm of his other hand, then grinned. "But, like, totally true. Why live life small when you can live it in style?"

"Mia, this is Lance and Sofia," Dylan said. "My school

friends. Guys, this is Mia. I know her from the other thing."

"Ah, the other thing." Lance winked hugely, then wiggled his fingers in the air.

Mia shot Dylan a worried look.

"I know it might not seem like it, but Lance is good at keeping a secret," Dylan said. "Or at least he has been so far, and if he wants to see the awesome new things I've found..."

"My lips are sealed." Lance mimed locking his mouth up and throwing away the key.

"That's not going to last half as long as I'd like," Sofia said. "Still, I'm gonna make the most of it. What have you got to show us, Dylan? Does it have to do with the cool stuff we dug up?"

"Oh yeah." Dylan grinned. "If not for that dig, I never would have found this. Come on. We'll go somewhere out of the way, then I'll explain it."

They cycled farther into the park and found a patch of low ground hidden from the world by trees. Dylan summoned a small magical light, which settled on the earth between them as they sat in a circle. The light illuminated their faces as the world grew dark around them, and Dylan explained the quest that the Mini Griffins had been on. The clues in the picture at the museum, the magical tree, the barrier beyond it, and eventually to the cave.

"...and that's where we found this." He drew the crystal bracelet out of his backpack. The light from his spell glinted off its edges and refracted as it fell through the irregular shapes of the crystal carvings, creating small spots of light in all the colors of the rainbow

"It's beautiful," Sofia said. She pulled out her sketch pad and started drawing the bracelet. "I'm going to have a wizard in my comic wear one just like it. I mean, if that's okay."

"It's okay with me," Dylan said. "Though technically this belongs to the Tolderai, so I guess I should maybe ask them."

"Can I have a look?" Lance asked, reaching for the bracelet.

"Not until you've seen its full effects." Dylan grinned. This was the part he'd been looking forward to. "Watch."

He put the bracelet on his wrist, then focused on a particular point along its edge. Over the past couple of days, he'd repeatedly practiced using the bracelet, and though he was only starting to understand how it worked, he had far more control than when he'd first picked it up. The magic didn't start feeding its light until he told it to, and when he did, it was in a controlled way.

First, the bracelet itself started to glow, letting out a clear, white light. Then that coalesced, gathering in a single point on the bracelet's surface. That point rose, a ball of light emerging from the bracelet, then changing shape, rotating as it turned into a mouse that hovered in the air between them.

"That's totally awesome!" Lance said. "Can you make it move?"

"Of course." Dylan focused on the bracelet. The mouse stretched out, twitched its nose, then jumped. As it landed, still in the air, an ear of corn appeared beneath its feet. "I can do much more than that."

The ear of corn became a row of corn, became a whole field as the mouse, and its perch shrank and a world of light expanded. The others gasped as the field rippled and transformed, becoming a jungle that lifted higher into the air so there was more space for more details. A tiger prowled between the trees, a monkey leaped from branch to branch, birds fluttered through the canopy, all painted in clear white light.

"This is way better than the displays at the planetarium." Lance stood and reached up to touch the images. They didn't waver or break up at his touch, but his fingers went straight through them. Then the images vanished as Dylan took the bracelet off.

"Show them what you can do." He handed it to Mia.

"Are you sure?"

"Sure, I'm sure. It's even cooler."

"I don't think so, but I'll do what I can." She put the bracelet on and focused her attention on it. Once again, the bracelet glowed, less brightly than for Dylan, but in a host of different colors. When a point of light emerged, it was a swirling marble in red, blue, and green, which turned into a brightly colored parrot.

"I can't do such big images as Dylan," she said. "Or as many at once. But I find it easier to refract the light than he does, to make something other than just white."

"When she says she finds it easier, she means I can't do it at all." Dylan looked at the others. "But I'm going to work it out, I hope."

The parrot took flight and vanished a few feet above their head.

"What should I make next?" Mia asked. "It has to be something out of nature, like a plant or an animal."

"Could you two make something together?" Sofia asked. "Combine Mia's colors and Dylan's power?"

The two magicals looked at each other uncertainly.

"I don't know," Dylan said. "We've not tried it."

"Then let's try it now." Mia slid the bracelet off her wrist and held her hand out palm down, the bracelet hanging from the backs of her fingers. She smiled. "What's the worst that can happen?"

"There could be a big magical explosion," Lance said, "and you could be—"

"Shut up," Sofia said. "I want to see this."

Dylan slid his hand into the bracelet, and he and Mia pressed their hands together, palm to palm. They each took a deep breath, then let their magic flow. Colors swirled around the bracelet.

"You make something," she whispered. "I'll add color."

"What should I make?"

"What animal do you know well? That'll be easier the first time."

Dylan paused for a moment. Then an image appeared above the bracelet, a bright white dachshund.

"It's Buddy!" Lance said. "Good boy."

Mia's magic flowed, and the image of Buddy changed color, his fur turning shades of brown.

"I've only seen him in passing," she said, "but I'll do my best."

"It's perfect," Dylan said.

The light Buddy hopped down to the ground and sniffed around Lance, who mimed patting him on the head. Then the dog walked off between the trees and disappeared.

"Now something more impressive," Lance said.

"Something magical," Sofia said.

Dylan drew a deep breath. As he exhaled, an image appeared in the air again. It was a bird, its wings spread wide and its tail feathers fanning out beneath it. Its majestic, beaked head stretched into the sky.

"What is it?" Lance asked.

"A phoenix," Mia said.

Colors flowed through the bird. Feathers turned red, orange, and yellow, all the colors of fire. Tiny white points glinted on green eyes. Sofia scribbled away furiously, capturing the image in her sketchbook.

"How about..." Dylan said, and the edges of the feathers started to flicker like they really were flames.

"I was just thinking that." Mia clutched his hand tight in excitement as she shifted the colors at those burning edges so that they shone like real fire.

Dylan waved his hand, and the bird soared into the air, flying above their heads.

"More!" Lance shouted.

With growing confidence, Dylan and Mia wove a fresh image from the air. This time they didn't contribute their parts one at a time but provided them together, colors flowing in even as the beast took shape. Soon, a green-scaled dragon was chasing the phoenix into the night sky, breathing flames as it went.

"Can you do flocks?" Sofia asked. "Or is that too difficult?"

"Let's find out," Mia said.

Birds started popping into the air between her and Dylan, dozens of them, each one no bigger than a child's fist. She gave them different colors, some soothing blues and greens, others bright reds and oranges. The birds took flight, fluttering around the phoenix and the dragon as they circled overhead.

Nearby voices made the kids all look around.

"It's coming from over here somewhere," a man said.

"It must be some sort of projector, right?" another man said. "Like, some box that shoots lights into the sky."

"Yeah, yeah, yeah, that's it. I wonder who built it?"

"It could be magic," a woman said.

"Shut up, Suzie," the first man said. "You're just stoned."

"So are you."

"Yeah, but... but... but let's go find the lights!"

Dylan and Mia looked at each other, then extinguished their powers. All the magic they had cast vanished: the phoenix, the dragon, the fluttering birds, even the soft light in the center of the clearing. Dylan let go of Mia's hand and stuffed the bracelet into his pocket.

The kids crouched in the darkness.

"What if they find us?" Lance whispered. "We could be in so much trouble!"

"For what?" Sofia hissed back. "Being near some lights a bunch of stoners imagined?"

"You think they're the only ones who saw that? It was unmissable!"

"He's right," Dylan said. "We got carried away."

"It was fun, though," Mia said.

"Yeah." Dylan squeezed his hand shut around the bracelet. It had been a lot of fun, but by showing off like that, he'd risked revealing magic to the world. That wasn't something he could do, especially not with someone else's artifact. He would return the bracelet to the Tolderai. Sure, it would mean no more light displays with Mia, but it was the responsible thing to do. It would make his mom proud.

"They've gone past," Lance whispered, peering out through the bushes.

"Then we should get going," Sofia said. "My mom will want me home."

They picked up their bikes and headed through the bushes, back toward the trail. Around them, all was darkness, but in their minds, animals of pure light flew.

CHAPTER THIRTY-FIVE

Dylan cycled up the driveway of the Heron family home. Sad as he was to say goodnight to his friends, he'd peddled extra fast for the last few minutes, knowing that he was already arriving home late. He knew how to take care on the roads, but he also knew that his mom would worry if he took too long.

He left his bike leaning against the garage door and walked inside. Buddy ran out of the living room to meet him, tongue hanging out and tail waving excitedly.

"Hey, boy." Dylan scratched the dog's head. "It's great to see you."

To his surprise, the whole family was still up and sitting in the living room, including Ashley and Eddie, whose normal bedtime had passed. Ashley was rearranging her string robots to hold up a digital camera while Eddie was changing through a variety of different lizard bodies, trying on different scales, claws, and bulging eyeballs to see which ones suited him. The air kept shimmering as he shifted from one form to the next. On the sofa, Dylan's mom and dad had a big book open and were talking excitedly about its contents. A telescope lay next to them.

"Hi there, sweetheart." Lucy smiled at her son. "We were waiting for you."

"Sorry I'm late. We got distracted trying out some spells."

"That's okay. We're all staying up past bedtime tonight." Lucy pointed at the book. "We're going to do some stargazing. Want to join in?"

"Sure." Dylan ran a finger along the telescope and came away with a thick deposit of dust.

"An old toy of mine," Charlie said. "I found it in the attic this afternoon, and I thought we could give it a go. Now that our science team's all here, shall we head out back?"

Charlie picked up Eddie, who had settled into the shape of a chameleon, and popped him onto his shoulder. Then he picked up the telescope and headed out the back door. They all followed, Ashley bringing her robots with her.

They set up the telescope in the middle of the back yard, with Ashley's robot and camera array next to it.

"I've made some adjustments to the camera," she explained. "A new lens array, some light filters, and a connection to the robots that will give me more control. I can even sync it with the telescope to take photos of whatever we're looking at."

One of the robots unraveled from the top of the apparatus and stretched out to lay its end against the telescope.

"That's so smart, sweetheart." Lucy kissed her daughter on the top of the head. "Honestly, the things you and your dad can do with devices amaze me."

"I can't do the things you do with magic, so I have to find another way."

"I suppose that's one way of looking at it, though I'm not sure what I would have done to take pictures of what we see."

"Drawn it?"

Lucy laughed and tapped her back pocket, which held a small sketchpad. "Okay, that is an option."

The air above Charlie's shoulder shimmered, and Eddie turned into an owl. He twisted his head back and forth a couple of times, then flapped down to the ground and turned into a small boy.

"Stars are back," he said, pointing at the sky.

"They never really went away," Lucy said.

Eddie shook his head. "Weren't there in the day."

"They were. We just couldn't see them. Their light was hidden by the brightness of the sun."

Eddie scratched his head and peered thoughtfully up at the heavens. "They're always there?"

"That's right. The stars were there long before you were born, and they'll still be shining long after we're all gone."

"Old."

"That's right. They're very old."

"Older than Mommy?"

"Much older than Mommy."

"Older than Grandpa?"

"Even older than Grandpa."

"Wow."

"Wow, indeed. They're so old that we have a special word for them. Ancient."

"Ancient." Eddie rolled the word around his mouth like

a connoisseur tasting a fine wine, then repeated it a few times for good measure. Eventually, he nodded and took Charlie's hand. "Daddy ancient."

Charlie laughed. "I don't think so, but some of my colleagues might disagree."

They took it in turns to look through the telescope while Ashley's camera fed another version of the same view to a laptop screen. Comparing the results with the book, they tried to work out which constellations were which.

"I feel like a professor teaching a class," Charlie said as he adjusted the telescope and turned pages to a new constellation. "Teaching my little physicists what's out there in the universe."

"Sorry, honey," Lucy slid an arm around his waist, "but if anyone here should be teaching science, it's Ashley."

"I don't think so, Mom." Ashley shook her head. "I have a stronger grounding in astrophysics than many undergraduates, but I lack the pedagogical expertise to transfer my knowledge in a classroom environment successfully. I would be better suited to a research position."

"What did I tell you? Prof Heron is on the case."

"You know she's going to earn that title for real one day?" Charlie asked.

"Only if she wants to."

"Of course I want to." Ashley gave Lucy a bewildered look. "Why would anybody not want it?"

"You might choose to do something different with your smarts, like design computer games, or campaign to improve the environment, or, I don't know, build a better pop-up toaster. The important thing is that you do whatever makes you happy."

"Becoming a professor will make me happy."

"Then you do that."

Lucy wondered if this ambition would last through her daughter's teenage years. A lot could change when the body and brain did, but it seemed likely that Ashley would always be on this sort of track, heading toward the intellectual heart of academia.

Dylan stared up at the stars. Something his parents said had caught his imagination. The light from some of those stars was incredibly ancient. It took so long to reach the Earth that it showed how those stars had been thousands of years before.

If he could use magic to travel to those other star systems, could he look back and see what the sun had been like all those years earlier? Might it even be possible to see light that had bounced off the Earth and so see images of life here in those days, however tiny and difficult to interpret? That could open up whole new possibilities for studying the past, like discovering a photo album from a long-lost age.

Like his sister, Dylan was sure of what he wanted to do with his life, even if the details were a little hazier. While Ashley built the future, he was going to help people understand the past. Perhaps the same tools and techniques could help them both, illuminated by the light of different stars.

Eddie frowned as he peered through the telescope. Something was bothering him.

"Always there?" he asked.

"That's right," Charlie said.

"Lights."

"Yes, stars are lights."

Eddie looked up at him. "Why can't see in day?"

"Because the light from the sun is far brighter. It hides them."

Eddie shook his head and pointed up. "Still see them."

"Think about it like this," Lucy said. "If you turned into an ant and crawled into a big nest of ants, could you hide from us?"

Eddie nodded vigorously. For a moment, the air around him started to shimmer, but the magic didn't take hold. For once, he was more interested in hearing what people had to say than in changing into whatever creature they'd mentioned last.

"Because there would be so many other ants, all we would see was a mass of ants, right?" Lucy said. "We couldn't pick you out. It's the same with starlight during the day. It's so small by comparison with everything that's going on that it gets lost."

"Actually, Mom, it's more complicated than that," Ashley said.

"This will do for now. Do you understand, Eddie?"

He wore his thoughtful look a little longer, then nodded.

"It even happens at night," Charlie said. "With light pollution."

"I was trying to keep this simple," Lucy said.

"I get that, but I think there's a useful lesson here." Charlie pointed at the heavens. "See how many stars you can make out? You'd be able to see many more if not for all the light that people put out. The houses, the offices, the street lights, the headlights contribute to this great haze that hides the light of many stars. All the amazing things we've built can sometimes hide the amazing things that were already there."

"So without the city lights we'd be able to see even more?" Dylan asked.

In his pocket, his hand closed around the crystal Tolderai bracelet, one more light source, if a very different one.

"That's right."

Dylan tried to imagine what it would be like if every light in the city went out, how much more might be visible. It stirred something inside him, the thought of the ancient light from all those distant stars, transformed to tiny points twinkling far above. A wave of wonder rolled through him.

Suddenly, the house lights went out, then the lights along the street, around the neighborhood, all across L.A. Darkness descended, and through it all, the stars above shone. Thousands of them. Millions of them. A sea of shining jewels that took Dylan's breath away.

"What's happening?" Charlie asked.

"I don't know, but I'd better call work," Lucy said. "This doesn't feel like an ordinary blackout."

"Sorry, I think this was me," Dylan said. Now that the initial moment of wonder had passed, he noticed the connection between his feelings, his desires, and what had happened. It wasn't just an emotion that had passed through him, was it? It was his magic, inadvertently triggered by his thoughts. This time, the results were even worse than overrunning the schoolyard with trees.

"Can you fix it?" Lucy asked.

"I'll try." Dylan's voice wavered as he spoke. He knew he had far more power than most wizards, but he'd never done anything so huge before. He drew a deep breath, gripped the bracelet, and pulled the magic back in.

Lights came up again in the house, down the street, around the neighborhood, and across L.A. Lucy breathed a sigh of relief.

"I should probably still call work," she said. "Let them know that there's nothing to worry about." She squeezed Dylan's shoulder. "That was amazing. I'm so proud of you for fixing it quickly. But please, try not to do it again."

Dylan looked up at the sky with its diminished field of stars.

"All right," he said reluctantly. "I'll try not to."

CHAPTER THIRTY-SIX

Gruffbar read through the documents for a second time. In some ways, it was hard to believe that he'd managed to get hold of something so useful. In another way, it made perfect sense. This was exactly the sort of thing that he'd thought Nuada Industries were up to. He just hadn't thought that they might have left a paper trail. Nuada had gotten sloppy, and now the consequences were coming.

Clerks and witnesses hurried past along the corridor outside the magical courtroom as Gruffbar looked up from the file.

"You're sure about this?" he asked.

"One hundred percent," Lucy said. "I'm doubly sure because they tried to cover their trail. The ironic thing is that I might never have found this if they hadn't done that. Nuada and his people have put their plans in jeopardy."

"Why are you sharing it with me? You have to be assuming that my client's a scumbag too."

"Two reasons. Firstly, because this is the truth, and the truth matters. It's not only a tool, however people like

Nuada try to twist it around. Sometimes, it's a matter of principle.

"Second, because we have to stop these people. They're not just liars and manipulators. They're murderers. They shouldn't be allowed to win, and if being beaten by you here throws them off their plans, maybe they'll make a mistake that lets me take them down."

"Who'd have thought I'd end up on the side of the angels?" Gruffbar laughed. "It's still not a sure thing, though. Depends on how I can sell it and how the judge responds."

"I can watch, right?"

"Yep."

"Then I'll do that. If nothing else, it might help me understand Nuada more."

At that moment, Kelly and Max Petrie walked past, heading into court. Max smiled at Lucy and gave Gruffbar a respectful nod. Kelly glared at them both.

"I hate that guy," Gruffbar said once they were out of earshot.

"He's a good person,"

"That's probably why I hate him."

"Wait, does this mean you hate me or that I'm not a good person?"

"You're the exception, so good it comes out the other side and becomes annoying. Annoying I can live with." Gruffbar glanced at his watch, then straightened his tie. "Better get in there. Justine Delvenine's a stickler for punctuality."

They walked into the courtroom. Gruffbar took his seat behind the defense desk, next to Chuck Leader, while Lucy settled onto one of the benches in the public gallery behind him. Across from her sat Kelly, immaculately dressed and ready at her husband's back.

Two seats over from her were Finn Nuada and Elethin Tannerin, the PR elf looking elegant as always. The CEO's skin had its familiar magical glow, a light that might once have been alluring but that now made Lucy feel sick, knowing how he'd used its power to kill. She fingered the bracelet she wore hidden under her Batman hoodie, the bracelet that Jenkins had given her, with its reflector spell. It made her feel more secure but far from truly safe.

A graying Arpak in judge's robes stalked into the room and took her seat at the front. She smacked her gavel down, and the room fell silent.

"Nuada versus Leader, reconvening after several post-ponements." Justice Delvenine looked sternly at Gruffbar. "Be aware, my patience for such tactics will only stretch so far."

"Of course, Your Honor, and I'm sorry for any inconvenience." Gruffbar rose from his seat. "If it pleases the court, I would like to present some new evidence into the record."

"Of course you would." Delvenine's gaze didn't get any softer. "Why didn't you inform my clerk of this in advance?"

"I received the evidence five minutes ago. I could have asked for a delay to process it, but I didn't want to stretch your patience any further."

"What is this evidence?"

"Records of communications with patent experts, relating to the intellectual property under dispute."

"Then I will allow you to proceed, for now. Tread carefully, Mr. Steelstrike. If I feel that you have stretched too far, I will see this evidence stricken from the record, and unlike many jurors, I am quite capable of disregarding what I have heard."

"Thank you, Your Honor." Gruffbar held up the folder Lucy had given him. "I hold here copies of electronic correspondence between a senior employee of Nuada Industries, Ms. Elethin Tannerin, and a clerk at the magical patent office.

"In this correspondence, Ms. Tannerin asks the clerk to falsify a patent from Nuada Industries relating to the technology under discussion today, backdating it to before my client's patent filing. When the clerk stated that this was outside his capabilities, the correspondent instead asked him for advice on the type of evidence that someone could use to overturn a patent filing. Some of his recommendations are remarkably similar to those used in this case."

Gruffbar reached up and laid some of the documents on Delvenine's desk. She put on a pair of half-moon glasses and read the papers, then nodded.

"This matches what you are telling me. Mr. Petrie, do you have a response?"

Max stood and smiled. "With all due respect, Your Honor, my response is that these documents should not be put in the record, at least not until we've had a chance to check their provenance. Electronic records are easy to falsify, paper copies of them doubly so."

Gruffbar slapped another sheet of paper down in front of the judge.

"Provenance, Your Honor. An affidavit from a technician in the Silver Griffins, that this correspondence came directly from the computer of James Hooper, an expert patent consultant, who had obtained these messages and written notes on their origins. According to the technician, the metadata and other electronic traces match the story as provided by Mr. Hooper."

"If this evidence comes from James Hooper, then he should be brought in," Max said. "To explain why he has private correspondence from a patent clerk and how we can be sure of its veracity. Until then, this is hearsay and should be excluded from the record."

"I'd like nothing more," Gruffbar said. "Sadly, Mr. Hooper was the victim of a homicide. In case you want proof of that, here's the Silver Griffins' report on the body."

He added another sheet of paper to the pile on the judge's desk.

"I note that this says Mr. Hooper was killed using light magic." She raised an eyebrow. "Are you trying to level a further accusation here, Mr. Steelstrike?"

"Not at all, Your Honor. Merely appraising you of the proven facts."

"I see."

The judge's gaze turned to Finn Nuada, as did the stares of everybody else in the room. Finn looked perfectly calm, but beside him, Elethin had gone ghostly pale.

"You know the rules, Mr. Petrie," Justice Delvenine said. "Mr. Hooper's notes may be considered a dying man's testimony, but you have a right to challenge that. Do you wish to do so?"

Max drew a deep breath, then shook his head. "No, Your Honor."

"Petrie..." Finn said quietly, the whisper drifting through the room.

"Mr. Nuada, do you wish to brief your attorney?" the judge asked.

For a long moment, Finn stared at the back of the lawyer's head.

"No," he said at last. "I wouldn't want to challenge a dead man's right to be heard."

"By my beard, neither would I, if I was a potential suspect in his murder," Gruffbar said. "That could look really bad."

"Mr. Steelstrike," the judge snapped.

"Sorry, Your Honor. I apologize for the interruption and any unfortunate implication. I did not mean to impugn Mr. Nuada's character."

"I'm sure." The judge shook her head. "Well, you've presented your papers. What now?"

"I would like to call to the stand one of the participants in this communication, Ms. Elethin Tannerin, director of public relations at Nuada Industries."

"Will that take long to arrange?"

"Hardly. She's here today." Gruffbar pointed at Elethin.

"Very well." Delvenine gestured to the witness stand. "Ms. Tannerin, please."

Elethin had regained her composure. Without a hint of recalcitrance, she made her way up to the stand and smiled from there to the judge.

"This is all a mix-up," she said.

"I'm sure." Delvenine gestured to Gruffbar. "Your witness."

Gruffbar placed two sheets of paper in front of Elethin,

then walked away from the stand, leaving plenty of space between him and the elf. It wouldn't do to look like he was bullying her, and there was no need to add any more pressure.

"Ms. Tannerin, is that your cell phone number on those messages?"

"Yes."

"And your address on the emails?"

"Yes, but someone else could have—"

"I'm not asking you to explain, Ms. Tannerin. In fact, let me save you and Mr. Petrie some time. I concede that, until we have evidence otherwise, someone else from within your company could have sent these messages. Although as Mr. Nuada acknowledged in previous testimony, you have very tight electronic security, so this wasn't an outsider.

"For my purposes, that doesn't matter. What matters is that this clerk received messages he believed were from you, the charming head of Nuada Industries PR. Someone at Nuada tried to establish a false patent, then asked for advice on how to undermine a real patent fraudulently."

"Your Honor," Max Petrie was on his feet again. He looked distinctly uncomfortable. "I understand Mr. Steelstrike's implication, but he has not yet provided evidence that anything my client has said in this courtroom is untrue."

"Actually, I have." Gruffbar held up one last sheet of paper. "The patent application. When I asked Mr. Nuada for proof that he created this technology, he said that he never even wrote up a patent. Yet here it is, with his signature, supplied by his company. It might seem like a small detail, given that the claim was withdrawn, but your client lied to this court. Who knows what else he lied about?"

Gruffbar turned to the judge.

"Your Honor, under the circumstances, I would like to call for this case to be dismissed. We could draw the battle out, create a he-said-she-said argument over who sent those messages and why, but you know where this is going. My client has a patent. The other side has the sworn statement of a proven perjurer."

The judge sat back, looking at the papers in front of her, fingers steepled as she thought.

"Petrie," Nuada hissed from the gallery, "do something."

"You want me to interrupt her?" Max whispered. "This isn't the judge to try that on."

Justice Delvenine leaned forward.

"Gentlemen, I do not like deceit, and I do not like lawyers who support it in their clients. I am having to hold myself back from letting my urges drive my decision here, in a manner most detrimental to you, Mr. Petrie, and to your client.

"The clarion call to do battle against dubious lawyers rings out strong, but for now, I will merely dismiss this case. However, I will be asking the clerk of the court to investigate your role in this, Mr. Petrie, and to advise on whether sanctions are appropriate. I will be passing a full record of the proceedings to the Silver Griffins in case they should shed any light on the death of the late Mr. Hooper. Mr. Steelstrike, should your client choose to counter-sue Nuada Industries, I will watch that case with interest.

"Court dismissed."

She slammed her gavel down.

The door at the back of the gallery flew open as a pair of bloggers raced to get their report on the case in first. While Chuck Leader showered praise on Gruffbar, Finn Nuada and his entourage stalked out without a word to Max.

Kelly Petrie turned to Lucy. "You did this," she snapped. "You gave that scumbag lawyer the evidence. You made Max look like a liar."

"I'm sorry it hurt Max, but the truth had to come out," Lucy said.

"You think you're sorry now?" Kelly glared at her. "Just you wait."

CHAPTER THIRTY-SEVEN

Charlie and Ringo were on the receiving end of many ugly looks as they drove their van into Gunther's auto shop.

"This is stupid," Ringo said. "They don't want us here."

"They're fine with having us here," Charlie said. "As long as we're respectful to the staff and of the rules."

Ringo snorted. "Respectful. You mean ignoring when people act like idiots and following rules that don't make no sense?"

"If that's what it takes, yes." Charlie drew a deep breath. "Ringo, what would your ideal life be like? If money wasn't an option and you didn't have to work."

"I don't know, probably lying on a beach somewhere, sipping mojitos and soaking up the sunshine."

"If you want that dream, you have to put the work in first, got to earn the millions that will pay for your sunscreen and rum. This business is our best chance for that, so if you're getting frustrated, or you're having trouble holding back a comment, just think of those mojitos and keep it in, okay?"

"I'll try, but I'm not making any promises, man."

While Ringo started unloading the van, Charlie went to talk with Gunther, who had the hood of a truck open and a wrench in his hand.

"Don't make me regret trying this again," Gunther growled, prodding Charlie's chest with a thick finger. "You talked me back into it. If your pal pisses everyone off, that's on you."

"Don't worry. He's learned his lesson. No magic except what's essential to change the car. No comments that will annoy your staff. We'll be good as gold."

"We'll see."

A yellow Mitsubishi Mirage drove into the shop and up to the Green Machine Conversions van. Charlie hurried over, in case Ringo found a way to offend the customer in place of their colleagues.

A witch emerged from the car and looked around.

"You guys really work here?" She looked with a dubious expression from Charlie and Ringo to the rest of the place.

"It might not look like much, but this is a great garage," Charlie said. "Right, Ringo?"

"Yeah, great. Fine people. Salt of the earth."

"Um, okay." She shrugged and handed Charlie her keys. "While you're fixing my fumes, could you have a look at the lights? They've gotten all flickery a couple of times, loose wire or something, and I'm tired of using magic to compensate."

"We can't fix the lights," Charlie said, "but Gunther's guys could look at that while we do our thing."

"Really?" The witch looked around again and raised an eyebrow.

"Sure, and it'll save you having to take the car in somewhere else later. I'll introduce you."

He took the witch over to Gunther and explained the situation, then left them to negotiate a price while he got to work. He and Ringo lifted the car on jacks and got underneath to assess the work involved.

"It all looks in good condition," Ringo said. "Should be an easy job, man. Use the original setup, maybe a couple of tweaks to suit the exhaust pipe. Job done."

"Cool. I'll get my wrench. You fetch your wand. Remember, only the absolutely essential magic, and do it out of sight if you can."

They set to work disassembling parts of the car, ready to replace or adjust them. Charlie was still underneath when someone walked over, boots thumping on the floor.

"You got some wiring needs fixing?"

Charlie peered out at a solid pair of boots. "One second."

He crawled from under the car and looked up at the redheaded mechanic he'd met on his last visit to the shop. "Hi, I don't think we met properly before. I'm Charlie." He held out his hand.

"Kaz." She shook with a grip like a wrench. "What you got for me?"

"Lights have been flickering, apparently a few times."

"And she only just brought it in?"

"She's been compensating, not driving around blind."

"You mean she used magic." The mechanic rolled her eyes. "Freaking witches, thinking the rules don't apply."

"Aren't you..."

"I've got a little touch of magic, don't mean I'd call

myself a witch. Certainly don't mean I'd drive around in a busted car with only my sparkling fingers to light the way." She slammed a tool caddy down next to the car. "All right, Charlie, you get back to your thing. I'll let you know if I need someone to hold my screwdriver."

It didn't seem like standing around chatting was the right way to bond with their new workmates, so Charlie climbed back under the car and got on with his work. Most of the removable components were out and with Ringo, but some parts were easier to do in situ, if only because they were a total pain to get out of where they were attached. He raised his wand and a soldering iron and directed them together to start inscribing magically empowered runes.

"Hey, Charlie."

He looked around. Kaz was crouched by the side of the car, peering in at him.

"Problem with the wiring?" he asked.

"Course there is, that's why I'm here. But I was wondering, did you try using that chill rune?"

"We're going to. This is the first chance we've had to make the change since you suggested it."

"Huh. Wasn't sure you'd listen."

"Like you said, we're amateurs. We'd be idiots not to learn from someone with experience."

"You could be idiots as well as amateurs."

"True, but we're not. If you want, you could go remind Ringo about the rune, make sure he gets it right."

Kaz glanced toward the van, then shook her head. "Nah, it's all good."

She got up and started working again.

A few minutes later, Ringo came over. He slid a tray of components to Charlie under the car.

"There you go, man. I've treated those."

"How's the rest going?"

"Not bad. We gonna do the enchantments together at the end?"

"I think so, yeah."

Ringo stood. Charlie saw his feet turn toward Kaz as he watched her work.

"What you doing?" Ringo asked.

"What does it look like?" she snarled. "I'm fixing the wiring."

"Like that?"

Hearing Ringo's tone, Charlie shot out from under the car. He could feel disaster heading his way, with all the blunt force of Ringo's personality.

"You got a problem with the way I'm working?"

Charlie looked up at Ringo, who glanced briefly down at him. Charlie mimed drinking a mojito.

"No problem."

"You think I should do it differently."

Charlie frantically repeated his mojito mime.

Ringo's face crumpled as the desire to show off, and the desire to laze on a beach fought each other in his mind.

"No," he said without a lot of conviction.

"Sure." Kaz shook her head and turned back to the wiring. "Whatever."

Ringo stomped off around the van, and Charlie hurried after him.

"That wasn't so bad, was it?" Charlie asked.

"She's doing it wrong, man. On our customer's car."

"Maybe she's only doing it differently. After all, she has experience. She knows what she's doing."

"You mean she should know what she's doing."

"Let's wait and see the results."

They got back to work, Charlie under the car, Ringo safely out of the way behind the van. The whole time, Charlie worked with his shoulders tensed, sure that the other shoe was about to drop. Sure enough, after half an hour, Ringo approached the car again.

"How's it going?" he asked.

"Slower because people keep interrupting me," Kaz replied.

Ringo leaned in closer to peer at what she was doing. Charlie scrambled out from under the car, ready to start miming mojitos again, but then he saw the look on Ringo's face. There was curiosity there, which hadn't been present before.

"I hadn't thought of doing it like that," Ringo said.

"No shit, Sherlock." Kaz shook her head. "If you had, you wouldn't have wanted to do anything else."

"Can you show me how it works?"

She looked at him out of the corner of her eye. "Is this some kind of wind-up?"

"No, I promise."

"You're not trying to hit on me? Because I know some guys get weird about the whole female mechanic thing like they've seen too many models leaning over car hoods and now all that grease turns them on, and let me tell you, I am having none of that shit."

"I just want to learn to fix cars better. Is that so bad?"

"I guess not." Kaz shifted over so he could see the wiring better. "All right, so..."

While Ringo was learning, Charlie went to retrieve the remaining components from behind the van. It seemed like Ringo wasn't making a hash of things this time, and he didn't want to get in the way.

By the time Charlie had done everything he could do alone, Kaz had the wiring fixed, and Ringo and Kaz were standing nearby, comparing tools.

"You ready for the enchantment?" Charlie asked.

"Sure." Ringo took out his wand and rolled under the car, where Charlie joined him.

"Mind if I watch?" Kaz crouched close by. "I've never seen anything like this before."

"Go for it."

Together, Charlie and Ringo cast the spells to connect and activate the components, making the engine run cleaner and greener. Spells connected, runes illuminated, gears tightened, and chemicals activated. Then the magic settled, its glow faded, and left what looked like an ordinary engine.

"That's pretty cool," Kaz said as they emerged. "Wish I could do that kind of thing."

"Maybe with practice?" Charlie asked.

"Nice thought, but I don't think I've got the power."

"You could help out next time. See how you get along."

"Maybe." She shrugged, and Charlie figured that was as close as they were going to get to an agreement. "I've got other work to do. Catch you later, boys."

An hour later, the customer came by to collect her car. By then, they were onto another one, the auto shop space and the practice they'd got on recent cars letting them get through each job quicker than the last.

"We might even turn a profit one of these days," Ringo said as they waved the customer off.

"Mojitos on a beach," Charlie said. "Keep that in mind."

Gunther came up behind them and laid a heavy hand on each of their shoulders.

"Seems like you're doing good today," he said. "And the extra work's appreciated. So, when do you want to come in again?"

CHAPTER THIRTY-EIGHT

For the second time in a week, Lucy pulled up in front of a house fenced off with police tape. This wasn't something she wanted to get used to. When magical crimes got so bad that they drew the attention of the mundane authorities, it was a lot harder to keep the results under control.

A familiar figure was standing amid the uniformed officers at the edge of the scene, a tall woman with auburn hair and a detective's badge hanging from her belt. A cigarette dangled from between her lips as she scribbled something on a clipboard, then handed it to one of the uniformed cops. She waved at Lucy as she approached.

"Glad you could make it," the detective said.

"You must be Detective Bendis." Lucy shook the woman's hand. "Jill, wasn't it?"

"That's right. And you're Lucy?"

"Yes. Is your partner not here?"

Jill shook her head. "Billy's kid's come down with some bug, and mom's a hotshot accountant, so he was left holding the baby. Which means that I'm left holding this mess." She handed Lucy a mask, like the ones worn by hospital staff to avoid infections. "Where's your partner?"

"On another case. We're pretty busy right now."

"I didn't realize there was so much demand for specialist science consultants."

"You'd be amazed." Lucy held up the mask. "Is this really necessary?"

"Not necessary, but it'll reduce the stink. It took a few days before anyone reported that there might be bodies here."

"Oh."

"You'll want these too if you're gonna touch anything." Jill handed Lucy a pair of blue rubber gloves. "Might be worth taking that bracelet off first, in case it catches on something."

Lucy's hand went to the bracelet of mirrors and silvery metal, with its reflective enchantments. She'd been wearing it for two days now, and after seeing Finn Nuada frustrated in court, she didn't feel any more like taking it off.

"It'll be all right."

Jill flicked away her cigarette, then lifted a section of the police tape so they could walk through. "Suit yourself."

She led Lucy up the steps of a two-floor house with an overgrown garden and paint that was just starting to peel. They went through the front door, down a hallway, and into the kitchen. By then, Lucy could already smell why they'd worn masks.

There were five bodies in the kitchen, all of them shot or stabbed.

"There was one more victim, sitting at the table," Jill said. "For some reason, they got rid of that body, and only that one. Maybe someone was interrupted while cleaning up." She shrugged. "They've still left us with some odd details, like this." She pushed back the long hair on one of the bodies, revealing a pointed ear. "Body mods."

Lucy nodded, relieved that the detective had found a way to explain away the elf. It would save a lot of messing around with memories.

"Why did you call me in?" she asked. "This looks like a gang thing."

"Because of this." Jill pulled up the eyelids of one of the victims, revealing shrunken pupils and bloodshot whites. "They're all like it, though it's not so bad on pointy ears here."

"Just like the other case," Lucy said.

A grim certainty had hold of her. This was Nuada again, or his people, using blinding light to take out his victims. When she dug deeper, she'd find some way that these people had been obstructing his business, whether by design or by accident. The pattern was too strong for it to be anything else.

However, she would need to prove it if she ever wanted her superiors to see the truth, to get past this insane idea that they ought to be working with Nuada and his murderous colleagues.

"You know something, don't you?" Jill said.

Lucy took out her phone and took photos of the eyes.

"Not yet," she said. "But I'll see if I can work out what sort of light could do this."

"Uh-huh." Jill took a step back from the bodies and stood with her arms folded, watching Lucy. "I'm not an idiot. I know that Billy gets himself onto a lot of the weird cases and that those are the ones you consultants turn up on. I don't know what kind of nonsense this is, whether it's cults or government science or some *X-Files* thing, but I know when someone's not telling me the whole truth."

Lucy's hand drifted to the pocket holding her wand. It sounded like she might need a memory spell.

"Are you asking me something?"

"No." Jill shook her head. "If I'm not being told the truth, there's probably a good reason. Just... I don't know. I don't get to say it to Billy. He thinks he's covering well, so now I'm taking my chance. Not all of us are too dumb to see what's happening. Sometimes we choose not to."

She pulled out a packet of cigarettes and headed out the back door.

Lucy took one last look across the bodies, then headed down the corridor and out through the front. She needed to get back to headquarters, to start putting her case together, to persuade Applegate that it was time to take on Nuada.

She got into her car and set off down the road. Soft rock drifted from the radio while she pulled her thoughts together. What she had right now wasn't enough. Yes, several killings used light, but the connection between them and Nuada still had to be proved.

Even the death of Hooper, which initially helped Nuada's court case then harmed it, wouldn't instantly connect to the man himself. He could point out how many other sorts of magicals used light magic, how governments and scientists were working with lasers. As long as he had the ear of senior Silver Griffins, that argument would hold sway.

As she headed for the nearest Starbucks, she noticed a car that kept appearing behind her. Was it following? It had tinted windows so she couldn't see who was inside, but if detective Jill wasn't content with not knowing, if she were determined to dig out the truth, this would be a good way to start. Watch Lucy, see where she went, find out what her business was about. Fortunately, Lucy had a foolproof way to throw mundanes off.

She pulled into the Starbucks parking lot, grabbed her Batman backpack and her Wonder Woman travel cup, and went inside. She joined the short queue for drinks and used a mirror behind the counter to watch who came in after her.

A few minutes later, they entered. Not Jill, but a pair of blond guys in suits and wraparound shades. Guys with the uncannily familiar appearance of Nuada's goons.

"What can I get you?" a barista asked brightly.

"Tea, please." Lucy handed over her cup, paid with a card, then waited while the barista made her drink. It never took as long as when they made coffee, one more reason why tea was great.

Clutching her cuppa, she headed to the back of the coffee shop and through the magical door to the subway. She hurried down the steps. She wanted to get away before those thugs caught up with her.

As she rounded the corkscrew turn of the stairs, two more people appeared ahead of her. Both were pale and suited, just like her pursuers.

"You made Mr. Nuada look bad in public," one of them said.

"You got in the way of his business plans," the other said, his voice identical.

Lucy turned. The other two were descending, surrounding her.

"Mr. Nuada doesn't like to be humiliated," one of the new arrivals said.

"It won't happen again," the last one said, raising his hand. The palm glowed brightly.

Lucy flicked her wrist. She'd only placed the lid loosely on her tea, and the scalding liquid flew out, hitting the guy in the face. He yelped in alarm, and a blast of light flew wide.

Another of the light thugs came charging at Lucy from below. She kicked him in the face, and he stumbled back. His friend caught him before he could fall down the stairs. She flung her travel cup, but it bounced off the guy's head and smashed against the wall.

One of the others grabbed Lucy from behind, wrapping his arms around her. She struggled to break free, but he was unnaturally strong. His companion, the one whose face she had hit with her tea, pressed his hand against Lucy's face.

"That burned," he hissed. "This will burn worse."

His palm glowed, then there was a flash. The bracelet on Lucy's wrist shook and glowed as its magic scattered light, reflecting it in every direction.

"What the...?" The attacker stepped back, disoriented by the flashback from his powers. The guy with his arms around Lucy was still hanging on, but his grip had weakened. She slammed her foot down on top of his, and he let go with a yelp.

Lucy flung herself across the stairwell, but they were above and below. There was no way clear. All she had was a second.

She plunged her hand into the backpack.

"I don't know how you did that." One of the thugs grabbed Lucy by the shoulder and yanked her around. "But I bet it won't stop this."

He swung a fist. Lucy ducked, and the punch missed her head. She took one of the string of dark grenades she'd pulled from her bag, twisted the timer dial down to zero, pulled the pin, and released the lever.

There was a wave of magic, and the whole stairwell plunged into darkness. Even her glowing attackers disappeared, though their plaintive cries of alarm were music to Lucy's ears.

Unable to see, she fumbled in the backpack until she found the power-absorbing manacles, then stood ready, waiting.

The light started to rise. In a gray gloom like the tail end of night, the four light magicals huddled, their power wiped away by the darkness, their strength gone with the light that made them whole.

She slapped a set of manacles on the nearest of them, then on the one next to him. The light was rising as the grenade's spell wore off, and the magicals' strength was rising with it. The third one grabbed her, but his hand on her shoulder gave her the opportunity she needed. She slapped a manacle on, then twisted around and cuffed his hands together.

The last one raised his hand, palm glowing as it pointed at Lucy.

"Your protections can't last forever," he said.

"They don't need to."

She slapped a manacle around his outstretched wrist. The light in his hand vanished, swallowed by the cuffs. As he stared at his lightless hand in horror, Lucy grabbed his other wrist and cuffed that too.

With their powers suppressed, all four attackers slumped against the walls, huddling in on themselves. They were creatures of light magic. When countermagic checked theirs, there was little left to hold them up.

"Got you." Lucy grinned. "Let's see Finn Nuada try to get out of this one." She looked down at the tea dripping off one stair and the shattered remains of her Wonder Woman cup. "What a terrible price to pay."

CHAPTER THIRTY-NINE

Twylan and Kix stood in an alleyway behind a hotel's dumpsters. They were both dressed to hide their non-human features, with hoods up and dark glasses covering the glow of Twylan's eyes.

"Are you sure about this?" Kix asked.

"I'm sure," Twylan replied. "But just to check, which part are you asking about?"

"All of it!"

"Could you be more specific?"

"Are you sure this is the right hotel?"

"Yes. I've been following Sunder for days, and she goes here every night."

"Are you sure this is the right time to break in? I mean, the middle of the day..."

"I can't do it at night. She'll be there."

"Well, are you sure you need to do this at all?"

That was the big one, the question that had been bothering Twylan. Was it really the right move to break into the hotel room of one of the most senior witches in the Silver Griffins, searching for evidence that might or might not be there?

In some ways, the answer was obviously no. Twylan wasn't just risking arrest. She was risking any chance of becoming a Griffin in the future, of fulfilling her dreams. And she was doing it without any certainty that she would find what she was after, proof of a corrupt connection between Margaret Sunder and Finn Nuada, or that one of them was up to no good. This was a stretch to reach for a scrap of hope.

"I have to do it," she said. "I can't leave bad people in charge of the Griffins, people who will put ordinary magicals in danger, who might even have had Leontine's uncle killed. If there's any hope of changing that, I have to take a chance."

"All right, then I'm coming with you."

"Kix, you don't have to—"

"Yes, I do. You said that Sunder's started going about with a bodyguard. That means she's ready for trouble. You need someone to have your back."

Twylan hugged her friend. "Thanks. You're the best."

"I try."

They walked up to one of the hotel's service entrances. Someone had propped the door open to let in air and counter the heat from the kitchens as if the air from a late summer L.A. day could be any cooler. Together, the two magicals crept inside.

Twylan held her wand at the ready in case. Her shoulders were tense, her whole body on edge. She reached a service elevator and pushed the button for the eleventh floor. A moment later, they were on their way up.

"Places like this are crazy," Kix said. "Imagine living in a place that goes up so far instead of going down."

"Imagine living above ground at all."

"It would be pretty cool."

"When I'm a Griffin, I'm going to buy a house we can all live in."

"Oh, honey." Kix patted her friend on the forearm. "Silver Griffins are public servants. You'll be lucky if you can buy a shoebox."

The elevator doors opened, and they crept out into the corridor. Twylan had been this way already once, but she still checked all the door numbers as they went past, counting off until she found where she needed to be.

"Recludo," she whispered and pressed her wand to the electronic lock. Its little light went from red to green, and there was a *click*.

"I'll keep watch out here," Kix said.

Twylan nodded and headed in.

The room was bigger even than she'd expected from the images of hotel rooms that she'd seen on TV. There was a huge bed with glossy sheets, a desk and chair, a giant TV mounted on the wall, a sofa under the window, and a painting opposite the TV. The en suite bathroom was all marble and gleaming metal fixtures. It was immaculately clean.

Twylan looked in the wardrobe, under the bed, then started going through drawers. She rummaged through Sunder's possession without any concern for whether she could put them back how they had been. There was almost no chance that she could do this without leaving a trace, so better to be thorough and hope that finding what she was after removed any need to cover her tracks.

There was a safe in the desk. When everything else had proved futile, Twylan turned to that. She wondered if she should have tried it first, as the place most likely to hold something secret. Maybe that was a lesson for the next time she broke into the home of a suspect. If there was a next time, and she didn't get caught here, then end up spending the rest of her life in Trevilsom Prison.

She pressed her wand to the lock. "Recludo."

Nothing happened. Twylan tried the handle, but the safe wouldn't open.

"Recludo." Still nothing. There was another spell on the safe, one that resisted her unlocking magic. Sunder must have cast it, knowing that her danger didn't only come from conventional burglars. Perhaps there was another way around it, instead of a direct unlocking spell. Twylan took a narrow seed from her pocket and slid it into the tiny gap at the edge of the safe door.

"Crescent plantae." She let her magic flow again.

Working with the Tolderai, she had gotten good at plant magic. With this one spell, she could make plants grow in different ways, to make them tall, or healthy, or beautiful, or to take on a certain shape. This time she went for strength.

The safe creaked as creepers flowed into its joints, then started to expand. The whole thing strained. There was a *crunch*, a *pop*, a moment where she wasn't sure what had given in, her plant or the safe. Then the door dropped out onto the floor.

Inside, surrounded by roots and creepers, were two brown envelopes. Twylan opened the top one. It held transcripts of interviews with magical business leaders and a thumb drive holding the recordings.

The interviews were in pairs. In each case, the first one was the executive complaining about Nuada Industries doing something to pressure them, using magic or blackmail to cheat in an attempt to close down or take over their business. The second of each pair was the same interviewee, days or weeks later, saying that Nuada was fine and there was nothing to complain about.

The pressure had done its job. They had recanted, but when you brought all of these together, the pattern was clear: Nuada using illegal tactics against its competitors, then scaring them into backing down.

The other envelope was thinner. Of the papers inside, the top one was handwritten. It said: "I know what happened, and I have the proof. Never forget that. FN." Under that were some grainy photos of a younger Margaret Sunder, apparently taken from security footage at a hotel, where she was entering and leaving a room. At the bottom of the pile was a report on a case in which the Silver Griffins had arrived too late to prevent a magical accident that killed over twenty people.

Nuada was blackmailing Sunder over a past failure, getting her to keep quiet about his wrongdoing, perhaps even to cover it up. This was the evidence Twylan needed.

The door burst open, and Kix rushed in. Twylan leaped to her feet, envelopes in hand.

"Someone's coming," Kix said.

They ran for the door, but it was too late. A wizard in a suit stood in the way. Twylan recognized him as one of the bodyguards who had started accompanying Sunder.

"Hands in the air." He raised his wand.

There was no time to think and plan. As Twylan brought up her hands, a tiny seed flew from one of them, and she whispered a spell.

The seed hit the wizard and expanded, turning into a writhing mass of roots and creepers. As he tried to pull it off himself, Twylan slammed into him, knocking him back into the wall, then dashed past.

"Come on!" she shouted.

Kix ran after her. As they reached the corner, the wizard managed to get his hand free and flung a spell. Twylan countered it, then ran on.

The Underfoots ran through a door and down a stairwell, their footsteps echoing all around them. They ran down a floor, two, three, then heard the door bang back above them. The mass of roots and branches that had been Twylan's seed tumbled down the middle of the stairwell.

"Refrigero!" the wizard shouted, casting a spell down at them. The Underfoots dodged, and it hit the steps in front of them, coating the hard surface in ice. Twylan slipped, but Kix caught her. They jumped over the slippery steps and kept running.

"Two can play at that game," Twylan said as the wizard's footsteps raced after them. She pointed her wand back. "Refrigero."

Behind her, three floors of steps turned to sparkling ice.

There was a yelp of alarm, a *thud*, and a cry of pain as the wizard slipped and landed on his back.

The Underfoots ran down the last few floors, along a corridor, and out into the alleyway. A junior cook, taking a smoke by the dumpsters, looked up at them in surprise.

"What you doing here?" he asked.

"We're, um, just..." Twylan desperately tried to think of an excuse to avoid having to use magic against him.

"Setup for a prank show," Kix said. "It's for YouTube. You know the pop star who's staying on the top floor?"

The cook shook his head.

"Oh no, I've already said too much!" Kix pressed a finger to her lips. "Please, don't tell anyone. We wouldn't want to spoil it."

"I guess." The cook shook his head. "Whatever."

He ground his cigarette butt under his heel and walked back inside.

Twylan and Kix hurried down the alley until they reached a utility hole cover. They lifted it, set it aside, and lowered themselves through the opening before pulling the metal back into place above their heads. Even then, they didn't stop moving until the hotel was several twists of the tunnel behind them.

At last, they stopped and stood staring at each other.

"That was so cool!" Kix exclaimed.

"I feel sorry for that poor wizard."

"He was chasing us."

"He thought we were bad guys."

"He'll get over it. Did you get what you needed?"

Twylan held up the envelopes. "I did."

"Then it was worth it, right?"

"If I can find someone who'll believe this is real."

"Who's that going to be?"

"One of our friendly Griffins, of course. Either Jackie or Lucy..."

CHAPTER FORTY

Jackie looked at the picture on her phone, then at the tunnel around her, then back at her phone. This was the place.

Sure, there were differences between the two versions. In the picture, the tunnel was full of living plants, including a huge tree with thrashing branches reaching for the magicals around it. In the tunnel now, the plants were dead, the tree dried out and still. Even with their branches withered and their leaves fallen, these were clearly the same plants, in the same space, a concrete tunnel where no plants should be.

If they'd sprung up while any mundane people were around, it would have been a nightmare to cover up. Applegate was right. This was very much a case for the Silver Griffins.

Jackie switched from the frozen image, a single enhanced frame from a video, to the video itself. Even on mute, she could tell that the people on the screen were screaming as they ran around in alarm, chased by branches, creepers, and roots. Apparently, these people were influencers, some of them big names on the magical web, others wannabes, although Jackie couldn't tell the difference. Judging by their reaction to the plant attack, they were all idiots, running around in a panic instead of working together to protect themselves.

One of them had shot the video, a tanned blond guy with a goatee who kept shoving himself into view instead of capturing the action. Despite his intrusions, the video was a hit, shared worldwide wherever magicals lived, from Kentucky to Koblenz. Which was presumably how it had come to Applegate's attention, though Jackie doubted that he'd found it for himself. The regional manager was too old to be spending his days on MageTube.

She paused the video again. There he was, the wild figure with the braided gray beard, wand waving as he directed the plant magic, bellowing in fury. A wizard Jackie had met at least once before—Mackam of the Tolderai.

Jackie pocketed her phone and headed out of this wide tunnel into a narrower one that led deeper underground. Magical light illuminated her way, and another spell guided her, picking out the faint trails of footprints on the ground, showing different colors where different people had walked. The older trails were fading, but according to Jenkins, who had developed the specialist spell, it should be good for at least a month after anyone had passed by.

Those trails interested Jackie. She was no expert tracker, so she couldn't tell which prints exactly were Mackam's, but she could see several sets of recent tracks running over and through each other as if several people had come up here around the same time. At a junction, they ran over each other, running up to the basement of a nearby business, then back down to a downward sloping tunnel.

Jackie had already talked to the business owners, learning that Mackam had also attacked them and some other magicals saved them. They'd been shifty about the whole thing, and Jackie suspected that their operation was leaking magic in a way the Griffins wouldn't approve of. But that was a problem for another day. Right now, she had a mad Tolderai to track down.

She followed the trail of footprints down the tunnel, deeper under L.A. It twisted and turned, branching and changing, as man-made concrete gave way to packed earth tunnels held up by interlocked networks of roots. Throughout, the trail of footprints led Jackie toward her goal.

As she walked, she ran her hand over the roots. This was clearly Tolderai work, using nature to fulfil functions that other people would have achieved with planks or concrete. The result was comforting, which surprised Jackie, a city girl who was more than happy living away from nature. Maybe something was missing from her life. Perhaps that was why she hadn't told Applegate yet that she knew who was behind the attack. She could always tell him later, once she'd worked out what this was all about.

The air changed as she went deeper. She'd expected it to become stale and unpleasant, locked away from the wind and the open air. Instead, it was becoming fresher, clearer, more pleasant than in the city above. Something distinctly weird was going on here, something more than

Mackam's beard. Voices emerged from the darkness ahead, and was that bird song?

Another light appeared. Jackie extinguished her spell and walked toward what looked like sunlight but couldn't possibly be this far underground.

The tunnel emerged into a cavern. It was huge, at least two football fields across, and held up by more intertwined roots. The place was full of plants, from tall pine trees to low-growing shrubs. Birds chased winged insects through the upper branches, and light shone down from magical orbs embedded in the ceiling. It took Jackie's breath away.

She was so busy staring in amazement that it took her a moment to realize there were people nearby and that they were looking at her. She recognized two of them as Tolderai and another as Leontine, the Arpak from the Underfoot Brigade.

"What is this?" Jackie asked.

"Heather!" one of the Tolderai shouted. "We have a visitor."

"What do you mean, we have a visitor?" Heather strode out of the forest, Mackam loping along behind her. She stopped when she saw Jackie. "Jacks. What are you doing here?"

"That's what I was about to ask. What is all this? And why don't the Silver Griffins know about it?"

Heather stiffened and sucked in her cheeks. Everyone was looking at her, waiting to take their chief's lead.

"You lot go," she said. "I'll talk with Jacks alone."

"Wait." Jackie pointed at Mackam. "He stays. We have some issues to discuss. Leontine, is Twylan around?"

"Isn't she with you? She said she had Silver Griffins business."

Jackie frowned. She must have missed her junior sidekick in passing. She could check up on her later and ask some pointed questions about why Twylan had kept all of this secret.

"All right, the rest of you go." Jackie waved them away. "Heather, what's this all about?"

"Tribe business."

"That's not a good enough excuse. The minute you start throwing magic around in L.A., it's Silver Griffins business."

"We're not in L.A.. We're under it."

Jackie sighed. "Heather, you're better than this. Stop splitting hairs and tell me the truth, or I'll go get backup, and we won't be talking anymore."

"Are you threatening me?"

"Yes, of course! How do you think we get rogue magic users to cooperate?"

Heather stood glaring at Jackie, feet firmly planted, arms folded across her chest. At last, she let out a sharp breath and sagged a little.

"Fine. This is a project we created to clean up the air in LA. These forests are lungs for the city, taking in the dirty, carbon-filled air above and refreshing it."

"These forests? There's more than one?"

"Yes."

"How long have you been doing this?"

"Weeks. Months. Not long."

Jackie rubbed her temple. Bluntness was one of the things she liked about Heather, and it would help cut through to the heart of this, but her confrontational manner wasn't making it easy.

"Why underground? Surely it would be easier to grow forests on the surface?"

"Where people could chop them down? Where we would have to compete for land with property developers and their investment fund backers?"

"Okay, that makes sense." Jackie looked around again. It was a beautiful place, magical in every sense. It ought to exist.

Behind Heather, Mackam shifted from foot to foot, the beads in his beard rattling. He looked at Jackie through narrowed eyes.

"As for you," she said, "would you like to explain this?"

She held up her phone, the screen showing the video of his anti-influencer rampage.

"Pollution." He said the word with disgust. "Noise. Degradation. Their stray magic spraying out into the world. They were damaging all this." He waved his arms to take in the surrounding plants. "They had to be stopped."

"If they were letting out too much loose magic, I agree. But that's not your problem to deal with. It's ours." She held out her Silver Griffins amulet. "Remember this? It says that I get to beat up rogue magicals, not you. It also means you're on my shit list for what you did."

"Come for me, then!" Mackam drew his knife. "I dare you."

"Mackam, stop." Heather pressed a hand against his chest. "You were out of line, and you know it. We were lucky to get to you first. Maybe we weren't lucky enough.

"Jacks, he was trying to protect his people and what

we've built here. If enough magic is coming through the ground to affect us, then somebody up there is being reckless, and it needs dealing with. But we're in your city. We have to accept your rules. If you want to punish Mackam, we won't stand in your way."

"What?" Mackam stared at her, open-mouthed. "You're my chief. You're supposed to protect me."

"I'm supposed to protect the tribe. So are you. You put it in danger with your rampage, making enemies of the Griffins and what they stand for. Now you'll make that good. Understand?"

Mackam hung his head. "Fine." He dropped the knife and held out his hands. "Take me to Trevilsom."

Jackie watched Heather. The chief of the Tolderai had a poker face to kill for, but after their recent conversation, Jackie knew she had to be torn up inside by this. If she thought Mackam was a menace, she would've dealt with him strictly herself, but she also understood the politics here, that a sacrifice might be needed.

Perhaps, though, there was a better way.

"There are better ways to punish him," Jackie said. "Mackam is going to sit through our corporate anger management seminar series. As a previous graduate of that program, believe me, it's quite punishing in its dullness. How does that sound?"

Mackam looked confused. "Seminars? That's all?"

"Let me be clear. This is your only get out of jail free. After this, it's prison. Understand?"

Mackam nodded.

"Thank you," Heather said.

"We also need to work out a future for these forests.

Heather, you should have told the Griffins about them from the start."

"You might have stopped them."

"Or we could have protected them. They're hidden, they're not doing any harm, and by the sounds of things, they could act as early warning systems for when people are over-using magic above. We can use that, and we can shut down problematic magic without ending up all over MageTube."

"This is our thing. We protect it ourselves."

"We're your friends. Protecting people is what we do best. Let us help."

Heather looked into the edge of the forest, where Tolderai and Underfoots worked to help the plants flourish.

"Very well." She held out her hand. "It will be easier to protect these forests with help, and their safety is what matters most. On behalf of the Tolderai, I accept."

"On behalf of the Silver Griffins, I'm glad to hear it." Jackie shook Heather's hand. "Now that's out of the way, can you show me around? This place is amazing."

CHAPTER FORTY-ONE

Ellis's knee bounced up and down so hard that it shook the table he was sitting at, making the surface of his coffee ripple. He wouldn't have minded, but he hadn't even drunk the caffeine yet. This was pure nerves.

He drew a deep breath and forced himself to be still. This was going to be okay. He wasn't facing a monster. He was talking to his old boss, to a friend even. They were both reasonable people. They both wanted to do good.

Or did they? That uncertainty was what shook him.

The door of the Starbucks opened, and Margaret Sunder walked in. She nodded at Ellis, then went to the counter to get a drink. His jittering started again. He slid his hand into his pocket and closed it around the thumb drive, reminding him what this was all about, why it was worth doing.

It would all be fine.

It would.

Sunder sat opposite Ellis. Steam from her coffee

wreathed her face, briefly blurring the edges of her narrow features.

"Do you have it?" she asked.

"Uh-huh." Ellis held up the thumb drive. "Everything I could find off their computer system, and photos of some papers as well."

"Thank you, Ellis." Sunder held out her hand. "You were always one of the best."

He placed the drive next to his cup. Sunder frowned.

"Is there a problem?" she asked.

"That's what I'm trying to work out." Ellis stared at Sunder, trying to read her expression. The sort of suspects he usually dealt with, he could rely on to give something away. They'd grin or grimace or shift in their seat, revealing their inner tensions. Not Sunder. She was as calm as he'd ever known her.

"Ellis, I don't have time for this." She flexed the fingers of her outstretched hand. "Give me the information, please."

"First, you tell me what this is about. Why target Living Sun Tech?"

"As I told you, I have concerns about the company. They use magic in their technology, and it's possible they're misusing it. More than possible, in fact."

"Really?" Ellis tapped the thumb drive. "Because I saw what I was stealing, and most of it seemed pretty benign to me. Little bit magical, but mostly just engineering work, making solar panels and the infrastructure around them. That ain't all that dangerous."

"There are things you don't understand here, ways in which that technology could be used."

"Used by who?"

Sunder stiffened. For the first time, Ellis saw something beyond perfect calm.

"What do you mean by that?" she asked.

Now it was Ellis's turn to maintain a poker face. He had no idea what he was driving toward, but he knew this was a road he wanted to travel, and he had to keep Sunder talking if he wanted to get to the end.

"You tell me," he said.

"It was you, wasn't it?" Sunder's voice descended to a hiss. "You sent those girls to break into my hotel room."

"You think I'd be involved in a burglary?" Ellis tapped the thumb drive full of stolen secrets. "Why would you think that?"

Sunder sank back in her seat.

"Fine. I admit it. Nuada has his claws in me, and the longer it lasts, the deeper they dig in. Everything I've done for him has given him more he could reveal if he wanted to ruin me."

"And the information is for him."

"Of course it's for him. This is how Finn Nuada works. Why build a better product or a better business when you can lie and cheat your way to the top?

"At first, I let myself buy into the lie, that it was for the greater good, that he was making up for his competitors' cheating, that everybody did it. The lies let me live with myself. But the years passed, and I stopped believing. What was the point? It wouldn't make any difference to what I did.

"Please, Ellis, give me the files. I'll hand them to Nuada, he can do whatever he needs to do, and we can all move on. I promise I'll never involve you in this again."

"You turned me into a criminal, tried to use me to help one business spy on another."

"I did what I had to."

"Maybe, but I'm gonna do the right thing instead." Ellis slid the thumb drive into his pocket.

"Please," Sunder said. "For my sake. For all we've been through together."

"Sorry, ma'am, but you'll have to look out for yourself this time. Sounds like you're good at it."

"Where's your loyalty?"

"You used me. Where's yours?"

He stood and walked to the back of the Starbucks. His wand trembled in his hand as he tapped it against the wall, which grew thinner, letting him step through to the stairs that led to the magical subway.

He hurried down them, not running from Sunder but running toward help. He felt like his chest was going to explode with the pressure of what he'd learned. He had to find someone he could tell about this.

He took the secure side tunnel that led to the Griffins' special platform and jumped aboard the train carriage waiting there. The doors slammed shut, and it rushed out of the station in a cloud of steam.

In the carriage, Ellis pulled out the thumb drive. It was like a lump of guilt in his hand, technology stolen from an innocent company, secrets he should never have had.

He pulled out his wand and pressed its tip against the drive. "Liquescimus."

The thumb drive melted. Plastic and metal dripped to

the floor, where they cooled into harmless, meaningless blobs.

The train reached the Griffins' HQ, and the doors hissed open. Ellis leaped out.

"Agent Ellis." Normandy waved to him from the station keeper's booth. "Always a pleasure to see you."

"No time." Ellis dashed past, up the tunnel, then around the winding stairs and through the secret door into the Griffith Observatory. Tourists gave him indignant looks as he pushed past them, rushing past the planetarium, the pendulum, and the other exhibits, to a particular stretch of wall. He glanced around to ensure nobody was watching, then opened the hidden magical door and stepped through.

"Good afternoon, agent," the receptionist said. "Wand, please."

Ellis slammed his wand against the security sensor. It seemed excruciatingly slow, the light blinking on and off as it worked to identify him. After a second that felt like an eternity, the light went green.

Ellis didn't even wait for the receptionist to send him in. He charged through the doors into the office. A pigeon fluttered past his head as he ran down to the desks where he and his closest colleagues sat.

No one was there.

"Dagnabbit." Ellis kicked the desk in frustration.

"Who are you looking for?" Sam called from in front of Applegate's office.

"Lucy," Ellis said. "Or Jackie. Either of them."

"Agent Kowal is out, but I believe Agent Heron is down in the transport room."

"Thanks."

Ellis dashed away, along a corridor and down another set of stairs. What was with all these stairs? It seemed like the world was determined to slow him down, to make it as difficult as possible to get out what he needed to say.

At last, he rushed into the transport room. The technicians were off to one side, holding a whispered conversation about portals.

"Lucy?" Ellis shouted.

The technicians glared at him.

"Ellis?" Lucy appeared from one of the holding cells along the right-hand wall. "What's the matter?"

As Ellis rushed over, Twylan emerged from the cell, clutching two large brown envelopes to her chest. Ellis skidded to a halt. He needed to tell someone about Sunder, but there was a difference between telling Lucy and telling the teenager who followed Jackie around.

"There's something I..." His voice trailed off as he noticed who was locked in the other holding cells, waiting for transport to Trevilsom. Four magicals with pale skin, dark suits, and manacles around their wrists. They weren't glowing, but their resemblance to Finn Nuada was still uncanny. "What in tarnation is happening?"

"Nuada Industries is what's happening," Lucy said. "They've been up to no good. Bribing, blackmailing, murdering their opponents. When I got too close to the truth, they sent these guys after me."

Ellis stared at the captives. This was even worse than he'd thought. And to think that he had almost helped Nuada had almost become part of his web of crime.

"There's more," Lucy said. "They've been putting pressure on people high up in the Griffins, forcing them to turn a blind eye. That's why I met so much resistance when I started looking into the company. He doesn't just have friends at the top. He has victims there."

She held out her hand, and Twylan handed over the envelopes.

"This is going to be hard for you to hear, Ellis, but your mentor, Margaret Sunder, she's one of the ones involved. He was blackmailing her, and she's been covering for him for years. I know you might find it hard to believe, but Twylan has proof."

Ellis sighed. "Sadly, it ain't half as hard to believe as you'd think."

He told her briefly about what Sunder had asked him to do and the results when he'd confronted her.

"I'm so sorry," Lucy said.

Ellis shrugged. "What's done is done. What matters now is fixing this."

The door to the transport room banged open, to the annoyance of the technicians, and Jackie strode in.

"There you all are," she said. "I need your help. Something big has come up with the Tolderai, and we're going to need to talk management into accepting it."

"We're in the middle of a problem," Lucy said. "I think it might be bigger."

"Well, you haven't heard about what I found yet. It's all over the city, and it's spectacular, but a huge use of secret magic."

"Is it the forests?" Twylan asked.

Jackie looked at her and laughed. "Of course you'd

know. Yes, that's it. So tell them, we need to sort this out, right?"

Everyone looked at Twylan.

She shook her head. "Sorry, Jackie, but the forests will have to wait."

CHAPTER FORTY-TWO

Light streamed in through windows in the roof of the factory hall, illuminating Finn Nuada where he stood on a stage, flanked by a pair of robotic assembly arms. A crowd of press and guests had gathered to hear him speak, with a few employees thrown in to bulk out the numbers. Elethin was proud of her work. She'd arranged the event with something close to perfection, and it was ideally timed, coming as they needed a distraction from the failed court case.

Unlike the court case, this event would get the attention of the mundane as well as the magical press. Trade journals, local TV stations, even a national newspaper had people in attendance. This was Finn's day, and she loved that she would help him shine brighter. He needed her, and she needed to be needed by him. She watched from the wings as he approached the end of his speech.

"The factory won't always look like this." Finn gestured at the robots to either side. "For starters, Benny and Bernie here will have work to do." The employees in the audience laughed as instructed, and some of the others laughed with them. "And let's face it, we don't need a stage on the assembly floor." More respectful laughter.

"Then there's the grime and grit that will eventually accrue, the scuffs and scratches of a working factory. Even then, I believe that this place will shine brightly, a beacon to our industry and to L.A. We're saying to everyone, there's a better way to make both lights and solar panels, and if you allow us, we'll light the way for you."

He took a step back and lowered his hands. The crowd burst into applause, louder and more convincing than the laughter. Not everyone might enjoy what passed for jokes in a corporate speech, but they all appreciated the brilliance, the charm, and the fame of Finn Nuada.

Elethin walked out onto the stage, holding a microphone. When the applause had died down a little, she spoke.

"Mr. Nuada will now be taking questions. So..."

Hands shot up. Elethin singled out a friendly journalist, one whose question she'd not so much vetted as written for him, in return for the chance to ask first.

"Yes, Bob."

"Mr. Nuada," the journalist began, "there are plenty of companies already supporting power generation in the city. What makes your solar panels so important?"

"That's a great question, Bob." Nuada beamed, and his face was just short of shining. "The truth is that L.A, like every modern city, sometimes struggles with power supplies. Just the other night, we saw a mysterious blackout across the whole city, and while it might have been brief, it's still a cause for concern. After all, it's not only our homes that are reliant on electricity. It's our communication systems, our water supplies, even our hospitals.

"The new solar panels we'll be producing here are fifty percent more efficient than those of even our best competitors. Not only do they generate power, but their built-in storage systems mean an efficiently managed electricity flow from the very moment it enters the network. That means a power grid that's more flexible, more responsive, and more resilient when something goes wrong. I think that's the sort of technology whose importance we can all appreciate."

With the warm-up question out of the way, Elethin pointed at another journalist. "Your turn, Jane."

"Mr. Nuada, your company has recently taken over several significant competitors. What do you tell people who are concerned by the consolidation of so much of the industry in a single company, and who are worried by the anti-competitive nature of such monopolistic practices?"

Elethin clenched. She knew how much Finn hated questions like that. When this was over, he would make her regret letting it through. For now, though, he was on public display, and he had to respond.

"That's an interesting question, Jane," he said. "I find that complaints about monopolies are often a sign that people are jealous of your success. Competition is valuable, but so are the efficiencies that come from combining companies. Who's next?"

While Finn fielded the next question, Elethin nodded at Halldora, who stood to one side of the room. The head of security quietly made her way through the crowd and took

Jane by the elbow. Unable to resist Halldora's strength, the unfortunate journalist had no choice but to accept the forced escort out and missed the rest of the launch event. Elethin made a note not to invite her again. Anyone who wanted to enter the privileged sphere around Finn Nuada had to learn to play by his rules.

After twenty minutes of questions, Finn nodded at Elethin.

"That's it for now, folks," she said. "There are plenty of refreshments and expert members of staff available to talk to you about their work. Please stick around. Mr. Nuada will be back out shortly. Then you can ask the really insightful questions you didn't want your colleagues to hear."

As the crowd broke up, she led Finn down the back of the stage and into a corridor beyond the main factory hall.

"Is he here?" the CEO asked.

"Yes, Finn."

"Good. I'm in the mood for some monopolistic practices."

A man sat at a table in a meeting room at the end of the corridor. His assistant stood behind him. The man wore a tailored suit and a frustrated scowl. He folded his arms as Finn and Elethin walked in.

"You're wasting my time again," he growled. "If you think I'm more likely to sell you my company after you've wasted an hour of my time while you went out there to show off for the crowd, you badly misunderstand who you're dealing with."

"I doubt that very much, Mr. Davies." Finn sat at the other side of the table. "Elethin?"

She handed him a large brown envelope.

"Whatever contract you have in there," Davies said, "whatever amount you're going to offer me, I'm not selling. I came here to tell you that to your face. Now I'm going."

He made to stand up, but one of Finn's guards appeared behind him and pressed him back into his seat. The assistant watched them all nervously.

"This is assault," Davies growled. "I'll report you to the cops."

"I doubt it." Finn opened the envelope. "Just as I doubt that you'll keep refusing my offers once you see these." He took out half a dozen photos and spread them across the table. "That's you, isn't it?"

Davies looked down at the photos, aghast. He tried to shake his head, to deny the truth, but he couldn't. Finn was glowing, and something about that light made it impossible to lie.

"Yes," Davies said. "That's me."

"That's not your wife, is it?"

Davies shook his head.

"Who is it?"

Davies mumbled softly.

"What's that again?" Finn leaned forward and cupped a hand to his ear. "I couldn't hear you."

"It's my sister-in-law, and you know it." Davies glared at the photos. "How did you find out?"

"The truth never eludes me for long."

Davies glanced at his assistant. "You never saw this, never heard this, understood?"

"Of course not, Mr. Davies."

"Good." Davies glared at Finn. "All right, tell me what you want."

"You know what I want. Your company."

Davies sank deeper in his seat. He rubbed his hands over his face, then let out a sigh.

"Fine. Give me the damn contract."

"For half of what I offered you before."

"What? That's outrageous!"

"That's why you should have agreed before. You made me jump through hoops to reach this point. Now I'm going to make you pay the price."

"I won't do it. Not for that little."

Finn slid one of the photos forward and tapped his finger against it. "This one's special. It's not in some anonymous hotel room. Where is it?"

Davies' looked at the photo, and the indignation fell from his voice.

"Our holiday home."

"Your holiday home. The one you bought for your wife's birthday, right? Imagine how she'd feel knowing that this happened there. Not just knowing it, but seeing it." He peered into the envelope and smiled. "There's another one here that includes the pool boy."

"All right, you win." Davies put his head in his hands. "Send me the contract. The company will be yours by tomorrow."

"A wise choice." Finn gathered the photos, put them back in the envelope, and slid it across the table. "A souvenir for you. I have plenty of copies. Maybe you could connect them, make an amusing cartoon strip about your adventures in no-pants land."

Finn got out of his seat and walked back into the corridor. Elethin followed him. When the door had closed, he burst out laughing.

"That was too much fun. I should do it more often." He looked at his watch. "Are the boys back yet? They should have dealt with Agent Heron by now."

"You'd have to ask Halldora. Security isn't my area."

"Of course not. Too tough for a woman like you." He stroked her cheek. "But don't worry, you still have uses to me."

"Thank you, sir. I try."

"You even succeed, most of the time. In the future, make sure you have the journalists under control. I don't want any more nasty surprises."

At that moment, Halldora dashed down the corridor toward them, a gun in her hand and a wild look on her face.

"Sir, you have to get out of here now," she shouted. "The Silver Griffins have come."

CHAPTER FORTY-THREE

Lucy dashed down the main hall of the new Nuada Industries factory, wand in hand, dodging around the journalists who stood staring slack-jawed all across the factory floor. Starting the raid with a huge "never was, never will be" hadn't been the ideal plan, but the alternative had been giving Nuada time to get away while the journalists got out, and Lucy wasn't going to allow that. The man was too dangerous. He had to be dealt with now before he did any more harm.

One of Nuada's guards stepped out in front of Lucy, hand raised and palm open. A blast of blazing light hit her and scattered off the reflector field, turning into a thousand smaller beams, like light bouncing off a disco ball.

She swung her fist and hit him right in the nose. He staggered back, light blasting from behind his dark glasses.

"Stupefacio." Lucy waved her wand, and a spell sprang forth. It hit the guard in the face, and he staggered, then fell to the ground, stunned.

Two more were already coming up behind him. One of them cast a blast of light at Lucy.

"Nice try, sunshine," she said as the beam scattered into fragments.

In that dazzling moment, the other one had time to reach her. He knocked the wand from her hand and grabbed her by the arm, flinging her to the floor, then kicked her in the ribs.

"Oof!" Lucy curled in around herself, then grabbed the guard's ankle as he tried to kick her again. She yanked on his foot, and he fell to the floor.

The other guard stood over Lucy, aiming a pistol at her head.

"Bet you're not immune to this," he said.

There was a *snapping* sound, and something dark hit him in the chest. He looked down in horror as it spread and the light radiating from him started to fade. Within seconds, his bright, shining body had turned gray. He sank to the floor, limp as a rag doll.

Jackie appeared, clutching a black pistol.

"Jenkins' shadow gun," she said, patting it. "I can't believe you said no to this."

She reached out a hand and helped Lucy to her feet.

"I'm not a gun person," Lucy said.

"Neither am I, but I'm definitely a 'beat the bad guys' person, and this is helping loads."

"Just be careful you don't come a cropper, waving that thing around in a confined space."

"Whatever you say, you big English weirdo. Let's go hunt some execs."

All around them, the Silver Griffins were battling

Nuada's minions, both his glowing guard clones and the other magical members of his security detail. An elf pointed a gun at Kelly, who made it melt with a blast of magical heat. Roger Applegate levitated a pair of guards into each other, then hung them over a robotic arm. A burst of light blinded Jim, but he still managed to fight back, sending out sprays of ice that kept his opponents from getting close.

Ellis fought with a ferocity he hadn't felt in years. The memory of Sunder's betrayal drove him on, as did a sense of hurt at the blackmail used against her. He fought for revenge, fought for justice, but mostly just fought to get the sick feeling out of his system.

A pair of dwarves in dark glasses ran at him, one waving a wand, the other with runes glowing in the air around her hand.

"Volant!" Ellis shouted the spell's trigger and flew into the air. A second later, he dispelled his power so he fell feet-first onto the head of the armed dwarf, knocking him out. The other one turned and unleashed a spell, but Ellis countered it, magic crackling away to nothing between them. She cast another spell, but this time he dodged, then came up to her side.

"Agglutino." A wave of his wand stuck her to the floor with magical glue. As she struggled to free herself, he walked around behind and hit her over the back of the head with his wand, a little magic giving it extra weight. The dwarf fell to the ground next to her colleague.

At one side of the hall, Twylan crept along, trying to get past the distracted guards. She felt honored and excited that the Silver Griffins had included her when planning the raid but also daunted. Would she be judged for her performance here? What if she didn't fulfil her part of the mission, if she failed from the very start?

She was almost at the end of the hall when one of the light guards appeared in front of her. His shades had fallen off, revealing eyes that glowed much like hers, though with light instead of the raw, crackling mess of magic. They stood for a moment, staring at each other, seeing something familiar and yet strange.

"Please," Twylan said. "I know that you're connected to Nuada, but you have to understand that he's bad news. Let me through, and maybe you can be free of him."

"He is my master," the guard said. He raised his hand, light glowing from the palm.

"You don't have to be bound to where you came from. You can make your own choices, find your way in life."

"He is the master." The hand glowed brighter.

"You don't have to accept a master. You can be—"

The light burst from his hand, a bright blast heading for Twylan. Instinctively, she responded with her magic, a beam of darkness rolling out of her eyes. It collided with the light, wiping it out, then hit the light guard in the middle of the chest. He looked down, his mouth opened in a surprised "O," then he keeled over.

Twylan didn't stop to check how badly she'd hurt him. She had a mission to locate Finn Nuada and let the others know where he was. She pushed open the door at the back of the room and stepped into the corridor.

Three people were there—Finn Nuada, Elethin Tannerin, and Halldora Helmsguard.

"I told you, sir," Helmsguard said. "We should have run as soon as they arrived."

"And give up on everything I've built?" Nuada asked. "Never."

"Then we fight for it."

Twylan waved, and a hedge of thorny bushes filled the corridor beyond the executives, a barrier of nature magic such as the Tolderai would use, made stronger by her time learning from them.

"Please give up," she said. "You can't get away."

"Like hell." Halldora pulled the trigger on her gun.

Twylan hadn't known that she could catch bullets, but there was no other way to describe it. A wall of shimmering magic appeared in front of her, with the bullets suspended in it. Her eyes ached from the power that had flowed through them, from the speed and force of it all, but she was still standing. The bullets shook with unspent energy as they hovered, caught by her power.

"Fraaakk," Halldora said.

"Nice trick," Nuada said. "It looks like it's taking you a lot of effort. I wonder what happens if I do this..."

A flash of light burst from him. Twylan's instincts took hold again, trying to redirect her power to protect her sight. The bullets flew free and hit the wall behind her as the shield failed. Despite it all, the magic came too late. There was a blinding flash, and her world went dark.

"Jackie!" she shouted. "Lucy! Anyone! Help!"

Out in the main hall, Lucy heard the cry. She dashed through the door and into the corridor to see Finn Nuada and his sidekicks standing over a fallen Twylan. Nuada was pointing his hand down the corridor, using light to burn through a thorn thicket. As Lucy entered, he turned to look at her.

"Of course," he said. "You would be here."

"How can you do this?" Lucy said. "All of it, just for the sake of a business? Just for the sake of profits?"

"How?" Nuada laughed. "How could anybody not do this? Profits are power. Business is power. The light might blind some, but it can empower me. Why would I not take what I can?"

"Because of other people."

"Other people are nothing to me. Just tools to my ends."

"All of them?"

"What do you think, Agent?"

"I think that you're going down."

Lucy raised her wand.

Light shot from Finn's eyes. Most of it scattered as it hit Lucy, casting bright points off the walls. But some got through, a slender beam hitting her in the shoulder, burning her. She remembered what Jenkins had said about the bracelet's protection, that it would hold off ninety-seven-point-one-eight percent of light attacks. Apparently, this was the two-point-something percent that got through.

Lucy pulled a dark grenade from her back pocket. After the fight at the subway and the initial assault on this place, it was the only one she had left, but it was the perfect weapon against Finn Nuada. She flung it straight at him.

Halldora leaped in the way, catching the grenade and landing with it underneath her. There was a soft sound and darkness pooled out around the dwarf, but it wasn't the globe of shadow Lucy had been counting on.

"I can't see," Halldora said. "Go without me, sir. Get out of here."

"Always the good soldier, eh, Helmsguard?" There was a sneer in Finn's voice. "Your strength and your weakness. But I don't need to run. There's nothing this witch can do to stop me."

"Oh yeah?" Lucy started flinging spells at him. Stun spells, sleep spells, glue spells, even darkness spells. As each one flew from her wand, a counterspell emerged from Finn's fingers, obliterating it.

"You think I got this far just with light shows?" Finn said. "I am power. I am light. I am truth. I am too much for any of you."

"Too much for anyone, right?" Lucy looked past him at where Elethin stood, clutching her handbag and watching the fight in horror. "After all, we're just tools."

"That's right, Agent. I am the light. I am power. Nothing can stop me, and nothing matters next to that."

"You really will use anyone."

"Of course. Why wouldn't I?"

"I don't know, ethics maybe, or loyalty?"

Finn laughed. "Those are for little people, Agent. Greatness goes to those who grab it."

"No loyalty to anyone." Lucy looked past him to Elethin again. "Is that what you want?"

"Of course it's what I want," Finn said, "you pompous, ridiculous—"

His words cut short as Elethin's handbag collided with the back of his head.

"I gave you everything," she howled, "but you'll still

throw us all away, won't you? Nothing I do will ever be good enough!"

"Never." Finn turned, one hand drawn back, ready to slap her. "And this is why."

"Stupefacio." This time, Finn wasn't looking at Lucy. He wasn't ready to counter her spell. The stun hit him in the back, and he stumbled just a little. He shook his head and turned toward her.

But in the few seconds it took him to gather himself, she sprinted down the corridor, pulling a pair of absorbing manacles from her back pocket. Finn reached out. Lucy reached out. A manacle closed around his wrist, and the magic faded from his hand. As the manacles absorbed his power, the CEO's glowing skin faded to nothing more than a sickly white.

"The truth's out, Finn," Lucy said. "You're a dickhead, and now you're under arrest."

CHAPTER FORTY-FOUR

It took a long time to clear up the mess at Nuada Industries.

First, there were the journalists and other guests from the grand opening. They all had to be ushered out and given appropriate snippets of information to let them fill in the gap in their lives where the Silver Griffins had wiped it away. A few had taken pictures or videos in the first few seconds of the raid, and Jenkins and Nigel went through all the electronics, carefully deleting those. With the time limit on "never was, never will be," that part was a race to the finish line, with everything else temporarily set aside.

Then there was the staff. They were all magicals, so at least they didn't need their memories wiped. The Silver Griffins had to interview them all to work out who knew what, who had been involved in which crimes, and who might deserve some time in Trevilsom. Sorting that was a slow, messy business.

It was all worth it to deal with Finn Nuada.

Lucy sat in a chair across from him in the factory's

conference room. His hands remained manacled, his skin was pale, like he'd spent all his life indoors. The suit that had seemed to fit him so perfectly now seemed too large. Without his powers, he had shrunk to a withered remnant of himself.

His confidence, however, remained untouched.

"You think you've got me?" He laughed. "Don't you know how rich I am? I can afford the best lawyers in the world, magical or mundane. By the time they're finished, you'll be the ones in chains."

"I doubt it," Lucy said. "Any lawyer has their limits, and you're not suing other people over patents anymore. We're talking about fraud, blackmail, multiple cases of murder. That puts a certain stink on the lawyers that many of them don't like, even when it turns out that their client is innocent. You're definitely not innocent."

"Prove it."

"That should be easy. We have the bodies. We have witness statements. We have a confession from your head of PR, although your security chief seems determined to keep defending you. Apparently, some people are loyal even to masters who aren't loyal to them."

"I told you, I still have power. Wealth will buy all the friends you need."

"You think you're still wealthy?"

"Oh, yes. Have you seen how much my company is worth?"

"No, but we have someone looking into that now."

There was a knock on the door. Jackie walked in, followed by Max Petrie.

"See?" Finn said. "My lawyer is here. Now, do you want

to take these torture instruments off my wrists, or do you want to be sued for your brutality?"

Max walked around the conference table, set a laptop down, and sat next to Lucy.

"Petrie?" Finn frowned. "What's going on?"

"I'm not your lawyer anymore, Mr. Nuada," Max said. "I've been hired by the Silver Griffins to assess your firm, to decide how we go about the legal process of winding it down."

"Winding it down?"

"Oh, yes. The Griffins are confiscating your firm as proceeds of illegal magic. It's going to be dismantled. There are parts worth preserving, of course. I wouldn't want the world to lose all the good work you've done developing solar panels. They'll sell off those parts and use the proceeds to compensate your victims and to support the Silver Griffins in their work."

"You can't do that." Finn leaned forward, a look of right-eous indignation in his eyes. "I built this company. It's mine."

"You didn't build it. You bought parts, stole others, then jammed them together and used cheap PR tricks to boost your image and fool investors into throwing you too much money. If you'd been mundane, it would have collapsed years ago."

"This isn't over. I have other resources. There are other lawyers."

"I'm sure they'll have a great time interviewing you in Trevilsom Prison," Lucy said. She nodded at Jackie. "Take him away."

"Gladly." Jackie hauled the protesting Finn Nuada out of

his seat and out the door. The door *thudded* shut behind them.

Max sighed.

"I made a fool of myself," he said, "standing up for Nuada in court. After all the scumbag corporations I've faced in the past, I should have known better."

"He tricked a lot of people," Lucy pointed out.

"Still, it was a mistake, one that could have made him even more powerful. Thank you for doing what you did, for digging out the truth and making sure I lost."

"No problem. Does this mean that Kelly's going to stop giving me the evil looks?"

Max's face screwed up. "I wish, but she's very protective of me, and she thinks you should have dealt with it differently. She's going to stay mad for a while."

Lucy shrugged. "I can live with that."

They got up and walked out through the factory, past Jenkins and Nigel playing with the robot assembly line, Twylan smiling as Griffins gathered round to thank her for her help, and Ellis leading the team of agents preparing prisoners for secure transport. Outside the factory's main doors, the sun was setting over L.A., with all the golden glory of a late summer evening.

"Mommy!" Eddie ran up to Lucy. The rest of the family was just behind him.

"What are you guys doing here?" she asked.

"Jackie called to explain why you were running so late." Charlie kissed her on the cheek. "We figured we'd come to make sure you're taking care of yourself, and of course, bring you some dinner." He held out a pizza box. "Ours are waiting in the car. We figured you probably wouldn't want us hanging around."

"Sorry, but no. There's still a lot to do here. Thank you so much for this."

Lucy hugged her kids, then took the pizza.

"What happened to this place?" Dylan asked, watching as Halldora was led shackled into the back of a van, along with half of her security team.

"The truth finally caught up with some very bad people," Lucy said. "It does that in the end."

"Only because you help it," Ashley said. "The truth can't expose itself."

"I suppose not. Now you lot run off home. I'll see you in the morning."

Her family climbed into Charlie's car and drove away, the kids waving out the back. Lucy opened the pizza box and smiled. Yes, that would help see her through the evening.

"Your family is great," Max said. "You must be proud of them."

"I really am," Lucy said. "Now come on, we need to get back to work."

Orange Upside Down Polenta Cake

I'm kind of over the standard cake – for now – and have been dipping into the more Mediterranean side of cooking. Cakes tend to be more dense and less sweet and in hotter weather that appeals to me more. This one is a fun take on pineapple upside down cake but with the fresh replacement of oranges. Enjoy and think of cool breezes off the Amalfi coast as you take a bite.

Ingredients:

- 1 ½ c instant polenta
- 1 ½ c whole milk
- 2 oranges and 2 t grated orange zest (get all you can out of those oranges)
- 1/3 c packed brown sugar
- 2 t cornstarch
- Pinch of salt

- 1 c all-purpose flour
- 1 t baking powder
- ½ t baking soda
- 3 eggs
- 1 c sugar
- 6 T extra-virgin olive oil
- 2 t vanilla extract

Preheat oven to 350 degrees. Toast polenta on baking sheet until you can smell it in the air – 5 to 10 minutes. In large bowl mix polenta with milk and orange zest and let sit until liquid is completely absorbed. Then break polenta apart into small crumbs.

Grease 9-inch round cake pan and line the bottom with parchment paper. Mix together brown sugar, cornstarch and pinch of salt and spread evenly in bottom of cake pan. Remove peel and white pith from oranges and cut into thin slices. Arrange on top of sugar mixture.

Mix well the flour, baking powder, baking soda and ½ t salt in a bowl. Beat with mixer - the eggs and sugar on medium speed till pale and tripled in volume – about 6 to 8 minutes. Reduce speed to low and slowly add oil and vanilla. Add polenta crumbs next until everything is thoroughly mixed. Next comes the flour mixture – add slowly and scrape the sides as needed. Make sure all ingredients are thoroughly mixed.

Pour into cake pan over oranges and sugar mix and spread into an even layer. Bake until the cake appears golden brown and a toothpick comes out clean. About 1 hour.

Let cake cool in pan for 15 minutes and then flip onto

plate or rack to continue cooling. Don't worry if a caramelized orange slice stuck to the pan. Carefully peel it off and rearrange on the top of the cake. Go for a little more and add a dollop of whipped cream to each slice. Enjoy your summer!

Get sneak peeks, exclusive giveaways, behind the scenes content, and more. PLUS you'll be notified of special **one day only fan pricing** on new releases.

Sign up today to get free stories.

Visit: https://marthacarr.com/read-free-stories/

AUTHOR NOTES - MARTHA CARR

AUGUST 3, 2021

I didn't think it was possible but 2021 has been a weirder year for me than 2020. Maybe that's because it was stacked on top of all the events from last year. This year started off with a broken elbow from tripping in a gopher hole while walking Leela, who didn't notice anything was amiss. She was too busy sniffing a particularly good spot.

The year picked up speed once I was diagnosed with 3rd stage melanoma – a recurrence from eleven years ago. No, I didn't know that was possible either. The oncologist at MD Anderson, where I eventually landed, said stress can make that happen. Well, check and check.

Now, once a month I travel to Houston for chemo and will be doing that till next June. I've learned to take my own snacks, use Uber Eats in the hotel and pick a really good, long book. I'll get through it.

Worst side effect so far is the feeling of always being tired. It's frustrating but I'm making myself get up and go do things. I have kind of figured out how to deal with this.

No drinking, no massages, move when I can move, rest when I need to rest.

But then the sweet pittie Leela started having trouble walking and I had noticed some other things were off. It was like her entire little body was going haywire. It took a while, but I finally got a diagnosis. The sweet girl has cancer and there's nothing to be done about it. It could be weeks, it could be months and it's already spread. She's lost a third of her body weight and her back legs don't always do what she hopes. There are other things too, but you get the picture.

So far, she's happy and eating like a champ so we soldier on.

I have a dog stroller and I walk her early in the mornings till she can't walk any further and then push her in the stroller.

Sometimes I have to remind myself not to go too far. I'm the other cancer patient in this picture.

What's to be gained from all this? It's the question I ask from time to time. There have to be gifts there and I don't want to miss them. It's an ongoing kind of open-ended question.

Self-acceptance is a big one. I want to work out more but I'm often too tired. I want to lose more weight but see previous sentence. Slowing down has helped me to notice things like all the dragonflies flittering through the garden out back.

Community is another gain. More people are offering to help by knitting a shawl, or stopping by to chat, or sending dinner or flowers or wonderful lotions. Best Fans Ever have sent postcards and handwritten letters from all over the world that I read slowly and pile up to read again at some point. I feel the threads of connection weaving themselves together all around me.

There is nothing sweeter. It's my definition of Love – capital L. It's finding ways to be there for someone to let them know, we will walk this together. It may be hard, but it won't be lonely.

You may have noticed that's kind of a theme in everything I write. Our hero may have a tough road but they don't walk it alone. There are always ride or die friends beside them, rushing in to the fray, fireballs at the ready.

That's why, even in the midst of all this turmoil, I'm still happy. I can see what matters and there are still things to do, at a slower pace, with so many people around me. More adventures to follow.

AUTHOR NOTES - MICHAEL ANDERLE

AUGUST 7, 2021

Thank you for not only reading this story but these author notes as well.

Taking time out to smell the roses (a metaphor, I have no roses here in the desert around Las Vegas) is something I'm considering a bit more.

Especially since I am taking medicine(s) that slow me down. I swear I had more energy when I was particularly unhealthy, and my heart was pumping blood out at a pressure that made the doctors look twice.

At this slower pace, I have to be thankful for so many of the wonderful people in my life and in this company that keep things moving along at a very steady clip. Everything from art to editing to publishing and marketing, the wheels keep going round and round.

Also, the request for author notes.

Back in 2015, when I started these things, I never would have thought I might end up doing hundreds and probably getting closer to a thousand of them in six years. Close, but I'm sure it's closer to maybe 700 or so, I think.

The way that Martha and I joke is usually pretty dark, so I won't share what I tell her when she mentions the troubles and travails that she deals with in her life. Suffice to say it's more than she shares.

She's a strong woman.

However, it's the grace and goodness that she exudes, which I am particularly amazed at as she goes through the gut-wrenching challenges she walks.

Out of the two of us, you would do much better to emulate her than me.

The two of us have talked long about a little bit of everything, including politics and religion, and still remain friends who know that on the other side of the phone is someone who will make you laugh.

How's that for an amazeballs human being?

(Yes, I mean her, not me. Trust me, I'm good to talk about myself; I'm just not doing it here.)

Anyway, if you have a down day, just take out your trusty Martha Carr books and read the author notes.

They will usually bring a smile to your face!

Ad Aeternitatem,
Michael Anderle

Solve a murder, save her mother, and stop the apocalypse?

What would you do when elves ask you to investigate a prince's murder and you didn't even know elves, or magic, was real?

Meet Leira Berens, Austin homicide detective who's good at what she does – track down the bad guys and lock them away.

Which is why the elves want her to solve this murder – fast. It's not just about tracking down the killer and bringing them to justice. It's about saving the world!

If you're looking for a heroine who prefers fighting to flirting, check out The Leira Chronicles today!

<u>AVAILABLE ON AMAZON AND IN KINDLE UNLIMITED!</u>

CONNECT WITH THE AUTHORS

Martha Carr Social

Website: http://www.marthacarr.com

Facebook: https://www.facebook.com/
groups/MarthaCarrFans/

Michael Anderle Social

Website: http://lmbpn.com

Email List: http://lmbpn.com/email/

https://www.facebook.com/LMBPNPublishing

https://twitter.com/MichaelAnderle

https://www.instagram.com/lmbpn_publishing/

https://www.bookbub.com/authors/michael-anderle